Annie Sparrow is in her thirties. Her background is in sales and marketing. She is the author of *Said & Done*.

Matchstick Love

Annie Sparrow

POCKET BOOKS
TOWNHOUSE

First published in Great Britain and Ireland by
Pocket/Townhouse, 2003
An imprint of Simon & Schuster UK Ltd and TownHouse Ltd, Dublin

Simon & Schuster UK is a Viacom company

Copyright © Annie Sparrow, 2003

This book is copyright under the Berne Convention.
No reproduction without permission.
® and © 1997 Simon & Schuster Inc. All rights reserved
Pocket Books & Design is a registered trademark of
Simon & Schuster Inc

The right of Annie Sparrow to be identified as the author of this work
has been asserted in accordance with sections 77 and 78 of the
Copyright, Designs and Patents Act, 1988.

1 3 5 7 9 10 8 6 4 2

Simon & Schuster UK Ltd
Africa House
64–78 Kingsway
London WC2B 6AH

Simon & Schuster Australia
Sydney

TownHouse Ltd
Trinity House
Charleston Road
Ranelagh
Dublin 6
Ireland

A CIP catalogue record for this book is available from the
British Library

ISBN 1-903650-36-4

This book is a work of fiction. Names, characters, places and incidents
are either a product of the author's imagination or are used fictitiously.
Any resemblance to actual people living or dead, events or locales is
entirely coincidental.

Typeset by SX Composing DTP, Rayleigh, Essex
Printed and bound in Great Britain by
Bookmarque Ltd, Croydon, Surrey

Acknowledgements

With heartfelt thanks to:
Audrey, Jackie, Rita, Susan and Tom, for all the laughter, drinks and support. It kept me going through some hard times.
Kim for your help and encouragement.
My mum, for always being there.
And lastly, my agent, Faith O'Grady, plus everyone who played a part at my publishers, TownHouse and Simon & Schuster, in particular Treasa, Suzanne and Jane.

For Derek

1

'I'm sorry . . . but it's over,' she said nervously.

He stared at her blankly.

'I'm sorry,' she said again, her gaze drifting downwards, as a heavy silence filled the room.

Simon remained sitting with his legs crossed on the sofa beside her, his hands resting in his lap. His eyes expressed mild confusion, as if she'd just told a joke and the punchline didn't make sense to him. 'What are you talking about?' he asked.

Amy swallowed. Her mouth felt dry and there was a slight tremble in her hand. She hated these scenes and had almost opted to tell him over the phone, but her sense of fair play had made her drive through the lashing rain late on a Sunday evening to his apartment. 'It's over.'

He screwed up his face and said, with self-assured disbelief, 'Are you being serious?'

Strangely, in that second her nervousness disappeared. Looking back up at him and seeing his perplexed little face almost brought a fit of misplaced laughter from her. Instead she let out a dispirited groan. Why was he shocked? she wondered. Hadn't he ever listened to her?

Simon Delaney was a classic commitment-phobe. Oh Shit! Another one! Amy felt she had an internal antenna that attracted them from miles away. Every time she got too close to him, he panicked and talked about needing 'space'. In her twenties she might have been more accommodating but now she couldn't be bothered with all that. Rightly or wrongly she had decided that a man asking for space really meant that the novelty had worn off and he wanted to keep his options open.

I will not be an option for any man, she affirmed. Not any more.

'I'd better go,' she said. She was clutching her car keys.

'*But why?*' he gasped. 'Why are you doing this? I didn't know you were unhappy.'

Her mouth fell open, her eyes closed, and a long, weary sigh seeped out of her. *I didn't know you were unhappy!* The words whirled in her head. What a joke! What a jerk! Hadn't she spent the last four months trying politely – and, at times, less politely – to express her upset and confusion about his increasingly distant manner and his refusal to commit to any arrangement more than a few days in advance? The more effort she had made to try to get things back to how they used to be had resulted in him pulling further and further away. How different it had all been in the beginning. How different *he* had been. A standard cliché. Amy found herself laughing.

'Jesus, Amy, what's got into you?' Simon tried to take her arm but she pulled it away. For the first time he looked hurt. She copied his expression, but the truth was she felt nothing. There was so much she could have said, but she was all out of words. All out of effort. She was angry with him – and with herself for being so patient with him, for trying to be who he had wanted her to be instead of just being herself.

'Amy, this isn't like you. Surely we can talk about this, work something out?' Simon was pleading for another chance.

Her eyes cut through him with their coldness. Her ability to cut off immediately, which had served her well in her life – possibly even saved her when she was growing up – still surprised her. Sometimes she questioned her ability to love. Of course she experienced all the chaotic, heady emotions of first attraction, and carried the pain of various hurts, but somehow at a certain point, something seemed to click inside her and all emotion ceased. There was no going back. Could the sun reverse its orbit?

Now part of her wanted to tell him to fuck off – and maybe she would have, but unfortunately, they worked for the same company and she didn't want him as an enemy. She was the sales and marketing manager and Simon was the IT manager. That was the trouble with office affairs: they were incredibly exciting to start with – the secrecy, the stolen embraces in the corridors, the knowing glances across the room, the flirty, humorous, sometimes X-rated emails – but when they were over, you still had to work with the other person. (Praying that they'd deleted everything!)

Thankfully she was in discussions with one of their sister companies about a possible new position. Work was her salvation. It was an area of her life in which confidence reigned. An area she could control.

'I'm sorry, Simon, but I think I should leave now.'

'But, Amy, I care about you. I – I—'

She watched him, sensing the revelation that might be coming.

'*I love you!*'

Wow! The L-word hadn't been used in ages. But it was just a word, she told herself. He didn't mean it. In fact, his reaction wasn't a surprise. Now that Simon had gathered he was losing her, the pressure was off so he could revert to the old behaviour in a last-ditch attempt to keep her. A textbook example of a commitment-phobe. Well, that was what she'd read in the psychology book that Tessa had loaned her.

Amy stood up. 'Take care, I hope we can continue to be friends.' She knew, of course, that they couldn't. They hadn't been friends to start with so why would they be friends now? He'd probably hate her by the morning. Probably sabotage her computer, send her hate emails, vote against her in management meetings. Paranoid, maybe, but it was still possible. Hell has no fury like a damaged male ego!

Amy stood in the doorway and said she was sorry at least three more times. Then with a final sad glance at him, she left.

Driving home through the rain she wondered if tears would come, but they didn't. At thirty-four she was all out of tears. Single again! Most of her friends were on their second baby by now. Some were on their second marriage! That meant they'd had two lots of wedding presents while Amy had had to buy every single kitchen utensil herself. Life was so unfair. Not that she necessarily wanted marriage and all that. The fact was she didn't know what she wanted. But she knew what she didn't want. That was the good thing about getting older: your tolerance for crap diminished.

She decided on two new rules – to add to the growing list.

1. No more men with commitment phobias – apart from George Clooney. He could be an exception. But only him.

2. No more relationships with men she worked with. That was a definite taboo.

2

Four weeks later

You won't unsettle me, she thought.

Two hours into her brand-new job Amy had been thrown into the lions' den. Poor lions! This was her arena.

The smartly suited man opposite her smiled, yet his eyes remained guarded. 'CEM has one of the highest profiles in the industry,' he said, in his deep, velvet-toned voice. He had just heard that part of her job specification was to raise it. He was Greg Hamilton-Lawrence, the senior business development manager – apparently excellent at his job. Yet she had the impression that he was threatened by her appointment.

While she considered her response, her eyes scanned the others present. Underneath their polite smiles and pleasant words of welcome, she wondered how many were hoping she'd fail. Out of the six suited men and two suited women sitting around the oval table in the boardroom, she believed that, given half a chance, at least four would stab her in the back. It would be down to her not to give them the opportunity to do so.

William Halson, the managing director, started to answer Greg's remark, but Amy indicated that she would like to deal with it herself. William had already given a ten-minute introductory talk on her future role and it was time she took control.

When she spoke it was in a strong, commanding voice, with a hint of friendliness. Being popular wasn't her main goal: that was to get the job done to the best of her ability. However, it wouldn't hurt to win some of them over. 'Of course within the corporate-hospitality and event-management industry, CEM has a strong profile among its existing clients, a proven track record. That's not in dispute. But the bottom line is, turnover and profit have to increase. There are ample new markets for growth. The company's client base needs to be expanded into *every* sector of industry. I—'

'The business-development team has already been addressing this issue,' interrupted Greg. Again he offered her a smile, but his cold, stern eyes suggested otherwise. He was a tall guy, athletic with broad shoulders and short, very neat black hair, parted on the side – probably mid-thirties. He had a square jawline, chiselled cheekbones and dark-hazel eyes beneath thick, arched brows. If you were into James Bond you'd probably think him good-looking, but Amy instantly felt wary of him.

'My role isn't to duplicate or detract from your work. It's to assist it . . . to assist you,' she replied.

William nodded. 'In addition to raising the profile of CEM, Amy will devise strategies on how we can do the same for our clients. As I explained, I see a gap between Sales and Marketing, and Operations. Amy will work with both departments. It'll be down to her to generate unusual and innovative ideas for product launches, conferences, corporate hospitality and PR, tailored specifically to individual clients.'

Amy continued, 'In a sense the strategic-planning department will be an extension of the client's marketing department. Instead of waiting for them to brief us on what they want, we'll—'

'*Waiting?*' One of Greg's eyebrows shot up. 'We're a very proactive team,' he added, and leaned back in his chair, totally at ease with himself.

That man has a powerful presence, she thought. Even Roger Cummings, the sales and marketing director, Greg's boss, who was sitting to his left, seemed resigned to play second fiddle to him.

'Maybe that was an inappropriate word to use,' she said. 'However, I was merely stating that the aim now is to present to the clients a fuller package, broader ideas on how they can spend their marketing budgets. We'll devise a whole series of events, publicity and PR. In a nutshell, we'll tell them politely what they need to be doing.' She had addressed everyone, but now she focused on Greg: 'Why accept ten per cent of their budget when we could win more?'

His eyes locked on hers, which refused to retreat. Neither moved, blinked or showed any emotion. She guessed she was probably a bit contentious for a first day but, hell, she wasn't going to pander to his or anyone else's delicate ego. When it came to work and business, she felt confident. Relationships might send her a bit wobbly but business grounded her.

William smiled. 'As you know, Amy joins us from Protea Software, another company within the group. As sales and marketing manager, she increased their turnover threefold over three years. She's an ideas person. I'm delighted she's joined us. I believe her contribution to CEM's growth will be considerable. She'll be working closely with all departments but will report directly to me.'

Amy broke eye-contact with Greg and looked at William, who was continuing to talk about her past achievements. Then he went on to his own ideas for the new strategic-planning department. He had warned her that the post for which he had headhunted her might not go down too well with some of the others – they would see her as stepping on their toes. Amy liked

William. He had only been with Centrex Event Management for two years, but he was ambitious and full of ideas to grow the business. He appeared strong, determined and fair. Without his full backing she wouldn't have considered accepting the offer.

She was sitting at one end of the table, wearing her new scarlet suit – a fitted jacket and skirt just above the knee. Her shoulder-length, highlighted blonde hair was blow-dried into a loose bob that curled up at the ends. At five foot seven she was slim, with a narrow, pale face that at times looked drawn. At other times she looked very attractive and she normally wore a large amount of make-up, brown eye shadows and peachy pink lipsticks, plus brown eyeliner to define the size and shape of her large blue, oval eyes.

At Protea she had headed a division of thirteen staff with a turnover of £120 million, but now she was ready for a new challenge – especially with the salary package and share options she had negotiated with William. Plus she wouldn't have to see Simon *ever again*.

'I await these *innovative* ideas with interest,' Greg said, and once again he was smiling at her, yet it was the coldest smile Amy had ever seen.

For the rest of the morning Amy set up her new office with Beth, a girl in her early twenties with long, mousy-brown hair, who had been employed as her secretary. Beth had been with CEM for a week, to learn the internal administration procedures in anticipation of Amy's arrival. Already Amy had a feeling they were going to get on well. Beth was from South London and seemed down-to-earth, organized and intelligent, with a good sense of humour. She drank her tea from a *Star Trek Voyager* mug. It turned out that they were both fans of the television programme and discussed it for a while. '7 of 9' was Amy's hero, emotionally in control.

Later that day William walked Amy round the whole office, which consisted of the top two floors of an eight-storey building just off Piccadilly in central London. He introduced her to every member of staff, fifty in all, of whom at least forty were female, mostly in their twenties and thirties. As usual in the event management and PR industry, everyone was pristinely turned out: beautifully tailored suits, expensive haircuts, flawless skin, nails perfectly manicured, and their teeth were incredibly white – capped, thought Amy. Even the office juniors and postroom assistants looked like they'd just stepped out of the pages of a magazine. And they all spoke with the same plummy accent – as if they'd spent a year at a Swiss finishing school. It was par for the course, thought Amy and she played the game, looking and acting the part also.

In contrast to the lukewarm reception from the management team, these women were over the top in their enthusiasm and sweeter-than-sweet smiles, welcoming her on board.

'We must do lunch,' said several. The word 'supper' came up too.

'I'm Isabel, call me Issy,' said one waif-like creature, in her mid-twenties.

Amy even met a Tinkerbell – could parents really be so cruel? 'Call me Tink,' she said, with a wink.

Extreme confidence oozed from every moisturised and pampered pore. They seemed so perfect. *The Stepford Wives* movie came to Amy's mind, in which living women were secretly replaced by faultless and impeccable robotic doubles. Amy smiled to herself, maybe the same had gone on here. She was used to high standards, but these women seemed a little too perfect to be true.

It was gone nine o'clock by the time Amy walked through her front door. Her tabby cat, George Clooney, trotted over to her and she picked him up to cuddle him. It was a cold February evening but her apartment was always kept warm: she hated the cold.

She lived on the top floor of a large, converted Victorian house in Crystal Palace, South London, which she had purchased three years ago. It was a spacious two-bedroom, split-level apartment. The lower floor was mostly open-plan, with whitewashed wooden floorboards and the original bare red-brick walls; it had been made to look like a New York loft conversion. She even had her own roof garden, filled with ivy and numerous pot plants; it had a stunning view over South London. A cast-iron spiral staircase led up to the bedrooms – one with an *en suite* bathroom. The living room was uncluttered, with few ornaments, personal mementos or even furniture. Apart from two stone-coloured sofas, at either side of an open fireplace, a television, stereo and desk with her laptop on it, there was little else. Some visitors wondered if she'd just moved in – perhaps her belongings were still in transit – but Amy liked it that way, with lots of space to think and relax. Her home was her refuge from the world. Once the door was shut she felt at ease. Her work persona faded and the face she showed to the world softened.

That evening, while George Clooney ate his fresh tuna, Amy had her ready-made Marks & Spencer microwave lasagne. She frequently sipped her glass of wine, which was refilled at intervals. All the while she thought about CEM – in particular, Greg Hamilton-Lawrence: there was something about him that unsettled her.

3

Amy looked up from her desk and saw Greg Hamilton-Lawrence leaning casually against her office door. Out of politeness, she smiled at him.

No smile was returned and, after what appeared to be a deliberate delay, he walked in slowly and sat down opposite her. Raising one eyebrow and with an undertone of amusement he said, 'I've just spoken to William. I understand you'd like to shadow me.'

'It's my intention to shadow someone from every department,' she replied matter-of-factly. 'I want to spend the next two weeks learning everything I can about CEM and how it operates.'

There was a brief silence.

'I'm presenting to a potential client this afternoon. I've been working on a deal.' He leant forward. 'The biggest, in terms of budget, for the whole industry this year.'

'The relaunch of Trans-Global Airlines.'

'*You* know about that?'

'William mentioned something.'

Annoyance flickered across his face but then he relaxed into his chair and smiled. 'You may be asked to submit some of your marketing strategies for the project. The appointment's at four. Thought you might like to tag along. We'll leave here at three. They're in Hammersmith. I'll drive. Sally Roberts, the operations manager, is coming too.'

'I'd love to *tag* along,' she said pointedly.

'That's settled, then. I'll brief you in the car.' He continued to sit there, without saying any more, and looked around the office. Just then Beth glanced up from her typing and caught his eye. Amy was surprised and a little unsettled by the huge beaming smile that the two of them exchanged. He then stood up, nodded at Amy and left.

Through the glass walls of her office, she watched him glide along the corridor and disappear. She didn't trust him, but she had gathered that she was the only person to feel that way. He seemed popular with everyone, men and women. Even William constantly sang his praises. She looked at Beth who had returned to her typing: 'He seems an interesting character,' she said.

'Yes, he's really nice. He took me and Clarissa, the other new girl, out for lunch last week. Sort of a welcome to the company. We really enjoyed it. He's so funny.'

'Hilarious, I'm sure.'

'All the other girls say he's so helpful. You can approach him over anything.'

'Sainthood is calling.'

'It's only your third day and he's already involving you with that huge deal he's been working so hard on,' said Beth.

Amy already knew that William had instructed Greg to take her along. 'So he gets on with everyone, then?'

'Well, there's been the odd person who clashed with him,' she said, 'but apparently they didn't last very long. They always left. They weren't the CEM type.'

Amy eyed her new secretary warily. It occurred to her that Beth seemed different today, less down-to-earth and, for want of a better word, *posh*. She even looked different: she was wearing her hair up, in a Princess Anne style bun.

Maybe my *Stepford Wives* theory is true, thought Amy. Maybe they'd swapped Beth with her robotic double last night. She wondered when they'd be coming for her.

At five to three, Amy was waiting on the leather sofa in Reception. A couple of minutes later Greg appeared. He was carrying his laptop and briefcase, and Sally was at his side. She was an attractive, aloof-looking woman, early forties, with short auburn hair, parted on the side, discerning green eyes and lashings of red lipstick. She was wearing a beautifully cut pinstripe trouser suit. Amy had been introduced to her briefly on Monday. Now Sally beamed a full-on smile at her for precisely two seconds, then as if at the flick of a switch, it vanished. She turned towards the lifts and pressed the button.

Soon the three were walking across the underground car-park, heading for Greg's new BMW. On reaching it, Sally got into the front next to him while Amy sat in the back. A few minutes into the journey Greg looked into the rear-mirror at her. 'How are you settling in?'

'Early days,' she replied.

'It's a great team here. The best.'

'Have you worked for CEM long?'

'Three years, but I've been in corporate hospitality and event management for around eight.'

'You must know the industry well, then.'

'I know every company in it, every event that happens, and pretty much every person too . . . Well, those worth knowing.'

'And you, Sally?'

'Two years here, four within the industry. Greg and I worked together for a competitor. It was his persuasion that brought me to CEM.' Sally shot a coy smile at him, which Amy glimpsed in the wing-mirror.

Matchstick Love 15

She guessed they probably had 'history' together – maybe it was still going on? He's probably got a harem, she thought.

The rest of the journey Greg spent briefing Amy about Trans-Global Airlines, or TGA, as he referred to the company. It was a recent amalgamation of three smaller airlines, Zurich Air, Anglo-Euro Jet and the American UDC. The new company was now the eighth largest airline in the world, with routes to every major European, American and southern hemisphere city. It was officially to be relaunched in June, four months' time, and there would be major television, press and radio commercials, handled by the chosen advertising agencies. To accompany the media campaign the company wanted to set up sixty major presentations and launch parties in most European cities. Travel agents, corporate-travel bookers and executive frequent flyers would be invited to attend, and would learn about the rebranded airline and the quality of service on offer.

That part of the package, which had a ten-million-pound budget, was what CEM was proposing to run.

On arriving at the TGA offices, the three were shown into an immense boardroom on the fourteenth floor, with a huge oval table in the middle, capable of seating at least twenty people. They were a little early, and were left alone to set up the equipment for the presentation.

'Impressive,' said Amy, staring out of the window at West London, sprawled before her.

Greg nodded, but she could see that he was focused on the presentation. He was attaching his laptop to the large television screen at one end of the table and, at the same time, testing Sally on her own presentation. He had gone over it with her in the car too, like a director briefing an actress. Amy had the impression that they had rehearsed it several times already.

Feeling like a spare part she said, 'Can I do anything?'

He glanced up. 'If you really want to help, bat your eyelashes at Mark Greenshawe, the managing director, but make it subtle. He's no fool.'

Amy examined his face, expecting him to laugh but he was serious. 'Have we accidentally gone through some time-warp or is this still the twenty-first century?' she asked.

Equally firmly he replied, 'First rule of selling, Amy: people buy from people. Mark Greenshawe likes pretty women. Good salespeople do whatever it takes. That's my motto, "Whatever it takes".'

'Maybe I should just take off my top and do some lap-dancing. Would that win the deal?'

Greg and Sally exchanged an obvious look of disapproval.

Surprised and angry that another woman didn't back her, Amy asked, 'So do you agree, Sally, that my role here is to flutter my eyelashes?'

With a stare that could kill she replied, 'I agree with Greg. Whatever it takes.'

Amy couldn't deny that she'd done some subtle flirting in the past to win business – she wasn't naïve and knew that people bought from people: that was the whole point of client lunches and entertaining. But for someone else to tell her to act the bimbo – no way! How demeaning! She was probably more experienced at winning contracts than both of them put together. 'That's not the way I operate,' she said determinedly, but neither of them bothered to look up.

Within ten minutes, Janis Halloran and Philip Jones, both senior marketing managers, joined them with

Matchstick Love

Mark Greenshawe. Greg had met them twice before and shook their hands warmly. They seemed genuinely pleased to see him.

Mark Greenshawe was a tall, strongly built American in his fifties, with a commanding presence and a pronounced Texan accent. He reminded Amy of Storming Norman Schwartzkopf.

Janis and Philip were both English. She was a skinny woman in her forties with short-cropped hair and an angular yet pleasant face, while he was studious-looking, brown-haired with narrow-rimmed glasses, probably in his late twenties. Greg introduced Sally immediately, and explained her background and role at CEM. Then his eyes scouted across to Amy. 'Amy has just joined CEM and is learning the ropes. Hope you don't mind if she sits in as an observer.'

Inside Amy fumed as she politely shook the clients' hands. Why hadn't Greg explained *her* position? *Learning the ropes!* She was hardly some schoolkid on work experience. He's done it deliberately, she thought angrily. He's trying to undermine me. She was about to speak up for herself, but decided against it. Always put on a united front for clients. She'd have words with Greg later.

They all sat down and, after some pleasantries over coffee, everyone fell silent and waited expectantly for Greg to begin – including Amy, who had concerns about how he was going to handle it. He got up, dimmed the lights, stood to the left of the large screen and pressed the remote-control in his hand. The first visual came up, showing the structural breakdown of CEM with its parent and sister companies. 'This presentation will cover our preliminary proposal for the events and how CEM will organize and run them. Having our own in-house production company is a huge benefit. They've made my life a lot easier by producing this short film showing our initial set designs and event environment. As the film runs, I'll talk you through it. Afterwards Sally will explain the logistics in more detail, plus the preliminary costs breakdown. As I mentioned, Sally will head the operational team and be responsible for co-ordinating the budgets. At CEM, Sales and Marketing work closely with Operations to ensure an innovative and professional approach to every detail.' He stared disdainfully at Amy as he added, '*Innovative ideas* are our business, and have been for many years.'

Amy got the message, loud and clear.

Greg started the film and spoke at various points. He was full of facts, no waffle. He explained that the production company would construct a dummy plane fuselage, which would be easily dismantled and transported between locations. The guests would be able to see the new interiors, the new seat design with in-built television screens, the spacious leg room and wide gangways. They would even be offered samples from the new five-star menus and carefully selected wines.

Amy had to admit that both he and the short film were impressive. She kept glancing at the clients discreetly. Greg had their full attention. They were obviously impressed too, and she could tell that they liked him. Why *does* everyone like him? she wondered.

After twenty minutes, Sally got up and, also to the backdrop of a short film, showed in more detail the operational side and how CEM would tackle such a large contract.

Towards the end, Amy's eyes met Mark Greenshawe's and she smiled at him. His face softened and he smiled back. Ignoring Greg's suggestion, she looked away, refusing to flirt. After more coffee and various questions from TGA, the meeting ended. Greg arranged with the TGA team that they would visit CEM the week after next and everyone stood up and shook hands.

'We'll have to have a round of golf soon,' said Greg to Mark Greenshawe, who agreed. Mark Greenshawe then turned to Amy and shook her hand slowly. 'Good luck with the new job, young lady. I hope to see you again.' He winked at her, then left.

Young lady, Amy cringed. He sounded like her uncle. She looked at Greg, who was grinning at her.

Back in the car Greg let out a cheer and punched the air. 'Yes!' he yelled. 'Yes, yes, yes!' Then he gave Sally a hug and kissed her cheek. 'You were brilliant, the best.'

'We both were.'

'This deal is ours. I can feel it.'

'Absolutely! They loved us.'

Amy watched them from the back seat and finally said, 'It went well. Very professional and creative.'

As if he had suddenly remembered she was there, Greg turned round and for a second his face grew serious before he smiled politely. 'Thank you.'

'I was however surprised that you didn't explain the reason for my own presence there. First impressions count,' she said.

His smile faded. He turned back and put his key into the ignition. 'I didn't want to confuse the situation at this stage. Obviously *if* we win the contract, and *if* you join the project team, then *of course* I'll explain your illustrious background and position at CEM.'

Amy's face tightened.

He looked at her in the rear-view mirror and again

smiled. 'It went well, Amy. That's all that counts at this stage. Winning the contract. Whatever it takes, remember.'

'I wasn't asking for my ego to be massaged. However, if they develop an incorrect opinion of my role and seniority, my credibility with them later on might be compromised.'

Still smiling away he added calmly, 'It went well. That's all that counts.' He started the car and drove off at speed.

Amy hated his goddamn smile, which said, 'Don't let it worry your pretty little head.' This guy was trouble with a capital T. She began to consider how to handle him. For now she'd bide her time. He was no fool. But neither was she.

4

Ben Brown made his way through Kudos, a busy, modern wine-bar just off Piccadilly Circus and a short walk from the CEM office. He stopped at a table in the corner, where Greg and Daniel were already seated, drinking champagne and laughing. When he saw Ben, Greg pulled the bottle out of the ice bucket and filled the empty glass they'd kept for him. 'Get that down you. You've got some catching up to do,' he said.

Their eyes were glazed and Ben guessed it was the second bottle of the evening. 'Sorry, guys,' he said, sitting down. 'William caught me on the way out. I ended up having to talk Amy Lambert through some client files.'

Greg frowned. 'When I dropped her back in the car park, she said she was heading home. Mark my words, that woman's trouble.'

'Every woman's trouble,' said Daniel. 'Planet Earth is hormone hell.'

All three nodded with subdued resignation and in unison drank some champagne.

'I take it we're celebrating the TGA presentation,' said Ben. He was a stockily built man in his early forties, with dark hair and beard, thick-rimmed glasses and an expanding belly – the result of too many client lunches.

Greg let out a long, satisfied sigh and leant back in his chair. 'It's in the bag. Life's too damn good. What's a man to do when everything he touches turns to gold?' He surveyed the goings-on in the bar. Four girls from CEM were at a table on the other side and one of them,

Tink, caught his eye. She raised her glass to him. Greg raised his in acknowledgement.

'Bit close to home,' Daniel whispered.

'Just window shopping.'

'Said the thief to the judge.'

They exchanging a knowing glance.

'Amy fired a million questions at me. She's certainly on the ball,' said Ben.

Greg's eyes narrowed and with total contempt he said, 'I'm about to win the biggest contract in the whole industry this year. Turnover has increased by twenty-five per cent year on year, profit not far behind, yet William still feels the need to bring in some pretty little ice maiden for some fancy *strategic planning*.'

'Huge salary, I expect. And why have her reporting to him? He's probably giving her one,' said Daniel.

'I expect he'd like to, but I've met her type before – totally focused on work. Career is god. No doubt the cobwebs have set in down below.'

'I wouldn't mind getting my duster to them.'

Greg and Daniel laughed, but Ben rolled his eyes at their schoolboy banter. They were always the same with a few drinks inside them. They had been the best of friends since boarding-school and Greg had got Daniel the job at CEM. Ben accepted that he himself would always be a bit of an outsider.

Soon Greg was scanning the room again. As usual it was brimming with loud, successful, excitable people, having a few drinks after work and overflowing with cocaine-induced happiness. Trendy dance music was playing in the background. He looked back at his colleagues and said despondently, 'Actually, cobwebs in women are a rarity these days. So few pose a decent challenge.'

'*Thank God*,' said Daniel. 'Here's to liberated

women – an endless supply of them. Luckily for us, City girls always say yes.'

Ben felt obliged to join in their laughter, but decided to finish his drink and catch the ten past eight train home. He knew they were up for another long drinking session. He didn't know how they escaped hangovers, but they always seemed to. In fact, most mornings they were in before him, seated at their desks, totally focused and keyed up for the day's work, like cheetahs preparing for the hunt, which was how they approached business. It was also how they approached females.

He wanted to change the subject so mentioned a problem with a contract he was working on. Instantly Greg sat up straight and answered it. Business was his religion, and it was this side of him that Ben liked. He made allowances for his somewhat brutish manner out of office hours.

While Greg and Ben were talking, Daniel was gazing out of the window at the people walking by. 'Look,' he said, interrupting them. Amy Lambert had turned the corner and was walking briskly past them on the opposite side of the street. She was heading towards the tube station and they eyed her long, shapely legs, underneath her short skirt, the sway of her hips and the way her blonde hair swung from side to side.

'Bit close to home.' This time it was Greg whispering into Daniel's ear.

'Cobwebs or not, I wouldn't say no.'

Ben expected them to laugh, but they stared after her until she was out of sight.

'You've got two chances,' said Greg. 'No chance and fat chance.'

'And I suppose you can improve on that,' mocked Daniel.

'If I wanted to. Which I don't.'

'Fuck you.'

Ben sipped his champagne, watching Greg with interest: he found him fascinating. He was a cocky bastard, all right, but he had reason to be. Greg was the best at his job: his sales figures always exceeded his and Daniel's, and even though Ben had been at CEM longer, Greg had been promoted above him. The clients loved him and William thought the sun shone out of his arse.

And, of course, there were the women. They loved him. Even the few who didn't fancy him saw him as a mixture of a loyal brother and supportive father. But they never saw the side of Greg that he and Daniel knew.

'Amy Lambert would never be interested in you. She'd see through you any day,' said Daniel, indicating with a wave to Tom behind the bar that they wanted yet another bottle of champagne.

Greg snorted. 'You give women too much credit. Most are like Plasticine, easily moulded in the right pair of hands. Even the toughest, most independent women have a gene that programmes them to please their man. You just have to know how to access it. What buttons to push, what to say.' He picked up the skiing brochure that he and Daniel had been looking through earlier and flicked through the pages.

Daniel got up and marched off to the gents'.

Ben checked his watch and realised he'd missed his train. He took out his mobile phone, rang his wife, Grace, apologized, told her he'd be on the next one, said a quick hello to his two young daughters, and hung up. Unlike the other two, he had responsibilities. They were single, supposedly, although Greg had an on/off relationship with girl-about-town Miranda, an assistant to the assistant of the deputy production assistant, in some film company that her wealthy father financed. She seemed to spend most of her time lunching with friends, shopping or throwing parties at her exquisite apartment in Knightsbridge – something else Ben guessed her father financed.

Despite his good intentions, two hours later Ben was slumped, bleary-eyed and dazed, on a sofa in a corner of a packed nightclub, with a half-drunk Tequila Sunrise in his hand. He looked at the glass and wondered how many he'd had. Too many. He felt woozy and he couldn't remember where the nightclub was, just that Greg and Daniel had bundled him into the back of a cab and told him not to be so boring and respectable. He didn't even want to look at the time.

Greg was sitting to his left and Daniel was on the dance floor, with a scantily clad French student he had been chatting up. Her friend was sitting alone at another table and kept glancing at Ben and Greg.

'What's up with you tonight? She's giving you an open invitation,' slurred Ben.

'Can't be bothered. Not in the mood. Why don't you go for it?'

Ben frowned. Even in his drunken state he knew Greg was trying to wind him up. He had always been faithful to Grace and was determined to stay that way.

A few minutes later an irritated Daniel collapsed into the chair opposite them. 'She's going home,' he said. 'Says she's got exams this week.'

Greg laughed. 'You've lost your touch, Danny-boy.'

'Bollocks I have.'

'I have to go,' mumbled Ben. 'I really do. Grace will kill me. I've an early meeting with that new woman as well . . . What's her name? Emily Lambert.'

'Amy?' said Greg, sitting up and placing his glass on the table. 'Be careful what you say. I don't trust her. She's got her nose into everything. She's got Beth printing off reports on nearly every event in the history of the company. Women like that won't play ball.'

Daniel folded his arms. 'Aren't you giving her too much credit? I thought you said all women were easily moulded. Why don't you start moulding her? That's unless you're saying she's unmouldable – or maybe *you've* lost your touch. Worse still, perhaps you've met your match.'

Greg looked unmoved. 'Every woman can be moulded. But it takes work and time. Why would I bother? Hopefully she won't be around that long – not if I have anything to do with it.'

'So if you did bother, she'd be putty in your delicate hands?'

'But *why* would I bother?'

Suddenly intense, Daniel leant forward, his eyes glistening.

Greg eyed him suspiciously. Ben sat beside them, rubbing the side of his head and trying to summon the energy to leave.

Daniel started to hum the theme to *Mission Impossible*. 'Your mission, should you decide to accept it . . . is to clear the cobwebs from Ms Amy Lambert.'

Greg laughed. 'Breaks the golden rule – a little too close to home.'

'Makes it more risky. Not averse to that, are you?'

Both men stared, poker-faced, at each other.

Ben looked from one to the other. They were drunk.

They didn't mean it. It would all be forgotten in the morning.

Greg crossed his legs and assumed a businesslike pose, the way he looked when he was striking a deal. 'I sleep with her just once, right?'

Daniel inclined his head. 'Yes.'

'I'd need some time.'

'Two weeks.'

'Three. This could take some strategic planning.' Their guffaw revealed that the irony hadn't escaped them.

'This is awful,' Ben protested. 'Even for you two.'

Greg ignored him. 'You still haven't answered my question – why I should bother?'

'Name the stake,' said Daniel.

Greg gazed into the distance pensively. Then his eyes fell to the skiing brochures. 'The loser pays for the other's skiing trip,' he said.

Daniel hesitated. Then he held out his hand. 'Agreed.'

'This is disgusting,' said Ben angrily. 'Count me out. It's juvenile. You're mad. You're drunk. Can't you go back to daring each other to jump out of planes or abseil down mountains?'

'There are only so many mountains in the world. Fortunately there are more women,' said Daniel.

'I want nothing to do with it. I'm off.' Ben stumbled up, holding on to the table for support. He stared hard at his colleagues. 'This had better be forgotten in the morning.'

They watched him stagger across the dance-floor and through the door on the opposite side of the club.

'He's right. It is disgusting,' stated Greg.

'Completely,' agreed Daniel.

They nodded at each other seriously, but gradually broad smiles appeared on both their faces.

Greg held out his hand. 'Three weeks.'

Daniel shook it. 'Three weeks.'

5

Amy tutted loudly. Who the hell did that belong to? She had pulled her Saab into the car-park at the front of her home and an old motorbike was in her parking space. This was not a good start to the evening. All she wanted to do was get into a hot bath with a large glass of wine and forget about CEM – especially Greg Hamilton-Lawrence.

As a temporary measure she parked in the visitor's space and was walking towards the entrance porch when a tall, scruffy, lanky man with a mass of dark blond curly hair and an unkempt beard came out. He looked like Robinson Crusoe: unwashed, unshaved, wearing ripped jeans and a faded black sweatshirt. In the dark he didn't see her and he headed straight for the battered motorbike.

'Excuse me, that's my parking space you're in,' she shouted.

He stopped and turned to face her. He had a wilful look in his eye, which unsettled her. 'Parking's just for residents,' she added, refusing to be intimidated.

He started to walk over to her. Amy wondered what he was going to do. He looked around forty and appeared wilder than a feral tomcat.

He stopped a couple of feet from her. Underneath his mass of floppy curls he had the most incredibly deep blue, crystal eyes, which appeared slightly glazed. He was either a crazed psychopath or high on drugs, she thought.

He gave a nod. 'Hello, I'm John. I've just moved into number two,' he said in an exceptionally well-spoken voice.

My God! He's the new neighbour, thought Amy. What was Helen playing at? Surely there were more suitable candidates to let your apartment to – like someone who combed their hair and washed occasionally. This guy looked like some drug-dealing hippie. Not that she minded smoking the occasional joint, but she didn't want a dealer living downstairs. Why not a handsome, wealthy young barrister?

With a guarded smile Amy shook his hand. 'Hi, I'm Amy. Welcome to the house. If you need anything . . .'

'Thank you.' He looked at her car. 'Which space is mine?'

She pointed to an empty space with a large number two painted in white across the Tarmac. 'They're all numbered. Apartment two has bay two. Apartment three, bay three, and so on. The V stands for visitor. We try to leave it empty. The gas meters over there are numbered as well. Same with the electric ones, just inside the hall.'

He was looking at her very strangely as she went on to tell him that the wheelie-bins at the back were also numbered – apart from the green one, which was for recycling: they all shared that one. 'It keeps things organized,' she said. 'Everything to do with you has the number two on it.'

'Thankfully I'm not number dyslexic. Are new tenants tested and graded?' he enquired wryly.

She was unsure how to take him – and the next moment he saluted her as if she was his commanding officer, then turned sharply on the spot and walked over to his motorbike. After several attempts at starting it, he rode off, giving her a nod as he went by.

What an odd bloke, she thought. He's probably anti-establishment. How clichéd! No doubt his parents are stinking rich. How extra-clichéd! As soon as he was out of sight she moved her car into her own bay. She liked everything in its right place.

As Amy walked into the communal hall, Tessa opened her ground-floor apartment door and beckoned her in with a wave. 'I've started on the wine. Care to join me?'

'Love to.' Amy followed her inside. Tessa disappeared into the kitchen and Amy sat down on the yellow sofa in her living room. The walls were covered with Buddhist tapestries and African paintings, multi-coloured rugs were strewn over the orange-painted floorboards, the shelves were full of crystals, and wind chimes hung from the ceiling. Sweet-smelling incense filled the air. It was too unconventional for Amy's taste but then Tessa was hardly conventional.

They had been neighbours for three years and in that time the two women had become good friends. Because of Tessa's 'little problem', as she referred to it, she didn't have many friends. In fact, apart from Amy and Hilda, another neighbour upstairs, and Derek, her meditation tutor from the holistic centre up the road, there was no one else.

Tessa came out of the kitchen with two glasses of red wine and handed one to Amy. 'You met him, then?' she said, sitting down cross-legged in a yoga style position on the floor. She was an unusual-looking woman: small, pleasantly plump with a smiley face and short, reddish-ginger curly hair – a bit like a forty-year-old Orphan Annie, possessing a child-like innocence about her.

'Who? Robinson Crusoe?' said Amy.

'I believe his name is John Smith.'

'Don't tell me *you* spoke to him?'

Tessa looked fraught. '*No!* Of course not. But he did knock. Must have wanted to borrow something. I pretended I was out. I hope he doesn't think me rude but you know I couldn't answer it.'

Amy nodded reassuringly.

'Hilda was chatting with him. She popped in later and filled me in. Apparently he's just back from Nepal and India. Spent three weeks there.'

Definitely a drug-dealer, thought Amy. 'Did she say what he does for a job?'

'It sounded like she did most of the talking. She said she was telling him about everyone in the house.'

Amy winced. 'Oh, no, I can just imagine it. Probably described me as a powerful career woman, wealthy, independent, but morally corrupt.'

Tessa laughed. 'God knows what she said about me then! Mentally unstable, institution case.'

'At least no men stay the night here, not like the den of iniquity that she thinks my apartment is.' Amy rolled her eyes. 'If only.'

'What's he like?' asked Tessa excitedly.

Amy shrugged her shoulders. A new neighbour was of no great interest to her, but Tessa's life was a lot less busy – very limited, in fact – so she said, 'All I know is he's a well-spoken, scruffy guy with unnerving eyes, who rides a beat-up motorbike.'

'You should do the neighbourly thing and invite everyone up for drinks to meet him.'

'Why me? Why not Hilda and Thomas? They're the Christians. Love thy neighbour and all that. In my book neighbours are for tolerating not loving. Apart from you, of course.'

'Oh, go on, please.'

'What's it to you? You wouldn't come anyway,' said Amy.

Tessa bit her lip. 'Derek thinks I need to start pushing myself more. He's drawn up a little list of things I need to face. An evening like that is one of them. It's totally terrifying, but it's only upstairs so I could leave at any time. It would be a little experiment.'

Amy looked at her supportively. It was true, Tessa did need to start pushing herself more. Amy had been urging her to do that for ages. Over the last year Tessa had hardly gone anywhere or done anything. There was the holistic centre where she was always enrolling on some quirky course and receiving some form of therapy, but her phobia was getting worse. Each therapist labelled it differently and concluded that a different set of factors had caused it. Over the years it had left Tessa with a broad knowledge of psychology – she seemed to know more than the actual therapists. However even with all the therapy and knowledge, Tessa's 'social phobia', as Derek calls it, was still affecting her. Finding herself in the company of anyone new, or in a busy place like a supermarket, or indeed in any social situation, especially where she felt trapped, resulted in her having terrible panic attacks.

Amy didn't really understand it. She saw Tessa's problem as a fear of people, and to Amy, people weren't worth being scared of. She was the opposite to Tessa. There were lots of things in her own past that, if inclined, she could look into, but she wasn't that sort of person: life was for getting on with. Of course, sometimes it was a battle, but you just had to arm yourself and fight your corner. It worked for her, anyway.

'I'm not sure he'd come. I think I offended him by telling him he was in my parking space,' said Amy.

'All the more reason to invite him. Plus it would be helping me. I'd really appreciate it.'

'Maybe I'll organize something for next week. But you'd better bloody come. An evening with Hilda and the others isn't my idea of fun.'

'I'll be there. How long I stay is another matter,' said Tessa, pulling her trademark fretful expression.

For the next hour they drank wine, ate home-made pizza and chatted. Even with her problems Tessa could still laugh at life. 'Any word from Simon Delaney, the king of commitment phobics?' she asked.

Amy sneered. 'Susan from Accounts told me he's dating the new receptionist, nineteen and just out of college. No cellulite but no sense either.'

'He's *already* seeing someone else!'

'I know. I hate it when that happens. It's like you never existed. You're just in a long line of women, filling time with them. Come in, number twenty-seven, your time is up.' Amy shook her head. 'She's very pretty but rather dim.'

'Dim is good. They're not taxing. After you he's probably having a break.'

'I'm *not* taxing,' stated Amy defensively. A moment later asking in a meeker voice, 'Am I?'

'Only in the sense that you're intelligent and complex. Unfortunately that's not always what a man's looking for.'

'So *that's* where I'm going wrong. I should be more dim.'

'Afraid so. When it comes to men, dim is most definitely good.'

Both women laughed.

A little later Tessa asked how the new job was going.

'Pretty good. I'm excited about the industry. There'll be a lot of travelling, mostly around Europe . . . Florence, Venice, Barcelona.'

'Seems a cushy number to me, organizing parties around the world.'

'There's lots of pressure, constant deadlines. The logistics for some of these events are incredible. Bottom line, it's all about generating more business. Big money demands big results.'

Tessa gazed downwards, her shoulders becoming heavy and round. 'You're so capable and brave. I wish I were more like you. Nothing fazes you.'

'That's not true. I just love business, doing deals, winning contracts.' She paused. 'There is something that concerns me – or rather someone. Greg Hamilton-Lawrence,' she said his name in a mocking tone. 'He's so threatened by my presence, it's ridiculous. He's out to make my life difficult.' She shook her head and her eyes narrowed, becoming unattractively severe. 'But the thing he doesn't realise is?' Her voice lowered an octave. 'I'm used to winning and if he crosses me, he'll come off worst.'

6

Amy was standing backstage, watching the comic Alan Davies go through his routine. Several times she burst into laughter. She'd seen him twice before and had been thrilled to discover that he was the post-dinner entertainment and compère for the awards ceremony that evening.

The corporate audience loved him. Obviously he'd been briefed on the internal affairs and gossip of Henson Insurance because he was cracking jokes about some of the directors, which were going down a storm with the staff.

Henson Insurance was one of Ben's clients and he had offered to take Amy along for the day so that she could see how CEM operated. He was standing next to her, glancing discreetly into the audience to check their reaction. There were a hundred and fifty guests mostly eight to a table within the magnificent eighteenth-century ballroom at Burbage Manor House, just outside Hemel Hempstead. 'They love him,' he whispered to Amy.

She nodded politely but was trying not to miss the punchline of a story Alan Davies was telling.

'I should hope so, for the amount we're paying him.' The voice was smooth, confident.

Amy spun round. It was Greg, and he smiled at her as a roar of laughter filled the room. Damn, she'd missed the end after all.

'Didn't expect you here tonight,' Ben said to Greg.

'Thought I'd show my face.' He whispered into Amy's ear, 'Could have got him for a quarter of the fee before he did *Jonathan Creek*.'

'That's the capitalist free market for you. Didn't think you'd disapprove.'

'Disapproving of capitalism is like disapproving of oxygen. The human race won't survive without either.'

She didn't respond – Alan Davies was much more interesting.

Greg smiled to himself, then turned and indicated for Ben to follow him.

Amy relaxed a little and propped herself against the wall. It had been a long day and she was tired. She had arrived on-site at eight this morning and it was now nine in the evening. The staff of Henson Insurance had spent the day on team-building exercises either in the manor house or outside in the grounds. There had been archery, clay-pigeon shooting, go-karting, four-wheel buggy races and a hilarious scavenger hunt.

The black-tie dinner and Alan Davies's forty-minute routine had followed.

CEM, and their usual suppliers, had organized the day and Sally had headed the operational team of five girls who had ensured that the contractors worked to plan. So far everything had gone perfectly. The team had included the excitable and exuberant Tink and Issy. Their sweeter than sweet smiles had never left their faces and by the evening, their makeup hadn't smudged or faded, every hair was exactly in place and not one perfectly manicured, painted nail had chipped. They hadn't even stopped for lunch.

'Aren't you hungry?' Amy had asked, feeling a complete wimp as she ate a sandwich.

Wide-eyed, waif-like Issy, flashed a white smile at her. 'We'll have a huge supper tonight.'

Tink nodded several over the top times then gave her usual wink of her eye.

Five peas and a carrot, thought Amy. And that's between them.

However, she had to admit that the CEM women were professional and efficient.

Within an hour the awards ceremony was over and Alan Davies was standing in the main entrance hall signing autographs and having his picture taken with various guests. Amy stood in a doorway opposite, watching him from a distance. Part of her wanted to go over, but she considered it tacky and embarrassing to ask for an autograph. Also, celebrities in real life were never as nice as you imagined them.

'Not queuing to shake his hand?'

She suddenly looked up and saw Greg standing a couple of feet away from her with a glass of wine in his hand. She shook her head wondering how long he'd been there.

'Can I get you a drink?' he asked.

She eyed him with a degree of caution, but eventually nodded and followed him into the kitchens where the staff were busy clearing up.

'White okay?' he asked, as he took a new bottle out of one of the huge chill cabinets.

'Fine.' It was her first alcoholic drink that day so she didn't care what it was.

As he opened the bottle she couldn't help noticing the label. Pouilly Fumé. Puzzled, she glanced to where some waitresses were opening several more bottles. It was the same wine. 'That's odd,' she said. 'The quotation from the catering company stated Pouilly Fuissé.'

Greg poured her a glass and handed it to her without comment.

'Ben showed me the client file this morning. There's at least two or three pounds difference between the two wines,' she went on, 'this being the cheaper.'

Unfazed, Greg topped up his own glass. 'I expect the budget got cut at the last minute. Happens all the time.'

Amy took a sip. It was still a good wine, and very welcome.

'You don't need to concern yourself with technicalities like that. I don't. Operations take care of all those boring details. We win the business and take the glory.' He beamed mischievously and, carrying his own glass and the bottle, gestured to her to follow him. He led her past the kitchens, through a side door and down a narrow, winding staircase. At the bottom Amy found herself in a long, cramped corridor with a low ceiling and several doors leading off it. She guessed this must have been the servants' quarters years ago – small and poky with little natural light. 'What are we doing down here?' she asked.

'I want to show you something. It's just along here.'

The corridor ran the length of the house, twisting and turning; it still had the original polished brown tiles. She felt uneasy to be there, especially alone with Greg Hamilton-Lawrence. 'Are we supposed to be here?' she asked.

'Sir John won't mind. I've got to know him quite well with all the events we do here. Anyway, he's away with his family until next week.'

Even so, Amy felt as if she was trespassing, and was considering turning back when Greg stopped in front of some double doors. He tried the handle. 'Good, it's open.' He disappeared inside, into total darkness.

Amy held the doors ajar to let in some light, but she couldn't see further than a few feet. In the distance she heard his footsteps, switches being pressed and the room lit up. She gasped at the sight of a huge rectangular swimming-pool, at least forty metres long, with two circular Jacuzzi pools at diagonal corners. The room was decorated like an ancient Roman bathhouse with a delicately patterned mosaic marble floor and frescos painted over the arched ceiling. Luscious tropical plants grew everywhere and life-size white marble statues of naked women stood in alcoves. A stone bridge crossed the width of the pool leading to a bar and seating area where four white sofas surrounded a large circular fountain of three cherubs at play, spouting water in every direction.

Greg was standing at the edge of the pool. 'Fancy a swim?' he said, with a glint in his eye.

Amy raised an eyebrow.

He crouched down and dropped his hand into the perfectly still water, running it up and down several times, as if caressing it gently, which caused a minor ripple effect. 'It's warm, just like a bath.' He stood up, walked over the bridge and sat down on one of the white leather sofas next to the bar.

Still wondering why he had brought her there, she followed him across the bridge and sat beside him on the sofa, crossing her legs and folding her arms. 'This is a bit different from the rest of the house,' she said.

'It's the new wing, where the family live.'

'Should we be here?'

'Relax. I told you they're away. If it wasn't for companies like CEM, most of these old manor houses would have fallen into ruin. New money rescues old.' He was surveying his surroundings as if they were his own. 'So, have you enjoyed your day?' he asked, swinging himself around to face her fully.

'I've attended numerous events like this before, so it's nothing new.'

'I love this industry. I love working for CEM. Never a dull moment. Once you get to know everyone, I expect you'll like it too.' He glanced downwards, seeming to hesitate. Then he stared directly into her eyes and said, 'Look . . . about the last few days. If I've been a bit off, it's nothing personal. I'm just incredibly serious about my job. It's everything to me. Winning the deal, getting the business. Maybe you're like that too.' He gave her a shy smile.

Disarmed by his little speech she said, 'I'm no threat to anyone here, Greg. I'm happy being a team-player. I was surprised that you seemed so unsettled by my appointment.' 'Unsettled' was the most diplomatic word she could find.

'As I said, it's nothing person. I just don't see the need for a strategic-planning department. You can plan all you like but the bottom line is, in this business you just have to get out and meet people.'

'Surely there's a need for both? Can't we work together?'

'But why should you report to William? You should be part of Sales and Marketing.'

'Reporting to you?' she said, with a half-smile. 'That's what really put your nose out of joint, isn't it?' she said.

'I suppose my ego didn't appreciate it.'

Amy was amazed by his candour. Fancy a man admitting he'd got an ego.

'However,' he continued, 'egos aren't confined to men.' Then he raised his glass. 'A little late, but welcome to CEM. I wish you all the best. If I can help in any way, just let me know.'

'Thanks,' she said, relieved, but somewhat suspicious of the change in his attitude.

Greg flopped back on the sofa and gazed at the

ceiling. 'I could spend hours looking at this. Each section represents a different story from the bible. Old Testament of course. Hell, fire and damnation, that's the most interesting bit. None of the "turn the other cheek" namby-pamby stuff.'

'Revenge and burning people at the stake,' she said wryly.

'Only women who step out of line.' Before she could respond he laughed, then added, 'That's my favourite picture, Samson and Delilah.'

Amy looked to where he was pointing and saw a huge depiction of a man in chains, his shorn hair lying on the floor, flanked by two soldiers. His expression was a mixture of shock, bewilderment, hurt and anger. A curvaceous woman, in low-cut robes, was standing beside him, smiling triumphantly.

'When his hair was cut, his physical strength went too,' said Greg, reflectively.

'I'm familiar with the story.'

'He trusted her and she betrayed him.'

Amy examined Greg's stern expression. It was as if he was accusing her of something. 'Well, that's women for you,' she said. 'You can't trust any of us.'

Fleetingly his stare intensified but then he sipped his wine and his eyes turned back to the now perfectly still blue water.

What an unusual character, Amy thought, and ran her hand through her hair.

They sat there for some time, gazing out across the pool. The sound of running water from the fountain was soothing. It was a peaceful place and Amy felt in no rush to leave. Occasionally they chatted about work or commented on their surroundings, and both seemed comfortable with the silences. While topping up Amy's glass for a third time, Greg said, 'So, you don't fancy that swim? It might be fun.'

'No, thank you, but you go ahead. I'll watch.'

'A spectator not a participant?'

'Depends on the activity.'

'No, it doesn't. There are two types of people in this world, those who spectate and those who have the balls to participate. Which type are you, Amy Lambert?'

'Pigeon-holing is so restrictive, I find. Don't you?'

His dark-hazel eyes narrowed. 'Which are you tonight?'

'If it's swimming, I'll watch. But please go ahead. Don't be shy,' she said, a note of challenge in her voice.

'Shy isn't in my vocabulary.' He took off his jacket and laid it carefully over the back of the sofa. With his eyes locked on hers, he loosened his tie, pulled it off and let it slide through his fingers on to the sofa beside her.

Amy forced herself not to show any sign of discomfort. If this was some sort of bizarre 'call my bluff', she'd call it. At the same time she wondered how far he'd strip down.

He undid the top button of his shirt, then the next, and had soon revealed his broad, muscular chest, which was lightly covered with dark hair.

Unconsciously Amy was holding her breath.

'Thought I'd find you here.' It was Ben: he'd come in without them noticing. 'I'm heading off now, Amy,' he called, from the other side of the pool.

She was unsure whether to be relieved or disappointed.

'Finish your wine,' said Greg. 'I'll drop you back.'

'No need. I'll go with Ben.' With one eyebrow raised and looking him up and down with deliberate indifference she said, 'Enjoy your swim.' Then, without looking back, she walked assuredly over the stone bridge, feeling Greg's eyes on her. 'I'll just get my things together,' she told Ben.

'I'll see you by the car.'

As soon as she had gone Ben walked across to Greg and stopped, shifting uneasily from one foot to the other.

Greg was now reclining on the sofa, with his wine. 'Is something up, Benny-boy? You look decidedly uncomfortable.'

'She's nice, Amy. I got to know her a bit today.'

'I was hoping to get to know her myself, before you came bursting in.'

Ben glared at him, then remembered that Greg was his manager and straightened his face. 'The other night . . .' he began.

'What about it?'

'You know . . . the bet thing.'

'Forget it. We were drunk. Go home to Grace.'

Ben's eyelids lowered. 'I'll see you Monday, then.'

'I expect so.'

Once he was alone Greg stood up and took a deep breath, outstretching his arms and smiling broadly. A few moments later he removed his shirt, shoes and socks. Then, as if undressing for a bath at home, he pulled off his trousers and finally his boxer shorts. Completely naked now, he stood at the edge of the pool. His body was toned from all the sports he did: rugby, squash, tennis, and occasionally, soccer. He breathed in deeply, then let out a burst of laughter, which echoed off the walls. The next moment he dived into the pool and swam the length under water.

7

'*I am relaxed around people. There is nothing to fear about people. I am relaxed around people. There is nothing to fear about people.*' Tessa repeated her mantra to herself several times, twisting her front-door key through her fingers as if it were a set of worry-beads.

'How are you feeling dear?' boomed Hilda, with a patronizing and over-sympathetic expression on her face. It was the third time she'd asked in the last twenty minutes.

Tessa felt everyone's eyes on her. She gave a quick jerk of her head.

'Have a mushroom vol-au-vent. I made them myself.' Hilda shoved the plate under her nose. She was a large woman in her early sixties with a round, chubby face, curly grey hair and pointed blue spectacles.

Tessa shook her head and glanced at Amy, who was in the kitchen area opening a bottle of wine.

Amy smiled at her. She could see that Tessa was anxious but tonight's drinks party had been down to her – it was hardly Amy's idea of fun. Thomas, Hilda's husband, a retired civil servant and the resident doom-and-gloom merchant, was discussing the local crime rate with Steve – or, rather, lecturing him about it. Steve hadn't spoken much so far. He never did. He was a man in his late twenties, with cropped hair and the physique of a beefy builder. Surprisingly he had the voice of a choirboy, and was a nurse in the gynaecology department of the local hospital. Call her old-fashioned, but Amy had decided to have her smear tests done privately when she'd discovered that.

Steve was already on his third can of lager. He had turned up with eight and Amy knew that as soon as they were gone he'd make his excuses and leave. Unless he was working, he spent every evening in the pub getting drunk, but he was never loud or a nuisance and kept himself to himself.

Amy looked at them all – such a bunch of oddballs: two devout Christians, who spent half their lives in church and the other half judging the decrepit state of the world, an alcoholic, a social phobic – and then there's me, she thought. Perfectly normal! She laughed to herself. *I just hide it better.*

They had gathered in her apartment to welcome John Smith, the new neighbour – he was already half an hour late.

'Maybe he got lost on the stairs.' Hilda chuckled at her little joke, then sipped her sherry.

'Maybe he forgot,' said Thomas. 'Reliability is a trait sadly lacking in the young today.'

Amy sat down next to Tessa. 'He's probably too embarrassed about the fishnet stockings,' she muttered under her breath.

Tessa smiled, and for a second she looked a couple of degrees less than terrified.

Apart from Tessa, Amy had decided to keep her second meeting with John Smith to herself. She still wasn't sure that she believed his explanation.

Last Saturday evening she had knocked on his door to invite him to tonight's gathering. When it opened she had been stunned by what greeted her: two women, dressed from head to toe in black leather underwear, skimpy knickers, uplift bras, suspenders, stockings and stilettos. Their faces were plastered in Gothic-style makeup and one even held a whip. On seeing Amy they burst out laughing.

Matchstick Love

Amy stood, mouth wide open and eyes lowered, embarrassed at having obviously intruded on *something*. She wasn't sure what. Maybe the new guy was a pimp as well as a drug-dealing hippie.

'We thought you were someone else,' the blond one said, giggling and hiding herself behind the door.

'Is that Paul?' said a man's voice from the bedroom. The next moment, John Smith strode out in a tatty brown dressing-gown, but underneath Amy could see that he had on black fishnet stockings through which sprouted a mass of blond hairs. He stopped dead in his tracks, gasped loudly and pulled an agonized expression.

She manufactured a polite smile. 'I'll pop back another time,' she said, and backed away.

'*Wait!*' He followed her out into the corridor. 'There's a very plausible reason for my attire.'

'I don't need an explanation – people are who they are. What goes on behind closed doors is no one's business but your own. I've lived in London long enough not to judge people,' she said, rather pompously.

He was looking at her as though she were the strange one and he'd walked in on some orgy of hers. His crystal blue eyes seemed to penetrate right through her. 'How noble of you not to judge,' he said sarcastically.

She huffed indignantly and began to climb the stairs.

'Was there something you wanted?' he called after her.

Again she stopped and looked back at him. Did she really want this man in her apartment? 'I was inviting you for drinks, to meet the rest of the house. Thursday night in my apartment.'

He looked taken aback. 'Oh. I thought maybe you'd come to tell me I'd broken a house rule. Used the wrong bin or something.'

The ghost of a smile curved her lips.

'I'll be there,' he said, and added an afterthought, 'Thank you.'

'Around eight, casual dress.' She went up two steps, turned and with an amused glint in her eye said, 'Fishnets optional.' His whole face lit up when he laughed, she saw.

As she reached the first landing she heard him shout, '*Rocky Horror Show*. Free tickets. Attending under duress. Apparently you're supposed to dress up.'

'Yeah, right,' she shouted down, and giggled.

Now Amy checked her watch again, and wondered where he was. Surely he'd turn up.

Thomas was relating the grim details of yet another mugging that had occurred a couple of miles away. She was surprised that he and Hilda ever ventured outside – but apart from going to church and the supermarket, they rarely did. Their lives were as limited as Tessa's. No wonder the occasional man staying over at Amy's place was such a talking-point.

She could hear Tessa's short and stifled breathing beside her. She glanced sideways at her and saw that her face was completely flushed and her eyes appeared dazed and stunned looking. She was obviously engulfed in fear.

'Try to relax, Tessa,' she said.

'Not sure I'm up to this tonight,' Tessa choked out. 'I don't feel well.'

Amy considered carefully what to say. Any pressure and Tessa would be out of the door before you could say mushroom vol-au-vent. 'You can leave at any time,' she said. 'You're doing great.'

Tessa bit her lip and glanced at the door.

'What's next on your target list from Derek?' Amy asked.

'Getting on a crowded bus and starting a conversation with someone.'

'Not a good idea in South London,' Amy observed. 'No one talks to strangers on buses. You never know what nut you're sitting next to.'

'I'm the nut, Amy.'

'You have issues, that's all. Truly nutty people don't know they have issues, but you do so you're only half nutty.' Amy smiled expecting Tessa to smile also, but she just nodded and looked away.

'Mushroom vol-au-vent, anyone?' said Hilda standing up and offering the plate around.

Everyone politely shook their heads, except Thomas who took a couple.

'Did you hear about that old pensioner and her drug-addict grandson who robbed all her savings?' he said, eyes shining with something akin to excitement. Amy gulped down her wine and topped up her glass again. Steve had the right idea: alcohol was the only way to get through this.

An hour later, the new oddball still hadn't arrived. In his absence, and at Hilda and Thomas's instigation, the existing oddballs resorted to a game of Charades. With a bottle of wine inside her and competitive by nature, Amy guessed the majority correctly.

'His absence speaks volumes,' said Thomas, a while later. 'Manners are lacking.'

Amy stumbled over to her window and looked down into the car-park. 'His bike's still not there.'

'What a shame,' said Hilda, who was still only half-way through her first sherry. 'I was looking forward to getting to know him. It's important to know one's neighbours.'

Steve was on his eighth can of lager and had hardly spoken all night.

'Another drink?' Amy asked him. She'd bought some cans herself.

'No, thanks. I have to be off soon,' he whispered.

At least, as the evening progressed, Tessa had relaxed. She was pleased that she'd managed to stay so long and murmured to Amy, 'I can always meet John another time.'

'Not in my apartment. I won't be doing this again.'

Within another half-hour everyone had gone except Tessa, who was celebrating her triumph with another glass of wine. She and Amy sat on the sofa finishing off the garlic bread that no one had touched – a whole loaf each.

'We're going to stink tomorrow,' said Amy. 'I'm presenting a report to the MD. He'll need a gas mask.'

'How's it been this week?'

'Everyone's been a lot friendlier to me, even Greg. It was strange. When he changed towards me, everyone else did too. Maybe it's a coincidence.'

'Sounds odd, though.'

'I know, but he's been really helpful the last few days.'

'Married?'

Amy frowned. 'No, but I'm not interested in him like that. And where did that come from? I told you, no more office affairs.'

Tessa rolled her eyes.

'What?'

'Well, look at you. You're strong, independent, intelligent and you know what you want, but men are your Achilles heel.'

'No, they're not. I don't have an Achilles heel.'

'We all do. You're just in denial. You want to feel like you're in control all the time.'

'But I am.'

'An illusion, Amy. Nobody's in control. We can't control anything.'

Amy screwed her face up. 'You're going all psychological on me again, regurgitating all that therapy stuff. Earth calling Tessa . . .'

'Just be careful.'

'There's nothing to be careful about.'

Tessa stared at her as if she was debating whether to add something but eventually she dropped her eyes and bit into another piece of garlic bread.

Later that night, some time after twelve, Amy was sitting up in bed and rereading her report for work the next day. She wanted to impress William so everything had to be exactly right. She was just about to switch off her bedside lamp when she heard a car pull into the carpark. She got out of bed and peered out of the window. A police car. The next minute the rear door opened and John Smith got out. He walked towards the front door, giving the occupants of the car a wave as it drove off. Then he disappeared inside.

Amy stood at the window for several more moments before she got back into bed. What was going on? Who *was* their new neighbour? Maybe he'd got busted for pimping or drug-dealing. Or maybe he was an undercover cop – or maybe even they were bent cops and John had supplied the girls and drugs for some police orgy. Then again maybe I've got an overactive imagination. She switched off her light and resolved to find out more about the mysterious John Smith.

8

'How is the Strategic Planning department this morning?' Greg was standing in Amy's office doorway, smiling at her.

'Fine, thank you,' she said. Actually, she had a headache and was popping Polos every ten minutes, paranoid that she stank of garlic.

'I'm fine, too, thank you,' said Beth, beaming at him.

In an overly formal manner he said, 'I'm here with an invitation. Sales and Marketing would like to invite Strategic Planning out for drinks this evening at Kudos.'

'Strategic Planning will confer and get back to you,' Amy said with mock disinterest.

'I'll take that as a yes, then. Six o'clock, and as it's Friday, no running off early.' He left.

Amy stared after him for a moment, then went back to the report she was preparing.

Her meeting with William was planned for eleven that morning and at ten forty-five, he walked into her office and dropped a bombshell. 'I've asked Roger, Greg and Sally to sit in. Your suggestions will have a knock-on effect on their departments.'

Amy was startled. 'My report is more of a discussion document at this stage. Shouldn't we wait until concrete proposals have been agreed between you and I before involving them?'

'They should be included in the discussion. That will speed everything along. Unfortunately I'm under pressure for results. Having a European finance house as a parent company is a recipe for high blood pressure. They want more profit from the group – and *fast*.' He smiled. 'I never said the job would be easy, Amy. See you in the boardroom.'

As soon as he had left, Amy leant back in her chair. A number if not all of her proposals might be deemed controversial, and with a hangover she wasn't in the best form to defend herself. Normally she liked a good battle, but not today.

At least she had William's backing, and she understood the pressure he was under: she had met Pablo Russolph, the MD of Lazlo Manco, the parent company, a few times through her work at Protea. Even though Protea's turnover and profit had increased considerably, Pablo was never satisfied. He had dismissed or downgraded a number of MDs for lacklustre performance. To him the share price was God. Luckily he saw Amy as a rising star.

Amy made an effort to pull herself together. 'You'd better print off three more copies of my report,' she told Beth. 'And don't get too excited about the drink tonight with Sales and Marketing. After they've heard what I've got to say, they may want to reconsider their invitation.'

Within fifteen minutes she was seated at the boardroom table, with William and Roger opposite. She could hear Greg and Sally walking up the corridor, chatting and laughing. On entering the room they became silent and sat down.

Amy glanced at each of them in turn and smiled, then spoke in a calm, confident manner: 'By way of an introduction, William asked me to put together an initial report, listing ways to grow the business and increase profitability.' She paused to allow her words to sink in. 'I have produced what I would call a discussion document. More detailed research is required on each area before any points are implemented. I would ask, however, that you all keep an open mind. Changes to the way CEM operates at present are necessary.' Both Sally and Roger twitched at the word 'change', but Greg sat perfectly still.

'I had expected this meeting to be a one-on-one with William, so I haven't prepared slides or a formal presentation. Therefore I'll read through each point and gauge your initial reaction. You'll all be given a copy of the report to take away. Thereafter I suggest a meeting next week when each point can be thrashed out and decisions made.'

Amy began to list her suggestions, with a brief justification for each. She mentioned the necessity for a better corporate image, improvements to the web pages, press releases for all events, selective advertising accompanied by editorial write-ups – she had a number of media contacts who would be willing to write some articles on the company.

Everyone listened and made an occasional comment. This was the easy bit, thought Amy. Wait till they hear what's coming.

'CEM needs to be a one-stop shop,' she started. 'At the moment we're losing business.' She gave examples of where clients had used CEM for a conference but a competitor for corporate hospitality.

'Is it really feasible to try to do everything?' asked Greg in an exceedingly friendly voice, as if he'd hate to upset her.

'It's true that we need to decide what our core activities are. However, if we can't organize, say, a day at the races, we should act as a third-party broker, branding someone else's package. We can't let our competitors have an inroad into *our* clients,' she replied.

'Easier said than done,' grumbled Roger.

What a negative comment from a sales and marketing director, Amy thought. How could he inspire anyone? No wonder Greg did his own thing. 'I never said it would be easy,' she reminded him, 'but it needs to be a definite aim of the company and implemented immediately.' She paused for a couple of moments, bracing herself for any hostility towards her next proposal.

'Pricing.'

'What *about* pricing?' interrupted Sally, her lips pinched. It was she who presently controlled the majority of budgets.

'I believe we need better control of it.'

Sally glared at her.

Amy continued: 'The profit margin on similar projects varies enormously. Some events had a large turnover but brought in a net profit of only five thousand.'

'Every client's budget is different,' said Greg.

'That doesn't mean our profit line should be compromised.' She went on to question the company's reliance on the approved-supplier list, which she felt needed a thorough overhaul. She recommended that every supplier should submit a new tender.

Greg glanced at William, then back at Amy. 'I didn't realize costs were in your remit.'

Her response was crisp and cool. 'My remit is very wide . . . very wide indeed.'

'I see,' he said calmly. They stared at each other for a moment. His demeanour was strange, she thought. Was he badgering her or flirting? She wasn't sure.

'We can discuss this in more detail next week,' William intervened.

Amy went on to mention another seven controversial

points. Sally and Roger remained quiet, but their taut faces, thin lips and creased foreheads betrayed their hostility.

Amy was trying to direct what she was saying principally to William – he was, after all, the MD and her boss – but her eyes were pulled to Greg. His reaction, or lack of it, surprised her. Occasionally he raised an eyebrow and murmured, 'How interesting,' but that was all. After fifteen minutes of this she became irritated. She was happier when he disagreed with her: at least she knew then where she stood. But her next proposal would get him going, she was sure. 'I believe CEM needs to be restructured internally. The ratio of operations staff to sales staff is disproportionate, especially as we subcontract a number of facilities and catering requirements.'

Sally's lips had all but disappeared. 'Absolutely not! I need every single one of my staff.'

'I propose we move some of the operations staff into a new department, Customer Liaison,' Amy said calmly. 'Others should become account managers. They will support existing clients, freeing the business-development managers to focus on winning new business. We need a concentrated proactive drive. I don't mean to dismiss the achievements to date of Sales and Marketing, but the structure of the company needs to reflect today's market.'

Amy turned to Greg, expecting to have her head chewed off, but he remained silent and unruffled.

'Unworkable,' said Sally.

'Quality would drop,' said Roger. 'Our clients come back to us time and time again because we deliver a high-quality product.'

Sally agreed. 'My teams are totally efficient. I will not have any of them poached for a new department.'

Matchstick Love

Amy was undeterred. 'There's no reason why quality should drop. With the amount of staff on the payroll we already have, there's no justification for employing more salespeople. We need to reorganize those we have. We don't just need turnover, we need profit.'

William asked Amy for a more detailed plan dealing with that point. Then he stressed to the others that everything was under consideration: they should come up with a line of defence based on hard facts. He acknowledged the great work everyone had already done, but added, 'Pablo wants more profit to drive up the share price, and buy more companies on the back of it. It's a pressure we can all do without but it's also a fact of today's world.'

Within half an hour the meeting had been brought to a close. William thanked Amy for some excellent work, which had got them all thinking, and she handed out the copies of her report, which covered twenty-five points. Greg took his without a word, and Amy watched him leave with Sally. Instantly they were talking in the corridor – she wished she could hear what they were saying.

Back in her office, she slumped at her desk, relieved it was over. Being the bad guy could be lonely. And there was something about Greg that unnerved her.

9

'After the meeting this afternoon I wasn't sure if the invitation still stood,' said Amy, sipping her wine.

Greg looked astonished. 'Whether I agree with you or not, I don't take things personally. It's good to meet someone with lots of ideas. Most people just follow the herd.' He took a swig of his Jack Daniel's and his dark-hazel eyes gleamed. 'I like people who have the guts to go out on a limb and speak their mind. Most just lick arses. Makes me sick.'

Amy nodded enthusiastically. 'I agree. I can take any amount of criticism as long as it's spoken openly. I prefer people in my face.'

'At least then you can answer them. Back-stabbers should be put on a boat and sunk in the middle of the ocean.'

She laughed. 'At least we agree on something.'

'I'm sure we agree on lots.'

They were seated alone at a table in Kudos. Beth had just left – she was meeting her boyfriend for dinner – and, surprisingly, Daniel had jumped up too, saying he had to be somewhere else. Only the four of them had come but it had been a pleasant evening. Apparently one of Ben's daughters was sick, and Roger had sent his apologies too – Amy guessed she wasn't his first choice of someone with whom to spend Friday evening. She could understand why. In a sense she had told him how to do his job.

Now she and Greg were sitting opposite each other in the busy bar. Amy pushed back her hair. 'What did you think of the points I raised?' she asked.

He frowned. 'Oh let's not talk about work anymore.

Matchstick Love

I love my job but even I sometimes need to forget it. Don't you?'

'Occasionally. I was just interested in your views. You were quiet in the meeting.'

'I shall read your report and get back to you.'

She nodded, and glanced around the bar. She'd already spotted a number of girls from CEM and throughout the evening they had been covertly studying her and Greg. 'I believe we may be the topic of conversation,' she remarked.

He followed her eyes. 'Yes, I've noticed that.' He looked back at her and asked, 'Are you hungry? There's an amazing Thai restaurant a couple of streets away. At least we can lose the prying eyes.'

She tapped the side of her glass for a moment, then said thoughtfully, 'I do love Thai food.'

'Another thing we have in common.'

Within half an hour they were eating spring rolls and cashew-nut curry and chatting comfortably away. Greg was asking her questions about herself. He seemed genuinely interested and was easy to talk to. They had in-depth discussions about life, religion and whether there was a point to it all.

'Half of me believes in destiny and fate, and the other half thinks it's all a random, chaotic mess, with no specific point or purpose,' she said, and bit into a king prawn.

'Random chaos is my theory. It seems much more interesting and eventful.'

'Yet you read the Bible – Old Testament, you said.'

'I've read the whole thing from cover to cover.'

Amy was perplexed. 'Why? What were you looking for?'

'Anything. Nothing. Just interested. One should look into something before discounting it.' He flashed her a devilish smile. 'I've looked into lots and discounted most.'

'Leaving?'

'Random chaos. Nothing more, nothing less. So we should just make the most of it by pursuing pleasure and avoiding crap.'

She leant forward and rested her chin on the back of her hand. With a devilish smile to match his, she said, 'And what pleasures do you pursue, Mr Hamilton-Lawrence?'

He leant forward too, whispering softly, 'I'm afraid you may disapprove?'

'Don't let that stop you.'

Blank-faced, he stared slightly beyond her, as if deep in thought. Eventually his eyes focused on her and he shook his head.

Disappointed, she frowned. 'At least tell me what crap you avoid?'

'All the usual – dishonesty, back-stabbing, two-faced bollocks, thick and narrow-minded people. And pretty much anything that I don't want to do.'

'A free spirit, then?'

'You could say that.'

'Another man scared of commitment.'

He scoffed and laughed loudly. 'My God, where did that come from?'

'It's a theory of mine. A man who calls himself a free spirit is usually suffering from commitment phobia.'

'Well, I can assure you that I suffer from no such thing. I just haven't met a woman I want to spend the rest of my life with.' In a more serious manner and staring at her through innocent, child-like eyes, he added, 'Hopefully that will change.'

Matchstick Love

With more wine and some gentle probing from Greg, she soon found herself talking about her ex, Simon Delaney. 'It got to the point where I wasn't even sure why I was with him. He was paranoid about being trapped! Like I was secretly planning to get him down the aisle.' She winced. 'He was the last guy I'd marry. Our relationship had deteriorated to such a point that all we did together was have sex, discuss work or play cards.'

'*Play cards?*'

'His way of avoiding conversation. Everywhere we went he brought his pack of cards. They were like his security blanket.'

Greg laughed, and Amy with him at the absurdity of it.

After he had calmed down Greg asked, 'Do you see yourself married one day?'

'Who knows? I'm in no rush, that's for sure. It's either going to happen or it isn't.' She suddenly realized she had spoken too openly. Usually she kept her private life to herself. But he was an excellent listener. It was as if he understood everything she was talking about without her having to explain every last detail.

'What about you? I seem to be doing all the talking here,' she said, determined now to be more reserved.

'There's not much to say.'

'Oh, I doubt that. You strike me as a person with an interesting past.'

He shrugged his shoulders. 'Less than you think.'

'Go on, spill the beans.'

'I've recently split up with a woman called Miranda. She was a nice lady, but in the end we weren't suited. Like you, I had to question why we were together. When you get to that point, it's already over.'

'Were you together long?'

'On and off for four years.'

Much longer than any of my relationships, Amy thought. The longest she'd gone out with someone was for two years, and that was when she was only twenty. Since then one had lasted eighteen months and there had been a string of year-long partners. Most of her relationships followed the same pattern: they were intense at the beginning, with declarations of love, lots of passionate love-making, and then gradually – sometimes not so gradually – the intensity diminished, the highs disappeared and she was left with a despondent downer; a love hangover, as Tessa labelled it.

Sometimes Amy was first to pull away, at other times it was the man. Simon Delaney had been just another in a long line of exciting hopefuls who had turned sour.

'You choose the wrong sort of men,' Tessa had said, but Amy didn't – her instinct did. You were either attracted to someone or you weren't. Of course she had tried nice, reliable, steady, supportive men. Undoubtedly, they were committed to her and were someone to plan days out with, long term futures and saga holidays. *But help!* There had to be more.

Peter had worshipped the ground she walked on and had been at her beck and call, ready to do anything she wanted. He was also the most boring man on the planet, an insurance broker, happiest when talking about his collection of antique matchboxes – over three hundred of them. Aaaaah! *And the sex!* Oh, please. It was OK. But when she found her mind wandering off in the middle to the next day's work and remembering who she had to phone, it was surely a sign that all wasn't right. Even so, she had been prepared to put up with it. Sex wasn't everything. Companionship, support, fidelity and long-term commitment were important too. Aaaaah! Stop! She couldn't wake up another morning next to him. Was this it? Growing old with him. He was nice. He truly was. But nice wasn't enough. Nice was boring! Everyone else seemed happy to accept nice, but she needed that extra something – the excitement, the drama, the flirting, an element of risk . . . *No!* No risk. She remembered, with a jolt, who she was with. She'd moved on. Mature, grown-up relationships, she told herself. I'm thirty-four and there's more to life than excitement. I want nice. Nice is good.

'A penny for them,' said Greg with a huge, sexy grin. *Shit!* When did his grin become sexy?

Go home, she told herself. Leave right now.

'More wine?' he said, holding up the bottle.

She shook her head.

'What about you? What pleasures do you pursue?'

'None, really. Pleasures seem to pursue me. And pleasures aren't always good for a person. A bit of crap can keep a person grounded.'

He looked amazed. 'Dear me, Amy. What's happened in your life to make you think like that?'

She wasn't going to elaborate.

The waiter appeared and offered dessert, which Amy declined.

'Some coffee, then,' suggested Greg.

'Actually I have to go.'

He looked disappointed but asked for the bill. She insisted on paying half, which he reluctantly accepted, and soon they were sharing a taxi home. It went first to London Bridge, where Greg had an impressive apartment overlooking St Catherine's Docks. Standing on the pavement with the cab door open, he said, 'Come in for some coffee.'

'Maybe another time.'

'Oh, come on. I'll call you a cab later.'

'No,' she said. 'I'd best be off.'

His eyes narrowed and some strange emotion flickered in them, then disappeared. 'Of course. See you Monday. Have a great weekend.' He closed the door and waved as the cab pulled away.

10

'Do you take this man to be your lawful wedded husband, for better for worse, for richer for poorer, in sickness and in health?'

Dorothy nodded, winked at the vicar and said aloud, 'You bet I will.'

All eleven of the small congregation laughed. Even the young vicar fought to suppress giggles before he turned to Ron. 'Do you take this woman to be your lawful wedded wife . . .'

As the vicar continued Ron's head turned sideways and he gave Dorothy the most adoring look that Amy had ever seen. Her heart expanded and fluttered.

Wiping a tear from his eye, Ron finally said, 'I will.'

Amy felt so touched by the ceremony. Weddings didn't usually get to her. In fact, call her cynical, she normally felt they were just a big performance for the day with two amateur leading actors making promises that everyone knew they had a one in three chance of breaking. Lots of money was spent; lots of stress was incurred in organizing it; people got drunk; and, above all else, *single women were made to feel there was something lacking in their lives*.

Sod's law that, in Amy's life, whenever a wedding came round, her most recent relationship had just ended. She would attend on her own and find herself shoved on a table with all the other leper single types who messed up the seating arrangements. In addition, every married relative would see it as their duty to make some over-the-top sympathetic comment about not worrying because it would be your turn next. 'I'm not worrying,' Amy would usually respond, with a forced smile.

But today was no ordinary wedding. Today was a celebration of life and love. Great Aunt Dorothy, aged sixty-two, was getting married for the first time to Ron, a sixty-three-year-old widower. They'd met less than a year ago and fallen madly in love. It was the first time that Dorothy had ever been truly in love. Now here was hope – not that Amy wanted to wait as long as she had.

'I now pronounce you man and wife,' said the vicar. 'You may kiss the bride.'

Ron and Dorothy were already sharing an impassioned kiss. It went on for so long that everyone cheered.

Amy looked at the plump, grey-haired woman with the big smile and even bigger heart. She loved Dorothy and was over the moon at her happiness. After all, Dorothy had been her saviour. Without her intervention, God knows what would have happened.

At the age of fifteen Amy had gone to live with her, in her two-bedroom terraced house in Wandsworth, South London. It had meant leaving the four-bedroom detached house in Surrey, but Amy didn't care. It was a relief not to have to tiptoe around someone's personality. With Dorothy you could be yourself, you were an equal, you could talk; you'd even be heard.

It was a far cry from the atmosphere at home. After the breakdown of her parents' marriage, which had left Amy and her mother, Pam, living in a rented leaky flat above a shop, Richard had appeared like a knight in shining armour. He was a wealthy dentist, and, Pam thought, should be for ever worshipped for taking on a woman with two small children. Amy had been seven and her brother Frank was six, but Richard didn't really take them on: if anything, when he married her mother he agreed that they could live in his house too. But there were rules, mostly unwritten ones, never discussed, just reaffirmed with every gesture, facial expression and sentence he spoke. On no account was he to be disturbed with matters relating to them. So he wasn't. Pam had kept the children out of his way. Amy and her brother soon learnt that, when Richard was around, they smiled, disappeared and kept quiet.

Everything ran smoothly for several years. Even teenage *angst* and moods were always hidden from him. If Amy was having heated words with her mother, they instantly stopped when Richard approached. That was the unwritten deal on which the marriage was founded. He was a cold, remote man and a slave to perfection, but in his way he loved Pam and took care of her. Neither child wanted to rock the boat so everyone behaved accordingly, keeping to their role within the perfect family.

But by the age of fourteen, Amy was far from quiet. At school she was noisy and disruptive. She started to miss lessons and hang around in the town with a dubious crowd of older boys. Teachers complained. She was even suspended for getting drunk one lunchtime in the playground. Luckily her mother managed to keep that hidden from Richard. After that episode her mother berated Amy for being so ungrateful for everything Richard had done for them. 'Can't you see how lucky we are? Do you want to go back to that squalid flat?'

Amy sneered, as only teenagers can.

'What's wrong with you? Richard's given us everything. Can't you show more appreciation?' Pam whined.

Amy promised to try harder, but if anything her behaviour grew worse and not everything could be kept from Richard. Just after her fifteenth birthday, in her large, comfortably furnished bedroom, with her own television, telephone, computer, sound-system and anything else her mother had thought might keep her there, Amy found herself crying. Her mother came in and tried to comfort her, begging her to pull herself together and stop crying because Richard would be home soon.

After several days of tears and tantrums, Dorothy, to whom Amy had always been close, offered a room in her house. So Amy moved in that very morning. Her mother and Richard dropped her there. It was the practical thing to do, said Richard. The tears and noise made an intolerable disturbance that was affecting his performance at work. Her mother apologized to him profusely and kissed her daughter goodbye. Just like that!

The tears stopped eventually and Amy got on with things. In fact, she excelled. She left school after A levels to get a job and earn some money. Money gave her freedom. Money gave her choices. Money gave her control of her own life.

At twenty-one she had bought her own flat and was sales manager for an office-equipment company, managing a team of four, smashing sales targets every month. She was now dependent on no one. She vowed she would never end up like her mother.

In keeping with Dorothy's no-fuss character, the reception and buffet lunch were held in a room above her local pub in Clapham. Thankfully Pam and Richard weren't invited. Amy hardly saw them now. Within an hour all of the guests and the bridal party were dancing to Rod Stewart. Streamers were thrown, songs sung, laughter filled the room, and not one person asked Amy about a man.

Probably because of the age of the parties involved, everyone was tired by ten p.m. and ready to leave. Amy kissed Dorothy and Ron goodbye – she wouldn't see them for over a month as they were having an extended honeymoon in America, staying with Ron's daughter.

She caught a taxi home and, drunk on cheap champagne and the prospect of true love, practically floated up the stairs to her apartment. She opened the fridge and poured herself a glass of white wine. The night was still young and she couldn't go to bed yet. She was in a carefree, mood, so she put on a Madonna CD and started dancing round the flat. It was several minutes later that she spotted her answering-machine was flashing.

'Hi, Amy, sorry I missed you. I was ringing up to invite you to a clay-pigeon shoot. I understand you're quite good at it.' He left a phone number, but not his name.

A bit presumptuous of him, thinking I'd recognize his voice, she thought. But she had, of course: it was Greg. She stood there, swaying from side to side, one hand on her hip, the other holding her glass. Greg was so goddamn confident. Too confident. There was absolutely no way she was going to phone him back. No way! *I'm not going to join his harem*. She pressed the message delete button. He was trouble, she said to herself. But why the hell did he have to be so sexy! And why the hell was her heart beating so fast? It was just the dancing, she told herself.

On the spur of the moment she decided to go down and see Tessa. For all her fears, Tessa was a grounded and sensible person. And she was always in. Amy dashed downstairs with the newly opened bottle of wine. She reached Tessa's door and frowned when she saw her hall light was off. That meant she was in bed and she was not the sort of person who liked to be woken up: she was a slave to her routines.

Amy plonked herself on the bottom stair in the hall and gazed around with a silly inebriated smile on her face. Her emerald silk dress was creased by all the day's activities, and had risen to her thighs, revealing her long legs, which were sprawled out in front of her. Her gelled hair had mostly fallen out of its clip and was now shooting off in every direction. She took a swig of wine from the bottle, and pondered what to do.

'Hello?' A perplexed-looking John Smith was walking through the front door. He stopped a few feet away from her, at his door and eyed her very oddly. She was sick of him eyeing her oddly, it was he who was the weirdo.

'Good evening, John Smith. Not that that's your real name,' she said, and gave him an exaggerated wink. 'It's OK,' she said. 'I won't tell anyone.'

'Tell anyone what?'

'Your real name, of course.'

'But it's John Smith.'

'Fine,' said Amy, nodding and winking again.

John looked bewildered and Amy took another swig of wine. She held out the bottle to him.

He shook his head. 'Were you waiting for me?' He seemed amused.

Amy giggled. 'Why would I be waiting for you?'

'Sorry. Just that you're sitting by my door.'

'I'm sitting on the stairs, which just happen to be by your door.' She rolled her eyes. 'Men.'

He took out his front-door key. 'By the way, sorry about the other evening. I popped up to apologize earlier, but you were out. Unfortunately I was delayed through work.'

Matchstick Love

Amy bolted upright, intrigued. 'Oh, really? Actually, I saw you getting out of the police car.'

'Oh, I see.'

'The whole house has bets on your occupation. I think you work for MI5, your scruffy exterior being merely a disguise.'

John laughed. 'I'm afraid this "scruffy exterior" is all real.'

Amy realized suddenly that he didn't look scruffy tonight. The dark blond hair had been given a good cut and was now short at the back, and his beard was trimmed tight to his face. He was wearing jeans – no holes – and a smart blue shirt that brought out the blue of his eyes. He still looked a bit wild, though, unconventional and nonconformist.

'If you don't work for MI5 maybe you were arrested, after all. Not that I'm one to judge but is pimping really politically correct?' Cheap champagne and white wine had got the better of her.

His jaw dropped open. 'I hate to disappoint you but—'

'*Then don't.*' She jumped up. 'Don't disappoint me. I'm so fed up with being disappointed.'

He stared at her for several moments, then said, quite seriously, 'You've caught me out. I'm an undercover MI5 transvestite, working to overthrow the Labour government by revealing that Tony Blair is really the illegitimate son of Margaret Thatcher and Terry Wogan.'

'I suspected as much.'

Silence ensued.

Suddenly she asked, 'Who are you, John Smith?'

His face remained blank. 'Nobody,' he said. Then he put his key in the door and disappeared inside.

11

'It's a pleasure to meet you again,' said Mark Greenshawe, smiling and shaking Amy's hand for longer than etiquette required.

'Likewise,' she said, and smiled back.

'How's the new job going?'

'Very well indeed.' Amy moved on to Janis and Philip who, with Mark, were visiting CEM's offices to discuss the final proposal and revised budgets for the Trans-Global Airlines relaunch. If today went well, hopefully CEM would win the ten-million-pound contract. As it was such an important meeting, William was also there, with Greg, Sally, Paul from the CEM in-house production company and Harry Jackson, the managing director of Benchmark Catering. Everyone was going to say a few words on their particular area. Amy thought it strange that Harry Jackson was there and wondered why it was a foregone conclusion that his company would be awarded the catering.

Eventually everyone sat down at the large oval table in the boardroom. Mark was opposite Amy and while coffee was being poured, he said, so that everyone could hear, 'I hope Greg's treating you well. A good secretary is hard to find.'

Amy glanced at Greg, who was trying to suppress a smile. She turned back to Mark and said politely, 'I believe there's been a misunderstanding. I manage Strategic Planning, reporting directly to William. I'm employed to submit corporate strategies on the future direction and expansion of CEM. However, my role regarding the TGA relaunch is to contribute ideas regarding the marketing, overall presentation and style of your events, including PR and publicity.'

Mark Greenshawe looked surprised and somewhat impressed. 'I didn't realize.'

'That's OK. It was our error not to convey this to you at our first meeting.'

'Perhaps we should start,' said Greg. 'There's a lot to discuss, and I hope you can all join us for lunch.'

His eyes still on Amy, Mark nodded slowly. 'Of course. It would be a pleasure.'

Greg chaired the meeting, giving a brief presentation himself, then inviting the various team members to speak about their own area of interest and responsibility. Each person was allocated a maximum of fifteen minutes and had prepared their own slides or a short film.

William spoke about the strength and financial backing of the Lazlo Manco group, of which CEM was proud to be a member. Sally submitted the budgets, gave updates on the most suitable venues around Europe and the logistics with regard to transportation and accommodation. Paul presented the latest designs showing the space-age setting, complete with executive lounges under a large metallic dome and walkways leading into the dummy aeroplane fuselage.

Then it was Amy's turn. She walked confidently to the large screen at the front and smiled. She began by talking about the necessity to guarantee a good attendance ratio from TGA's guests. 'There's no point in having an excellent presentation if we don't get the required numbers showing up to see it.' She went on to give examples of how to attract their target market, which included numerous attendance incentives. There would also be market research carried out on guest feedback. She explained how CEM would contribute to the overall look, style and feel of the events, by working alongside TGA's marketing department to ensure maximum publicity in trade magazines and the national press. She finished her talk by handing out a short report she had prepared at William's request.

'You have some impressive ideas,' said Mark Greenshawe, as she took her seat.

'Thank you.'

After a short pause Greg said, 'I'd now like to invite Harry Jackson to talk about catering.'

Harry went up to the front and gave a brief history of his company, then described how they would provide the catering around Europe. In some cases this meant working alongside a venue's in-house caterers. 'Whether we use our own team or not, each venue will have a Benchmark catering manager to ensure continuity of approach and guarantee quality.' He explained that the new TGA five-star menu would be sampled all over Europe at the product launches.

Amy listened to him intently. Having examined most of CEM's past records and client files, she had found out that, over the last two years, Benchmark Catering had been awarded nearly ninety per cent of CEM's catering requirements – several million pounds' worth of business. It wasn't a sister company, and it was risky to put all your eggs in one basket. In her view CEM should have been using a handful of top caterers. Although it wasn't her responsibility, she thought it inadvisable to award any company the whole catering part of the TGA contract, which was worth over two million pounds.

'As I said, your ideas were impressive,' said Mark Greenshawe, topping up Amy's wine over lunch in

Quaglino's just off Piccadilly. It was a large, ultra-modern restaurant with a lively buzz.

'Thank you. I hope this means we'll have the opportunity to work together,' she said, with a flirtatious glint in her eye.

He smiled. 'A final decision will be made early next week. Time is limited. There's a lot to do before the relaunch in June.' Then he said, for her ears only, 'But I, too, hope we'll be working together.'

Amy raised her glass, and they clinked in a private toast.

Greg was sitting opposite them talking to Janis and Philip, but Amy felt his eyes on her from time to time. Occasionally a smile passed between them.

The meeting had gone well and there was an air of relief and excitement around the table. Mark seemed happy to spend a lot of his time talking with Amy, who welcomed his attention: any edge you had on your competitors helped, and this contract could not be allowed to go elsewhere.

'So, you don't miss Protea Software?' he asked.

'I never miss anything. Life moves on and you have to go with it.' Then Amy asked about his own career and interests. Successful, powerful men like Mark Greenshawe always liked talking about themselves, especially when there were attractive women to listen and act suitably impressed – 'act' being the appropriate word.

Eventually the three from TGA had to get back to Hammersmith for further meetings and, after polite farewells, they departed, leaving the CEM team and Harry Jackson at the table. It was then that the celebrations started. Greg ordered two bottles of champagne, and even William, cautious by nature, had a glass, confident of the outcome. 'Well done, everyone.

Although we shouldn't count our chickens just yet, let's celebrate the impressive teamwork,' he said.

Everyone cheered and clapped, high on adrenaline and the scent of success.

At two thirty, Harry stood up to leave. As he shook Amy's hand he said, 'If you're ever in the area, call in and I'll give you a tour of our premises.'

'Thank you, I will.'

Greg walked with him to the main entrance and Amy watched with interest as they stood talking and laughing. Eventually they parted and Greg returned. He took the now empty seat beside Amy. With a mischievous grin he said, 'Have we accidentally gone through some timewarp or is this still the twenty-first century?'

'I was just being friendly,' she replied, mock-indignant.

'I'm not complaining. Mark is obviously enamoured of you. I was just surprised by the change of heart.'

'There was no change of heart. I was professional yet friendly.'

'A touch flirtatious also?'

With a half-smile she said, 'For the life of me, I'm at a loss as to what you're going on about.'

His dark-hazel eyes locked on hers. 'You're more like me than you care to admit,' he said. 'You believe in "whatever it takes" too. You just don't like being told how to play it. You want things on your own terms.'

'Nothing wrong with that.'

He leant towards her and whispered, 'You never rang me back over the weekend.'

'Clay-pigeon shooting didn't appeal to me.'

'We could have done something else.'

'Greg, we work together.'

He frowned.

'You're no fool,' she went on. 'You know exactly what I'm saying.'

'So we work together? Why the limitations? Life's too short.'

'That old chestnut.'

He gave a resigned shrug.

At that moment William stood up. 'We still have work to do,' he said, rather pointedly.

'We'll finish off this bottle, then follow you up,' said Greg.

Amy grabbed her handbag. 'I'll walk with you, William. Catch you later,' she said to the others.

Outside it was raining so William and Amy caught a cab for the five-minute journey back to the office.

'Why is it a foregone conclusion that Benchmark get the whole catering part of the contract?' asked Amy.

'I don't believe it is. I'm sure Sally's invited other companies to quote.'

'I haven't seen or heard anything.'

'I expect she has some details. But Benchmark are a good company with a proven track record. Why are you asking?'

'We should be inviting more competition in to keep them on their toes. And, if there are in-house caterers at some of the venues, why hire Benchmark to oversee them? Surely someone from Operations could do that. It's an unnecessary expense to use Benchmark.'

William was quiet for a moment. Then he nodded. 'Yes, that's something I'll discuss with Sally. But let's win the contract first, then have this conversation. By the way, you gave a most impressive presentation and report,' he said.

'Thank you.'

*

Later that afternoon, Amy was researching details for some of the proposals she'd made at the meeting last week and Beth was typing in the corner. Amy couldn't get over her transformation. She was looking more like the young Princess Anne every day, and sounding like her too. The London accent had disappeared. What had happened to her? She was completely different to when Amy had first met her, what with her now permanent smile, the manicured nails and the stylish, expensive clothes. But there was a strong culture in the organization, a CEM way of doing things. Sally interviewed the majority of staff and she obviously employed little clones of herself.

Most of the staff stayed at their desks up until eight or nine every evening, before hitting Kudos wine-bar. CEM wasn't a job, it was a way of life – a religion.

Her computer bleeped, indicating an incoming email, which she clicked to open.

```
Amy,
So we work together! Which commandment is
that breaking? Would it be so bad to go
through that timewarp into a past century? A
time when there was no confusion between the
sexes — when females were cherished! OK
. . . so you didn't get to vote! With such
low turnouts at elections, did the
suffragettes achieve anything?
Greg.
PS Fancy a trip around Brands Hatch motor-
racing circuit? Excessive speed is
guaranteed.
```

Amy laughed at his outrageousness and chewed the end of her pen while she gazed at her screen. CEM

Matchstick Love

was organizing corporate hospitality and guest participation at Brands Hatch tomorrow.

```
Greg,
Only a few women were cherished. Most had
shit lives and no say in them. However, I am
not opposed to stepping through that
timewarp!
But let's step forward in time. Politics
isn't working so in the late twenty-second
century, with automated muscle, artificial
intelligence and the creation of synthetic
sperm, the role of the male diminishes to
one of pure entertainment and pleasure for
the female race. The vote is taken away from
them and the world is ruled by women's
intuition.
Amy.
However, Brands Hatch sounds fun.
```

Within two minutes she had received a reply.

```
Amy,
A world ruled by women's intuition? God help
us! I think I'd catch a space ship to Mars
in search of some logic and rationale.
Little green men being preferable to little
green-eyed hormonal women.
Greg.
PS We'll leave here at 1 p.m.
PPS I hope you don't scare easily!
```

12

'How's that feel?' asked the dark-haired man in orange overalls after he had placed the helmet on Amy's head and secured the strap.

'Fine,' she said. She felt queasy with nerves.

He tapped the top of her helmet, then led her across the pit lane towards a customized Audi sports car. Greg was in the driving seat. As she climbed in she saw that his eyes were glistening and he looked like a man possessed.

The guy in the overalls strapped her into the full body harness, gave her a thumbs-up and shut the door. Greg started the engine and revved it. The noise tore through her like a knife and she regretted her decision to come. 'You have done this before, right?' she shouted.

He laughed and winked at her, then looked ahead, waiting for the yellow flag to drop.

Amy gripped the sides of her seat. Thankfully it wasn't a race and each car was separated by five minutes.

They had arrived at Brands Hatch twenty minutes ago, just as Havisham Engineering, CEM's client, was starting the afternoon session. Those who had the skill to do it were allowed to drive round the circuit unattended, but there were speed restrictions. Greg had immediately approached Jack, the owner and a friend, and asked to take a sports car round. Jack seemed hesitant but finally agreed. His parting words to Greg were 'Don't overstep the mark.'

Before Amy could refuse, she was getting into the blue overalls.

Matchstick Love

The flag dropped and they shot off. Within a terrifying sixty seconds they were doing ninety m.p.h. Her whole body tensed as they went into the first corner, which appeared out of nowhere. She closed her eyes and held her breath. The G-force was now pushing her against the door. The aggressive engine noise grew louder as Greg pushed it to its limits. Only when she felt able to sit upright again did she open her eyes, and saw thankfully that they were back on the straight.

Amy glanced at the road, then at Greg and then at the speedometer. When they hit 110 m.p.h. she glared at him. He laughed, but over the two-way radio they heard, 'Car seven, slow down.'

Greg eased off the accelerator and their speed dropped to ninety-five but soon they were heading into another long, curved bend. She expected Greg to slow but he kept his foot down, ignoring the brake. Another radio message: 'Greg, slow down to eighty immediately.' It was Jack in the control room.

Relieved, Amy glanced at the speedometer but was horrified to see it was still going up. She glared at him again, but he was focused on the circuit. They were taking the right-hand curve so fast that she was pinned against the door. If felt as if the car was going to flip over and it occurred to her that her life was literally in Greg's hands. She hated to be reliant on a man and at this moment she was totally dependent on his driving skill and his sanity.

Amy pushed herself away from the door and experienced true fear. Her heart was in her mouth and she prayed that he'd slow down. Pride prevented her shouting at him to do just that.

'*Greg, slow your arse down right now or you'll never get into one of my cars again,*' screamed Jack over the radio.

He slowed very slightly, but as soon as they exited the curve his foot floored the accelerator and they shot off again. For most of the circuit Amy's eyes were shut, except when the motion of the car made her feel sick and she had to open them. They caught up with the previous car, which wasn't supposed to happen, and Greg was informed over the radio that under no circumstances was he to overtake it. Finally he eased down and at long last the pit lanes appeared. Amy sighed with relief.

An angry-looking Jack was waiting for them, hands on hips, but Greg drove past him and parked a little distance away. He turned off the engine, took off his helmet and punched the air with delight. 'Fantastic,' he yelled, elated. 'What a buzz! Who needs drugs for a high when you can do that?'

'A tranquillizer might be more appropriate,' said Amy, mustering a smile.

He laughed at her. 'I love life, Amy. Don't you?'

'At times.'

Thankfully the man in orange overalls helped her out. Her legs felt wobbly, and she held on to the side of the car as he undid her helmet and took it off. She glanced over at Greg and saw that he was with a stern-looking Jack, so she headed off to the changing rooms, relieved that it was over and her limbs were still intact. Once dressed she headed for the hospitality suite, where she ordered a large vodka and orange.

At five o'clock the fifty guests sat down for their four-course meal in the large restaurant. The room was electric with everyone high on adrenaline and wine. Issy, Tink and some other CEM girls were there and would stay until the event ended at around nine or ten that evening. Greg took Amy's arm. 'The fun part is over so it's time for us to leave,' he said. Thankfully, his driving on the way back to London was a lot more sensible, although still too fast for Amy to relax. Within an hour he was approaching Crystal Palace.

'Fancy a bite to eat?' he asked.

Amy was famished so she agreed, and soon they were pulling up outside a Tex-Mex restaurant. They were seated at a table for two in an alcove and ordered rum cocktails. They had ribs as a main course and ate them while they chatted – Greg was a good dinner companion.

'So, you think women shouldn't have the vote?' Amy said.

'Voting is merely a PR exercise, so whether you're male or female it achieves little. There's no power in politics, these days. Power lies with the multinationals. Power comes from money.'

'What a cynical view.'

'Factual, not cynical. I'm not complaining. I accept my minuscule role in the world. I accept the inevitability of man's destructive streak, that we're ruled by hate, greed and pride. I accept my glory. I accept my demise. I accept my life. I accept my death.'

'You sound like it's a brave thing to accept, what's wrong with the world. Surely if you care, you should try to change things,' she said.

He stirred his cocktail. 'You're right, of course, Amy. It's just that this life can sometimes beat you down.'

'You don't look beaten down to me.'

'Appearances can be deceptive.'

'Can't they just!'

He sighed, as if frustrated. 'You think you're pretty clued up, don't you?'

'Do I?'

'I think you're only half living.'

'*Bollocks*. Where the hell did that come from?'

He sipped his drink. 'Forgive me, I thought you said that you like people in your face. Was that too in your face?'

Amy glared at him. He was like a Pandora's box of contrary yet perceptive comments. She knew she would probably regret allowing him to lure her into this conversation but she couldn't resist asking, 'Why am I only half living?'

'Because life is about throwing off the rules, yet I expect you gather them around you like a snow ball gathering snow.'

She leant forward so that her face was just inches from his. 'If a person never learns from their past, they would be very foolish.' For a moment they stared at each other, neither blinking nor moving. It was Amy who broke the silence. 'You're an interesting guy, Greg, but don't insult me by playing psychological games with me. I'm more clued-up than you think.' She sat back and sipped her drink.

He looked shocked. 'No offence was intended. I sometimes play devil's advocate, and I've done so with you because I'm interested in your views. I joke around a bit. It's not meant as an insult. I know you're nobody's fool, Amy.' He offered her a placatory smile.

Eventually she nodded.

'I feel you're wary of me. As we're both adults who appreciate honesty, let me explain my intentions concerning you,' he said. 'The fact is, I don't have any.'

Amy shifted in her chair, puzzled by this.

'Well, not in the way I think you think I do. You're attractive, intelligent and interesting. Why wouldn't I want to get to know you better? But CEM is filled with women like that, who are mostly friends, nothing more. Maybe we'll develop an enjoyable friendship too. Maybe more. I don't know. At the same time, to have predetermined rules and limitations on this or *anything* seems preposterously restrictive. I instinctively fight against it. If you've translated that into thinking that I'm after you, well . . .' He smiled. 'As a gentleman I'll accept the blame for your presumption.'

'I didn't presume anything,' said Amy, defensively. 'I just didn't want to mislead you. You have to be careful with people you work with.' She smiled. 'I'm glad we've sorted that out. I can relax now.'

He smiled broadly and whispered softly, 'Good. That's exactly what I want you to do.'

She raised her glass. 'To friendships.'

'To friendships, and fewer rules,' he said.

Later that night he dropped her at home. While she was getting out of the car, she considered inviting him in for some coffee, but before she could make up her mind, he said, 'See you tomorrow.'

'Thanks for a nice evening.'

As he drove off she waved, but he didn't look back.

Maybe I have been a bit presumptuous, she thought, then turned and went inside.

The next day at the office Amy was instructing Beth on some research she wanted carried out, when Tink and Issy burst into the room waving a magazine and giggling. Between all the gesturing, hullabaloo and cacophony of oohs and aahs, Amy gathered they were showing Beth a page in it. Eventually Issy came over to Amy and pointed to a photograph of herself at the wedding of Lord Henry Faulkner and Lady Annabel Havisham-Grieves. There she was, stick-insect Issy, in some hideous purple dress and hat, smiling unusually demurely. 'I've made it on to the society pages,' she said proudly.

Issy had arrived! Issy the new It Girl!

'Absolutely everyone will see it,' she went on rapturously.

'That's wonderful,' said Amy politely.

'I just know Charles Davenport will want to take me out now.'

Tink and Beth nodded in agreement. Thankfully the CEM girls' efficiency meant that the scene ended within three minutes and they headed obediently off to do some work.

The rest of Amy's day was fairly routine. There were meetings with media agencies, lunch with an old friend who was now working at *The Times*, and in the afternoon she was in discussions with a consultant about designing the new web page.

At six o'clock, with the beginnings of a headache, Amy decided to go home – criminally early for CEM. As she walked along the corridor, a few pretty heads looked up and said goodnight to her. Like a row of dominos it triggered every other head to pop up to see who the guilty party was, leaving so early.

As she passed Sales and Marketing, Greg called and asked her to pop in. She went over and stood in the doorway. Daniel was seated at his desk and nodded at her.

Greg flashed her a wicked grin. 'Pack a bag – tomorrow night we're staying in Florence.'

She raised an eyebrow.

'Just heard from Mark Greenshawe. He's most impressed with us, and it's now between CEM and one other company – I'm guessing Thomson Events. Apparently TGA are having a management meeting this Wednesday in Florence. All their senior managers are going and we've been invited to do a presentation at midday, but we'll stay over and take them out. And . . .' he smiled broadly '. . . I get to see Florence, one of the few places I haven't already been to.'

'Sounds good to me.'

'Have you been there?'

'Twice.'

'Good, you can show me around.'

'We'll see. I might get a better offer.' She smiled and walked away.

Once Amy was out of sight, both men looked at each other.

'Wednesday night,' said Daniel nonchalantly. 'You do realize what that means?'

Greg nodded.

'Three weeks. Doesn't time fly? And such a beautiful setting. Who'd have thought it?' added Daniel.

'Haven't you any work to do?' asked Greg, gruffly.

13

The switch was off. She could see quite clearly that it was. She stood still for a couple more seconds then carried on with the next procedure, which was checking that all the plugs had been removed from the sockets. As ever they had been, but she still had to check. 'We develop habits and then our habits develop us': Derek, her meditation teacher, reminded her constantly of this, but if Tessa didn't go through her routine, she couldn't relax outside. It only took seven and a half minutes, so what was the problem?

Six minutes into the routine, she was happy to conclude that every light was off, every electrical item had been unplugged, apart from the fridge, and every window was closed and locked.

She put on her coat and picked up her handbag. Before she went to the door she checked its contents once again: extra sets of keys, some emergency money, the miniature first-aid case and her driving licence – not that she drove any more but it would identify her if anything happened. Lastly there were the oat cookies to stop her blood-sugar level dropping, not that she was diabetic but you had to be careful. The sight of them made her smile. At least she could laugh at herself and her idiosyncrasies. Some people took life far too seriously.

Tessa stood by her front door and took a deep breath, preparing herself for her crucial excursion: to buy a loaf of bread at the local shop.

After double-locking her apartment door and carefully placing this set of keys in her zip-up coat pocket, she went out of the front door, into *the outside world*!

'I am relaxed around people. There is nothing to fear about people,' she repeated, under her breath, as she walked along the street, head down, eyes glued to the pavement, observing the different types of shoe that passed her: black stilettos, scruffy moccasins, a bright blue pair of Doc Martens. At one point she danced round two pairs of brand-new trainers – she had to step into the road to get past. Only then did she glance up to avoid being run over.

No matter how hard she tried, Tessa didn't feel comfortable in this world. It didn't represent who she truly was or how she felt the world should be. She was like an alien lost on some foreign planet. How had life evolved like this? People rushing endlessly to insignificant jobs, or out clothes shopping, to have their hair styled? It was a world obsessed with celebrities, money, looks, sex – *if you're not having multiple orgasms every night, you're obviously a failure!*

No, this world wasn't for Tessa. At times she beat herself up over not being like everyone else. Everyone else seemed so part of it all, happy with their role, or at least unquestioning of it. Was she the only one who was scared and unsure of where she fitted in?

Amy was always encouraging her to get a job, if only part-time: at least it would get her out of the flat and take her mind off herself. But that was impossible. The thought of going for an interview was like being asked to read the six o'clock news live on air. Fortunately, or unfortunately, she didn't need money so the motivation to push herself wasn't there. Anyway, her life wasn't that bad. She still had a laugh. It saddened Tessa that she didn't have a partner – *but what man would put up with me?*

It was a grey, drizzly London day and she pulled up her coat collar as she walked along the street. She reached the little shop and peered inside. It wasn't busy so she took the bull by the horns and marched in. She grabbed her usual loaf and dashed over to the till, holding her money. Thankfully there was no queue. Stuck in a crowded shop, surrounded by people brought on waves of irrational fear. She was grateful to Amy for driving her to the supermarket for the weekly shop every Tuesday night just before it closed.

Within less than a minute she was back outside with the bread under her arm. She sighed with relief, and started the eight-minute walk back to her apartment, humming as she went. She was passing the pillarbox, which indicated she was five minutes from home when she heard, 'It's Tessa, isn't it?'

Tessa froze. She didn't recognize the male voice behind her. Head still lowered she turned slowly and spotted a pair of leather biker boots less than three feet away from her. Her pulse raced. Her legs felt weak.

'I've seen you in the garden a couple of times,' said the man. He was well spoken.

Tessa plucked up courage, and looked upwards slowly, over a pair of jeans, then a black leather jacket, until eventually she saw a dark blond, curly-haired guy with piercing blue eyes. *Those eyes!* It seemed they could see right inside you, leaving you nowhere to hide. That distressed her even more.

'I'm John from the apartment opposite,' he said.

Her eyes darted sideways and she blushed.

'Are you heading back? I'll walk with you, if you like,' he added.

Terror-stricken, Tessa dropped her eyes to the pavement. Her heart started to pound and she prayed she wouldn't have a heart-attack and collapse – how embarrassing. Without a word she took off, marching head down along the street, praying she wouldn't make a fool of herself. Only five minutes to go, she told herself, hopefully four at this pace.

John jogged beside her. 'Power-walking, is it?' he asked.

'Yes . . . Keeps you fit,' she mumbled.

They marched on in silence, like two soldiers on exercise. Tessa didn't look up once: her only focus was to reach the safety of her home. A million thoughts rampaged through her – all negative, all fearful. The biker boots were matching her pace, stride for stride, like a stalker invading her space. And all the while she hated herself, knowing how unfriendly and odd she must seem. She wished she could stop and chat and laugh. But the fear drove her on.

At the old red telephone box, she knew there was barely a minute to go and allowed herself to breathe again. Soon they had entered the hall, where Tessa went straight to her front door and pulled out her key.

'Is everything OK?' he asked, seeming concerned.

Now in her safe environment, she braved a look at him. He was standing in the middle of the hall, breathing heavily. He wasn't scruffy, she thought. What had Amy been going on about? In fact, he was attractive in an unusual way, a strange mix of innocence and experience. His eyes had such depth, and she sensed a strand of suffering in him. Others might not spot it but she could. His eyes looked as if they had seen too much in life – things a person wasn't supposed to see. 'Sorry, in a hurry,' she said, with a smile. 'Just in a hurry.'

As if unconvinced, he stared at her for a couple more seconds, then went into his flat.

Tessa stumbled into her own and leant against the wall, then slid down it. Soon she was sitting on the floor gazing, trance-like, into space. *So that was John*

Smith! Wow! He was really nice. And he only lived across the hall. Very handy for a social phobic.

Then she cringed at the thought of how she must have appeared to him and her head fell into her hands. Overcome with frustration, she promised herself that the next time she saw him, no matter how scared she felt, she'd make an effort to talk to him. Who knows where it might lead?

Her determination surprised her. But there was something familiar about John Smith: a damaged soul can always spot another.

14

Greg gazed out across the city of Florence like a conquering warrior. 'I can't believe I've never been here before. I've been almost everywhere else on this little ramshackle planet of ours.'

'Earth too small for you, is it?' said Amy.

He cast a sideways glance at her, then looked away again.

She and Ben exchanged a discreet smile.

It was late afternoon and incredibly warm for March, even in Florence, so the three were drinking cappuccino on the hotel veranda. Amy stood up, walked over to the decorative railings and breathed in deeply. She loved this place. As they were three floors up they had a magnificent view of the old city, with its mass of yellow and tan buildings, and the distinctive dusty red roofs. No building stood above five storeys high and some dated back to medieval times with the remainder being built around the late fourteenth and fifteenth centuries. The huge red dome of the Duomo cathedral, which they planned to visit later, dominated the skyline.

'How about something stronger?' said Greg.

'Not just yet, thanks,' said Amy.

'I'll wait until dinner,' added Ben.

Greg frowned at them and ordered a bottle of the local Chianti and three glasses. When the waiter was out of earshot he said, 'You two are fun. We're in this amazing place, the capital of Tuscany, and we should be having fun, getting drunk and dancing in the square down there.'

'We've only just come out of the presentation,' Ben

pointed out. 'Shouldn't we be discussing it? I hope it went well – they were very quiet.'

'Relax, Benny-boy. As a betting man I can assure you that the odds are all in our favour.'

'I hope so. I wasn't sure I carried off Sally's part well enough. She knows this project inside out and it was nerve-racking to have to step into her shoes for such a major pitch,' said Ben.

'*Nerve racking!*' scoffed Greg. 'You're such a wimp. You're in sales – it's hardly brain surgery or space travel.'

Amy tried to hide a smile.

'There's a lot riding on this deal,' protested Ben.

'Don't *you* ever get nervous?' she asked Greg.

'I'm totally devoid of fear.'

'You're lucky.'

He stared at her with an almost haunted expression. 'Am I? Fear is *thrilling*. Without fear there isn't much thrill in life.'

'That's why Greg throws himself out of planes and canoes down whitewater rapids, even when the conditions are too dangerous,' said Ben.

'*Especially* when they're too dangerous.' Greg had recovered his self-assurance.

'The average life is too damn boring for him.'

Amy tutted. 'Addicted to the adrenaline rush. That has proved many a person's downfall.'

'Something to look forward to, then,' Greg said, and leant back, his hands behind his head.

He and Amy stared at each other, blank-faced and distant, as though they were locked in some odd combat. It was a welcome interruption when the waiter appeared with the wine.

*

The three had arranged to meet in the hotel lobby at six p.m. Amy was there first, but soon Ben was at her side.

'You look nice,' he said.

She was wearing a clinging calf-length light blue dress. 'Thank you,' she said. 'I thought we'd be entertaining clients tonight and that's why I brought this.'

Amused, he rolled his eyes.

'What?' she asked.

'I suspect Greg knew all along that Mark and the others would be flying straight back. No doubt he wanted an evening in Florence.' He added, mockingly, 'He has to make sure that he's seen everywhere on this little ramshackle planet of ours.'

They both laughed and at that moment Greg strode purposefully towards them. 'Amy, you look delightful. But, Ben – you could at least have changed your shirt.' Ben was still in his work suit.

'I did.'

Greg had changed into black trousers and a sharp blue V-necked jumper. At the revolving glass door, he stood aside to allow Amy to go through first, then jumped in front of Ben, who scowled at him behind his back.

Amy led the way through the maze of narrow old streets, which were partially lit by ornate lanterns. On nearly every corner they came across either a sculptured statue or gilded bronze figurine built into the wall. They passed at least four small churches and chapels, each with large stained-glass windows depicting a religious scene. Greg surprised them both by explaining the biblical story on which each was based. Outside one church while he was retelling the story of Samuel, Amy shook her head.

He stopped talking. 'What?'

'You,' she said. 'I can't figure you out.'

'Try harder.' It was said like an order, and he continued with the story.

Florence was brimming with people, mostly without coats, some even in shorts. The streets were lined with restaurants, already filled with Florentines and tourists, sipping wine, talking and laughing. The smells of wine, rich sauces and freshly baked bread hung in the air. The atmosphere was carefree, and instantly contagious – corruptingly so, thought Amy. You could forget yourself, lose yourself in dubious fantasies, in the past, when time didn't need to be captured and every second filled. In Florence, you fell into an acceptance of time, understanding all who had gone before and those who would follow. Rushing was futile. Stress was folly.

That evening the three meandered through the ancient streets. It was almost as if the spirits of the great artists, sculptors and architects, Michelangelo, Donatello, Brunelleschi, were alive and wandering with them, casting a mystical, romantic spell on anyone passing.

They entered Piazza San Giovanni, one of the grandest in the city. The Duomo stood in the centre and was a hive of activity with hundreds of people milling around.

Having been tempted all the way by delicious smells, they decided to eat immediately and crossed to the east side of the square where they could see a row of street cafés. They sat down at an empty table outside, under a covered terrace, and a waitress came over. Soon they were drinking wine and eating pasta.

'Who'd believe it? It's only March and we're eating outside,' remarked Ben.

'The benefits of global warming,' smiled Greg.

Amy checked her watch. 'I had hoped to go inside the Duomo but I expect it'll be shut by now. The ceiling of the dome has an amazing painting of the Last Judgement.'

'What's that?' asked Ben.

'When God judges the earth and condemns us all to hell,' said Greg flippantly.

'Speak for yourself,' said Amy.

'I was.'

'You like to make out that you're worse than you are.' She topped up all their wine glasses and ordered another bottle. 'I doubt you're that bad – just suffocating under the constraints of the supposedly strong, macho-man stereotype that's been forced on you. No doubt you went to an all-male-school? Probably boarding?'

'There's no fooling you.'

Ben was frowning. 'He's suffocating under his own ego, nothing else.'

'Like Amy said, I'm just a product of society's conditioning.' He added, 'I need *help* to break out from it.'

'I wasn't offering,' Amy retorted.

'I wasn't asking.'

'Good.'

'Good.'

Ben glanced away, eyelids lowered.

They had drunk three bottles of the local wine by the time they left the café a couple of hours later but they weren't ready to go back to the hotel. Instead they went into a lively bar where everyone was dancing to the music of two young guitarists. Pleasantly drunk, Amy and Ben joined in while Greg stood in a corner sipping Jack Daniel's. Now alone, he appeared sober and serious. His eyes were fixed on Amy, and he was watching the way she moved and how her dress emphasized her figure. She tried to do a twirl under

Ben's arm and almost got stuck, which left them both giggling. Eventually Amy beckoned Greg to join them, but he shook his head and continued to sip his whisky.

At half past eleven, he suggested they return to the hotel, and reminded them that they had to be up early for their flight. He had picked up Amy's handbag and took her arm gently, leaving her little choice but to go.

With all the alcohol, she had difficulty finding her bearings so Greg led the way back, retracing their route exactly. They were at the hotel within twenty minutes. He waited for Amy to go through the revolving door first, but when Ben tried to follow, Greg grabbed his arm. 'Benny-boy, it's time for your bed, *OK*?'

Ben looked confused, but then his face tightened. 'But you said—'

Greg pushed him through the door, then followed him in. 'Who's for a night cap?' he asked, in the foyer.

'Definitely,' said Amy. 'The night is still young.'

Greg glared discreetly at Ben, who looked away nervously towards the lifts, but didn't move.

'Aren't you having one, Ben?' asked Amy.

He seemed to hesitate, glancing at her then at the lifts. 'OK,' he muttered, then walked straight into the hotel bar, avoiding further eye-contact with Greg.

There were only about ten people in the bar, which had marble floors and old paintings on the walls. While Amy and Ben sat down in a little alcove by the entrance to a courtyard, Greg went up to the counter.

'You look tired, Ben,' he said, returning with three brandies and sitting down.

'I'm fine, thank you.'

'Haven't you got to phone Grace?'

'I rang her before we came out. Haven't you got to phone Miranda?'

Amy stared hard into her glass.

'I told you that's all off,' said Greg.

'Did you?'

'She's now dating some Swedish hunk.'

Amy sipped her drink. 'Fingers crossed for Monday,' she said. When she received no response from either of them she added, 'TGA's announcement?'

Surprisingly, they only nodded indifferently.

Twenty minutes later, puzzled by the change in atmosphere and what had been stilted conversation, she stood up and told them she was off to bed. 'I'll walk with you,' said Ben, standing up also.

Greg downed the remainder of his brandy. 'I'm going to have another.'

'On your own?' Amy asked.

'Looks that way.'

'Well, I'll stay a bit longer. You head up, Ben, if you want.'

Ben didn't move.

'Yes, you head up.' Greg grinned at him smugly. 'You need to make sure you're firing on all four cylinders. You're considerably down on your quarterly sales target. We'll have to have a serious chat when we get back to the office.'

Ben looked at Amy, then back at Greg. 'Good night,' he said, and walked away. He glanced back once before he disappeared.

'That was a bit over the top, wasn't it, talking about sales targets at this time of night?' said Amy.

'It's good to remind a person who they work for, who's in charge.'

'I'm glad I don't work for you.'

'That might change.'

'Never. Why should it? Unless you're planning to take over from William. But I doubt that . . . or are you?'

He smiled, and gestured to the barman for two more brandies.

'Are you?' she asked again.

'Anything's possible.'

'What are you up to, Greg Hamilton-Lawrence?'

'I am up to having fun. What are you up to, Amy Lambert?'

'One can tire of fun.'

'Then what?'

The barman appeared with the brandy bottle, poured some into their glasses, and returned to the bar.

'Then what?' he asked again.

She ran her hand through her hair. 'Oh . . . just everything.'

'Not much, then.'

'Aren't you?'

'Of course.'

She eyed him curiously. 'But can you give everything?'

'Yes, everything.'

She crossed her legs, and smiled uncharacteristically coyly. 'I'm not sure what we're talking about here.'

'Oh I think you do. Isn't this what life is all about? Sitting, pleasantly tipsy, in a beautiful city, miles from home and work, and all those boring limitations?'

'What boring limitations? I thought you did what you wanted.'

'I do. I was talking about you.'

She propped her elbow on the table and rested her chin on her hand. 'I've warned you, reverse psychology doesn't work on me.'

'What does?'

She grinned. 'Depends.'

Amy thought this was one of those conversations she would be embarrassed about in the morning. But right now she didn't care. There had been moments like this throughout her life, when sensibilities slipped away, and she had wanted to experience what she knew probably wasn't right for her. But on a night like this who cared?

Greg and Amy leant back in their chairs, and smiled at each other. Every now and then one of them would burst into a flutter of laughter, which triggered off the other. This went on for a few surreal minutes but then Greg's face grew intensely serious and he seemed troubled. Amy looked at him but said nothing.

He fidgeted with a beer mat and said nervously, 'I really like you, Amy.'

She sighed. 'Shame we work together.'

Silence descended. The quiet before the storm? Amy ran her hand through her hair again. Greg kept tapping the side of the beer mat, with increasing speed.

Amy crossed her legs, then uncrossed them.

He tapped the side of his glass. 'Does that really matter?' he blurted out.

Her eyes connected with his.

Greg put down his glass and stood up. 'It's getting late. Shall we go up?'

She nodded and followed him through the bar, across the lobby to the lift. Greg pressed the button but it took ages to come. In that time they neither spoke nor moved. Eventually the doors opened and they walked in, a foot apart.

Greg pressed the fourth-floor button and, as the doors closed and the lift moved, they looked at each other and grinned. Then Greg grabbed her and pinned her up against the wall, pressed his mouth into hers and kissed her.

Amy knew that this was all wrong, but strangely it just added to the excitement. Her heart was racing, and her lips moved fast under his. Her hands were under his jumper, caressing him. Greg's right hand was under her dress, travelling determinedly upwards, pressing with expert ease between the top of her legs. Amy groaned, and he pulled away to press the 'door open' button, which brought the lift to a stop. The door opened to reveal a brick wall.

'What are you doing?' she gasped.

He pulled her to him with force. 'I dare you,' he whispered, eyes glistening.

'Jesus, Greg, not here!'

'I hate limitations, Amy. I embrace open-mindedness.'

She freed herself, and pressed the 'door close' button, which sent the lift on its way. 'My room,' she said breathlessly.

Almost immediately the lift stopped again and he grabbed her hand, pulled her down the corridor and stopped at her bedroom door. Amy took out her key and pouted. 'I don't have anything,' she said.

'Back in two minutes.' He dashed away.

Amy went into her room and sat on the corner of her bed. She closed her eyes and waited.

Greg burst into his room and made for the bathroom. He opened his shaving bag and pulled out a packet of condoms. He grinned, flicked it into the air and caught it. On leaving the bathroom he spotted his mobile phone on the side table and picked it up. He typed in a text message: 'Daniel, get your credit card out. Skiing is on you! Women are so easily moulded!' And pressed 'send'.

15

Greg glided down the hotel corridor like a cheetah. When he got to Amy's room, he stood outside and smiled broadly, before composing himself and knocking twice.

'Greg,' exclaimed Amy, as she opened the door. 'My room's getting like Piccadilly Circus.'

As the door opened wider, Greg's face hardened into a vicious glare – Ben was sitting in one of the two armchairs and on seeing Greg he looked away.

Marching in, Greg stopped barely two feet from him. 'Good evening, Ben. What brings you here at this time?' he said, with an edge to his voice.

'Ben had some concerns about the presentation,' said Amy. 'I was reassuring him that it went well.' She was moving from one foot to the other. 'I expect you've come for that report,' she blurted out to Greg, cringing inside at the obvious lie. You'd think with all her years in sales and marketing she could have come up with something better.

Greg ignored her and continued to stare menacingly at Ben, so Amy went over to her briefcase, took out her file on TGA – it was the only one she had – and shoved it into Greg's hands. Then she went to the door and opened it. 'Don't stay up all night reading that.'

He didn't move.

'We can talk later about it. I'm sure you have to go,' she said insistently.

He still didn't move. He stood erect and stony-faced, like a gunfighter preparing to draw. But suddenly, out of nowhere, a smile shot across his face. He started to laugh, but it wasn't a joyful sound. Ben and Amy stared at him. Then he joined Amy by the door. 'I hope Ben doesn't mope here all night. That wouldn't be very exciting,' he said, and left.

Confused, Amy shut the door, hoping her face wasn't as crimson as it felt. She sat down opposite Ben in the other armchair. 'It went well, Ben. You handled the presentation great. If we don't win the contract it won't be anything to do with you. Stop looking so worried. I didn't realize how worked up about things you got.'

She had nearly died when he had appeared at her door. When he knocked she had assumed it was Greg and had jumped when she saw Ben, unable to hide her shock. He had said he needed to discuss the presentation and walked straight in without invitation. She'd tried to get rid of him — they'd discuss it in the morning — but he had practically pleaded to stay for a while. Amy wondered if he was planning to make a pass at her. He might be happily married but, after years in business and staying in hotels, nothing surprised her about men. *Nothing!*

Now she really wanted him to go. 'It's late, Ben. Can we continue this tomorrow?'

Eventually he nodded and stood up. Relieved, she went to the door and opened it. He was staring at her and biting his bottom lip.

Oh, God, she thought. *He is going to make a pass.*

'Amy.'

'Good night, Ben.'

He didn't move.

'It's late. You have to go,' she said.

'But, Amy . . .'

'I'm very tired.'

'*Listen.*' He paused. 'Just be careful of Greg.' He said it almost as though it were blasphemous to utter his name in such a context.

'There's nothing to be careful of. There's nothing going on between us. I hope you don't think there is,' she said, sounding overly defensive.

'Greg's really intelligent,' he said.

'So?'

'In a lot of ways he's OK.'

'And?'

'But he does stuff. Nothing means anything to him. *Nothing*. And no one will change that.'

She was frowning. 'I'll see you tomorrow.'

'I've really put my neck on the line telling you this. Watch yourself.' With that he left.

Amy shut the door and stood with her back against it, breathing deeply.

Five minutes later there was another knock and her heart began to race again. She revolved on the spot and opened the door. Greg tried to walk in, but Amy didn't move so he stepped back.

'I really like you, Amy,' he said soothingly.

She smiled at him, but she didn't move. 'I like you too, but maybe this isn't a good idea.'

She thought she saw many emotions flicker across his face, but none seemed to settle. Eventually, a wounded child-like innocence seemed to emerge.

'There's no hurry, is there? We can continue getting to know each other back in London. See what happens,' she said reassuringly.

'Of course. Whatever you want.' He looked hurt, which made her feel guilty.

'Shall we have one more drink?' he said.

'I've had enough. Early flight and everything.'

He nodded, but at the same time he reached out and took her hand, gently squeezing it in his. 'At least let's talk, then. I really want to get to know you, Amy. I want to know everything about you.'

She was staring at her hand in his, which he was stroking now: his index finger was moving round her palm and her body tingled. Soon his fingers were moving over her wrist and slowly up her arm.

'This is a funny sort of talking,' she said.

He smiled and took her other hand. She was about to protest when, in one sudden, forceful movement, he had turned her round, stepped inside, kicked the door shut and pressed her against it, pinning both arms above her head.

'I don't think this is a good idea,' Amy began, but, as if he hadn't heard her, he started to kiss her neck. His lips travelled up to behind her ear and he gently sucked the lobe. It tickled, and she smiled. Next she felt the tip of his tongue glide down and along the neckline of her dress to the top of her breasts. He blew across her chest and a warm sensation spread through her body. She let out a little groan, but she tried to free her hands.

'Greg. No. Not like this.'

His head jerked up and he looked into her eyes. 'You want it, Amy. I know you do.'

'I—'

Before she could say any more his lips were on hers and his tongue in her mouth. His body pressed hard against her and, letting go of her wrists, he slid his right hand up the inside of her thigh and tugged her knickers down. In a split second he had yanked her dress up to her waist and fallen to his knees. He began licking her with his firm tongue.

She gasped and let out a cry. She knew she should stop him and walk away, but what he was doing felt so good. Her hands were now free yet they remained above her head against the door for support. Her heart thudded.

Walk away Amy, said a little voice in her head.

But her body refused to move.
What are you doing, Amy?
It's just sex. We're both young and single.
It'll complicate things.
I'm in Florence. I don't care.
You'll regret it in the morning.
Go to hell, Conscience!

When she screamed – so loud she was sure that the whole hotel heard – Greg stood up and kissed her lips. And a short while later, there against the door, he entered her.

16

'I bet you never expected this as part of your tenancy agreement – hard labour in sub-zero temperatures,' said Amy, jumping up and down on the spot. 'Forget green fingers, mine are frost-bitten.'

John Smith smiled and picked up the rake. 'With my SAS Arctic training I don't feel the cold,' he said matter-of-factly and began to rake the chopped conifer branches into a pile by the wheelbarrow.

She picked up the other rake and made a half-hearted attempt to help him. 'Every year I suggest we hire a gardener, but I'm always outvoted. Like a friend said recently, democracy is overrated.'

Unfortunately for Amy, her neighbours wanted to keep the house maintenance costs to a minimum, so any suggestion to spend money on something unessential brought a firm refusal from everyone. She knew she shouldn't complain because Thomas did most of the work. Every week he mowed the large communal lawn, which was encircled by trees, bushes and flower-beds, but twice a year, spring and autumn, under his supervision, it had become a ritual for everyone to lend a hand and clear away old shrubs, weeds and any other rubbish. Unfortunately, after the recent mild spell, winter had returned with a vengeance and it was freezing today. Amy checked her watch. Another two hours of this torture. Thomas was ordering Steve around at the other end of the garden. 'I suspect in a former life, Thomas was a Siberian work-camp commandant,' she told John. 'Any form of power goes to his head. Hilda's just as bad. She was probably some Viking warlord. No doubt they make love with military precision.'

John grimaced, which made her laugh. 'Sorry – I have to amuse myself somehow or a day like this would send me doo-lally.'

'And what were you in a past life?' he asked, with a grin.

'Joan of Arc? Florence Nightingale?'

'I feel unworthy to rake leaves with you.'

'It's OK,' she said. 'I asked to be a fairly average person in this life. One can tire of putting the world to rights.'

'I can imagine.'

A little while later, wearing a pair of rubber gloves, Amy started to scoop the wet branches and leaves into the wheelbarrow. She wrinkled her nose at the stench. When she glanced up, John was laughing at her. She shot him a dirty look. 'So, go on, put us out of our misery. What do you really do for a living?' she asked.

A few feet away, Tessa, who was weeding, stopped to listen.

'I thought you didn't want to be disappointed,' he said.

'I'm used to men disappointing me.'

'That explains it.'

'Explains what?'

He continued to rake the rubbish towards her.

'*Explains what?*' she said, hands on her hips.

From the opposite corner of the garden Hilda shouted, 'Amy, can you help over here a minute?'

'It seems my expertise is needed elsewhere,' she said. 'You'll have to save your disappointment until later.' With that she strode off with a defiant air about her. Half-way across the garden when she glanced back he was still staring at her.

Odd bloke, thought Amy. John had hardly spoken all

day and had spent most of his time digging the flower beds with Steve, who had been equally as quiet. They'd both worked impressively hard, shaming everyone else. John was wearing several layers of tatty jumpers, jeans and large black biker boots, with an old Mexican-style riding hat.

'Check out Clint Eastwood,' Amy had said jokingly to Tessa, when he appeared on the hazy horizon that morning.

'Ssh, he might hear you,' she remonstrated, anxiously.

Tessa had spent the morning constantly darting back into her apartment, before plucking up the courage to reappear, sometimes as many as fifteen minutes later. After 'Good morning,' she hadn't spoken another word to anyone and had spent the day pulling up the same patch of weeds. Amy had told John that Tessa had an upset stomach: it seemed the easiest way to explain her disappearances.

By four o'clock everyone was freezing, so the day's activities were brought to an abrupt close and they arranged to meet up in John's at half five for drinks and food. They usually met up after the day's exertions at Hilda and Thomas's, but John had offered this time to make up for his absence at Amy's.

Half an hour later, Amy had had a hot shower and was wrapped in a large white towel. She went to her answering-machine. Nothing! She stared at the red light, willing it to flash. Why hadn't Greg called? She'd woken up in Florence the next morning to find that he had already slipped back to his own room. On the flight back he had hardly spoken to her, instead issued Ben with a million tasks – companies to contact, reports he wanted on his desk by first thing Monday. Greg had had appointments for the rest of Friday so,

Matchstick Love

after leaving the departure lounge, she hadn't seen him again. She had telephoned his mobile phone on Friday night but it went straight to voicemail: 'Hi, Greg, it's Amy. Call me when you get a moment.'

It was now Sunday evening. She grunted indignantly, yet the memory of their night together brought a smile to her face, then a blush. They'd made love three times – once against the door, once in the shower and once outside on the secluded balcony. Ben's room was underneath hers, and she hoped he hadn't heard anything, although he probably had, as they had been noisy. The only time they had gone near the bed was to finally sleep.

Amy concluded that Greg was one of the most exciting men she'd ever met.

But why the hell hadn't he rung? She prayed that he wasn't another commitment phobic like Simon Delaney. But even Simon, at such an early stage, had still been keen. Anyway, she'd see Greg at work tomorrow and they could have a chat then.

After blow-drying her blonde hair, she put on a low-cut red top over a short black skirt, then pulled on her black knee-length boots. She felt a bit dressed-up for John's but she had arranged to see some friends later. She put on some makeup, including red lipstick, grabbed a bottle of wine and went out. As arranged she knocked on Tessa's door: there was no way her friend would go in alone. After a few minutes Tessa opened it, and Amy had to suppress a smile. Her friend's expression was more akin to that of a condemned woman about to face a firing squad rather than a social event. However, she was also wearing twice the usual amount of makeup and her reddish hair had been gelled – it appeared both longer and straighter than usual.

'Don't think, just come,' ordered Amy. If that didn't work she'd try the nicely-nicely approach.

'I am . . . just . . .'

'Just nothing.'

'But—'

'No. Just come.'

'But I like him,' whispered Tessa.

'Who? John Smith? He's all right, I suppose. A bit odd.'

'No, I *like* him,' she repeated.

'As in fancy, attracted to, kissing, that sort of stuff?'

Tessa nodded, and her head drooped between rounded shoulders.

'You haven't liked anyone in ages,' Amy exclaimed.

'I haven't met anyone in ages.'

'True. So just get your things. We're going in.'

Tessa stared across the hall at John's front door.

'Tessa, if I have to drag you kicking and screaming, you're going in there tonight. You're too young to climb into your coffin so hurry up and get out here.'

Tessa vanished into her flat for another six minutes. When, finally, she appeared, Amy said, 'Ready?' She knew exactly what Tessa had been doing.

'I suppose.'

After she had double-locked her door, both women crossed the hall to John's and knocked. A moment later the door opened and he was standing there in a pair of tan trousers and a black T-shirt that looked as if it had seen better days. While Amy stared at the whole on his shoulder, she felt his eyes travel over her own outfit. Both their eyes then met and each one offered the other a discerning smile.

'Good evening.' Amy handed him the bottle of wine.

He thanked her, then led them to the living room where Hilda and Thomas, who were sitting on a two-seater sofa, greeted them. Steve was sitting in a chair in the corner, drinking from a can of beer – one of the eight he'd brought as usual.

'Hello, you two,' boomed Hilda, holding up her sherry glass. 'We wondered where you'd got to.'

'Just defrosting,' said Amy, sitting on the other sofa. Tessa sank down beside her and stared at the wall. Her right foot started to tap the floor and she fidgeted with her front-door keys. She was breathing deeply, and had blushed dark red.

John disappeared into the kitchen and Hilda sighed contentedly. 'Isn't this nice? All the house together again.'

Everyone nodded politely.

'We're lucky Helen let her apartment to someone as nice as John. We've heard some nightmare stories about neighbours.'

'Nightmare stories,' echoed Thomas. 'There's a lot of strange people in this world. Very strange indeed.'

John returned, handed Amy and Tessa glasses of red wine, and declared that the food was ready. They all went into the kitchen and helped themselves to pasta and spicy vegetarian tomato sauce. Back in the living room, Amy tasted hers. It was delicious. Everyone else thought so too, and compliments filled the air.

'I was eating pasta in Florence on Thursday night and I have to say this compares very favourably,' Amy said.

John was sitting on the floor beside her, his back against the fireplace. His penetrating blue eyes seemed to stare right through her.

'Amy jets around the world like it's a trip to the local shops,' said Hilda.

'Through your job?' he asked.

She nodded.

'What do you do?'

'Event management, corporate hospitality.'

He made no acknowledgement.

'Parties, product launches . . .' she explained.

'Yes, I'm familiar with the industry,' he replied, a touch dismissively.

She sipped her wine, eyeing him furtively. 'And so, John Smith, do the honours and finally tell us what line of work you're in.'

'I bet you're a chef!' bellowed Hilda.

'A gardener?' laughed Thomas.

'A musician?' said Steve, pointing to the three different guitars lying around.

John looked at Tessa, whose eyes darted away. She declined to hazard a guess.

'A drug-dealing pimp,' said Amy. Thomas and Hilda looked aghast, but John smiled wryly.

He took a deep breath and shook his head. 'I do a lot of things, but from nine to five I work as a benefits supervisor.'

Everyone looked at him questioningly.

'I work at the local unemployment office, supervising a benefits section. Dealing with people's unemployment claims,' he added.

The rest nodded but Amy screwed her face up in dismay. 'The *dole* office,' she said loudly.

'Yes.'

What an anticlimax, she thought. 'And the police car?'

'A drunk claimant struck one of my staff, a young girl in her twenties. I was at the hospital, then had to give a statement. They dropped me back.'

'No spying, then.'

'Disappointed?'

'*Very*.' She sighed. 'No one is ever who you think

Matchstick Love

they are,' she said, almost to herself, and glanced at the clock on the mantelpiece. She decided to stay another half-hour then leave. Her thoughts drifted to Greg and she wondered again why he hadn't telephoned. An unsettled feeling descended on her. Unbeknown to her, all the while John was staring at her. Her eyes eventually met his and she mustered a polite smile and asked half-heartedly, 'So what's it like working at a dole office? I've never even been in one.'

'How fortunate of you.'

'Hardly fortunate. More a decision.'

'Deciding what?'

'To be independent. To rely on no one, least of all the state,' she said.

'I've found, over the years, that life is never quite so clear-cut.' He sounded exasperated.

'I've found the opposite.' Their eyes locked briefly, but Amy couldn't be bothered to pursue it.

'Was the girl who got hit OK?' asked Hilda.

'Fine, just shaken up,' said John.

'What about the guy who hit her? What's happening to him?' asked Thomas.

'Nothing. Just a warning, I think.'

'Tsk,' said Thomas. 'Doesn't surprise me. A bunch of softies run the Government.'

'Drunk, first offence,' said John. 'It's not usually violent. Some people get angry but you learn how to deal with them. Quite often they're just angry with their lives and it gets directed at you. But I can understand that. Not everyone's life is one big *corporate party*.'

Amy's jaw dropped. How rude! But John raised a defiant eyebrow at her then resumed eating.

'Isn't this nice?' said Hilda again. 'We should meet up regularly.'

The others nodded, but Amy's eyes strayed once

more to the clock and then to Tessa. Her friend was gripping her front-door key so tightly as if it was a hand grenade ready to go off.

The evening dragged on. After they finished eating, Hilda persuaded a reluctant John to play 'Morning Has Broken' on his guitar. She sang her heart out, totally out of tune. Then he sang Cat Stevens' 'Father and Son'. Even Amy had to admit he was very good. All the while Tessa, who hadn't said a word all night, stared at him as if she was in a trance. She'd actually let go of her key and it was on the floor beside her. Her face had relaxed and there was even a hint of a smile.

When John had finished he looked at Amy, who shook her head vigorously. 'I'll leave the entertainment to you.'

When Thomas started to recount a story of a friend of a friend of a friend who was blind, dying of cancer and had been mugged, Amy and Tessa took the opportunity to clear away the plates. Alone in the kitchen Tessa whispered to her, 'He's amazing, isn't he?'

'He's OK, I suppose.'

'Why? What's wrong with him?'

'Nothing.'

Tessa glowered at her. 'Just because he's not into world domination like that flash guy Greg doesn't mean he's not worth bothering with.'

Amy was startled by her forceful tone. 'Sorry – I didn't mean anything by it. If you like him that's all that matters. In fact, for you he's perfect, what with living across the hall.'

Tessa put the plates into the sink. 'There's more to life than ambition and excitement, Amy.'

'I know. Maybe I could help get you both together.

How about—' At that moment John walked in, and she switched to him: 'Thanks for a lovely meal. It was delicious. You'll have to come up to mine one night.'

He didn't reply.

'Unfortunately I have to be off now. I have to meet some friends.' She smiled at Tessa. 'But we'll definitely do this another night.'

'I have to go too,' said Tessa, 'but thank you, it was lovely.' She followed Amy back into the living room, and after they had both said goodbye to the others they went out to the hall, where John was holding open the front door.

'Thanks again,' said Amy. 'Hilda and Thomas have the right idea, love thy neighbour and all that.'

'Your compassion moves me,' John said wryly.

She eyed him dubiously, nodded and left. Tessa ran out behind her.

17

Amy was sitting at her desk, chewing her pen and gazing into space. It was now one o'clock and she still hadn't managed to talk to Greg. He'd been in a meeting with William and Roger first thing, but that had finished ages ago and he was now at his desk. Amy knew this because she had deliberately walked past his office twice. Each time he'd been on the phone and both Daniel and Ben had been there so she hadn't wanted to hang around. She had decided to send him an email.

```
Hi, Greg,
How was your weekend? Hope you got my call.
Any news on the TGA deal? Want to discuss it
over some lunch?
Amy.
```

She had sent it over an hour ago and there had still been no response. *Something was wrong.* She grabbed her handbag and went to buy a sandwich. I'm not approaching him any more, she thought. The ball's in his court. *I don't care either way.*

Amy spent most of the afternoon compiling evidence to support her proposals for the internal changes at CEM. She expected a lot of resistance so she needed a watertight defence, especially as the others would have had time to prepare their own response. She felt a growing unease about Greg and the way he might play it.

Matchstick Love 119

At four o'clock Amy was just finishing a report on increasing sales turnover, when Charlotte, William's PA, walked into her office. With the trademark CEM insincere smile, she said, 'Hello, ladies, just to let you know, William wants everyone in the conference room at five this evening. He's going to make some important announcements.' With that, she left.

Amy wondered if the meeting had something to do with the TGA contract. But surely, as a member of the management team, she would have been informed first of any news.

At five to five, Amy and Beth left their office and headed for the conference room. As they walked in, the expectancy in the atmosphere hit them. All sixty staff were there, standing around in little huddles, champagne glasses in hand, excitedly awaiting the announcement as if it was the Second Coming of Christ. Amy smiled to herself as she took two glasses of champagne from the table and handed one to Beth. They made their way up the side of the room, and stopped a few feet from the front.

She froze. Greg was standing a few feet away, all smiles as he chatted to William and Roger, all three looked happy and relaxed. Just then Sally appeared at Greg's side. He patted her back and kissed her cheek. Amy's mouth tightened. Obviously they all knew something that she didn't and she felt like an outsider again.

'Isn't it exciting?' said an exuberant Issy, who had bounded over to them with her dazzling smile and sparkling eyes.

Tink was at her side, bouncing on the spot as if activated by an electric current. 'I understand there's a *few* announcements. What fun!'

'Isn't it?' enthused Beth, her eyes and smile matching theirs.

Amy nodded politely. She was convinced someone put cocaine in the coffee machine every morning. That was the only explanation for the perpetual high of the CEM women. She only drank tea, which she guessed was why she wasn't affected. She sipped her champagne and glanced at Greg, hoping to catch his eye but his back was towards her.

At last William made his way on to the podium. 'Excuse me, everyone,' he said loudly. 'May I have your attention, please?'

There was instant silence. Every pair of eyes was on him.

'Thank you all for coming. As you know, CEM has been working to win a very large contract.'

There was a communal gasp.

'We have been up against the best of our competitors. However . . .'

The whole room held its breath, apart from Amy who continued to sip her champagne and watch Greg. He was standing erect and proud, with a satisfied, authoritarian smile.

'. . . I would like to announce that we have been awarded the TGA contract.'

A huge cheer erupted. Several women squealed. Kisses, hugs and elated smiles spread like malaria. Tink and Issy embraced like long-lost sisters.

'Yes, it's great news,' continued William, over the frenzy, 'but if I may have your attention again . . .'

Silence.

'Although a number of people have worked hard on winning this contract, I must pay due respect to one person. If it wasn't for him, we would never have been in the running. I'd like you to raise your glasses to—'

Everyone was nodding, already knowing who it was.

'– to Greg.'

Matchstick Love

Another huge cheer erupted, followed by rapturous clapping. Greg turned and acknowledged the applause.

'To Greg,' said William, raising his glass.

'To Greg,' everyone repeated.

Amy raised her glass also. Again she tried to catch Greg's eye to congratulate him, but he seemed to be looking everywhere except in her direction. She wasn't sure if he'd even spotted her yet.

William raised a hand to quieten everyone. 'I have three more announcements.' His previous smile faded. 'Unfortunately, an important and valued member of staff is departing. Roger has been offered a position at Tanner and Domec, one of the sister companies. He'll be leaving us with immediate effect.'

Everyone pulled the requisite sad expression.

'I would like to take the opportunity to thank him for all that he's done and wish him the best of luck with his new position.'

Again glasses were raised.

Roger got toasted and William invited him up on to the podium to say a few words. Roger thanked everyone and said he had enjoyed his time at CEM.

As Roger stepped down from the podium William continued.

'Although Roger will be greatly missed, work goes on, so it gives me great pleasure to announce his successor.'

Amy noticed that the whole room was already smiling, apart from Ben who was standing at the back looking ill-at-ease.

'The new sales and marketing director is Greg.'

Yet more cheers, more squealing and more rapturous clapping. An instant queue formed to pat Greg on the back and congratulate him. Amy joined it. He deserved the promotion, she thought, and her attraction to him grew. There was something about ambitious and successful men that she found irresistible.

She was nearing him when William gestured for him to come up on to the podium, which he did.

'I'd now like to make the final announcement,' said William. 'And, I warn you, this may disappoint a number of the ladies out there.'

Greg beside him, started to laugh.

Amy stood upright, smile somewhat faded but still intact.

'Finally, and long overdue, I might add,' said William, 'Greg and Miranda have announced their engagement.'

Amy's smile vanished. The cheers and clapping around her felt miles away. In that moment she could only focus on Greg, who was sipping champagne now and occasionally waving from the podium, as if he'd just received a gold medal at the Olympics. For nearly two minutes she stood vacantly. Then her lips narrowed, and lines developed on her forehead.

'Amy.' Beth was tapping her shoulder. 'Wake up! I said, we're off to Kudos. Are you coming?'

As if in slow motion, Amy turned to face her. No words came. Instead she shook her head.

'That's a shame. Should be quite a night, with all we've got to celebrate,' said Beth, and she turned to go.

'Ciao.' Issy waved at her.

'Toodle-pip,' said Tink, with her trademark wink.

Amy remained standing by the wall, waiting for the room to clear. Her fists were clenched and she was flushed with rage. The veins in her neck throbbed. Greg was chatting with Sally and three girls from Operations.

'He looks in his element.'

Amy turned. Ben was beside her. 'Miranda's father is

extremely wealthy.' He sighed. 'Like I said, Amy, nothing means anything to him.' He walked slowly away.

Several minutes later Sally and the other girls wandered off. It was then that Greg looked up and, for the first time, stared directly at Amy. He walked over to her and asked, 'Did you want something?'

'Just an explanation.'

He put on a look of confused innocence.

'*What the hell's going on?*' she snapped. 'You were sleeping with me in Florence, and now you're engaged.'

For several seconds he just stared at her and then in an unruffled yet cold and contemptuous voice he said, 'Some women are for marrying, some just for *screwing*.' He smiled and walked calmly away.

'*How fucking dare you?*' she yelled.

But he was gone.

18

'*He actually said that!*'

Amy gulped down the remains of her third vodka and orange, then slammed her fist hard on the kitchen table. Through clenched teeth, she said, 'He took pleasure in saying it.'

Tessa, who was sitting opposite, shook her head in disbelief. 'What's he playing at? The guy must be insane.'

Amy got up to fix herself another drink. Tessa watched as she flung ice into her glass, followed by a double measure of vodka and a splash of orange juice. Seething inside, she slumped down at the table. 'He's not insane. He's just a first-class shit. And I fell for it.' Her head fell forward into her hands.

For the last hour she had paced up and down her kitchen, swearing and gesticulating as she relayed the scene over and over again to Tessa, as if she might come up with some reasonable explanation for Greg's behaviour. Amy had met her fair share of bastards but this was way beyond her comprehension. It was only during the last ten minutes that she had calmed down enough to sit down.

'All the warning signs were there, Amy. I remember at the beginning you couldn't stand him. What changed?' asked Tessa.

'He's a clever shit and I'm a damn fool. God knows what he was playing at.'

'Sex, Amy.'

'He could get that anywhere.'

'He sounds dangerous to me. You should be careful.'

She sat bolt upright. 'Fuck him. He's the one who

needs to be careful. That bastard won't know what's hit him.'

'He's now sales and marketing director, he could make life difficult for you.'

'Wake up and smell the coffee, Tessa! He's going to make life difficult for me anyway. That's a given. Thank God I don't report to him.'

'Maybe you should say something to William.'

'Of course I can't. You don't involve your MD in something like this. It's nothing to do with him. It's not an official matter.'

'Not yet.'

'Not ever. I can look after myself,' Amy said defiantly.

'Look, don't scream at me again, but you did flirt with him,' Tessa said cautiously. 'You encouraged him, too. I think you need to have a good think about what attracted you to him – what type of men you're attracted to.'

'Tessa, this isn't the time to go all analytical on me. He's the screwed-up bastard, not *me*!'

'I know . . . But what about Simon?'

'What about him?'

'Well, it was obvious *that* was never going to work. He'll never commit to anyone. He has more issues than *Reader's Digest*.'

'Hindsight is marvellous,' said a scowling Amy.

'I just think that you can be dismissive of perfectly nice men. You're too judgemental.'

Amy let her head drop so far forward that it nearly touched the table. Sounding defeated she said, 'This really isn't the time to go on at me. I'm sure John's a very nice person. I'm glad you like him. Ignore me, it's obvious I have crap taste in men.'

Tessa sighed. 'In a way you've had a lucky escape. I

wonder what Miranda's life will be like with him. He'll probably be screwing around on their honeymoon. All you can do is put it down to experience and learn from it.'

Again Amy slammed her fist on the table. 'If he starts giving me a hard time at work, I won't take it lying down. He chose the wrong person to make a fool of.'

'What will you do?' asked a worried-looking Tessa.

'Whatever I have to. There must be lots of dirt on a man like him. I'd say he's crossed the line a few times. It's just a case of looking hard enough. In fact, there's something at CEM that doesn't add up. I think it's about time I started to look into it discreetly.' With a manic look in her eye she added, 'As God is my judge, Greg will regret the day he messed with me.'

19

Amy was at her desk by seven thirty the next morning, going over her proposals for the internal changes and restaffing. She was even more determined to push them through, but her watertight defence now had to be bomb-proof, radiation-proof and, above all, Greg-proof.

Make no mistake, this was war. And he had more allies than she did. She wondered if she had any allies at all. Apart from William, who was neutral, everyone else was well and truly in Greg's camp. Even Beth had become a super-duper CEM type, confident, posh and impeccably turned out.

At half past eight Beth bounced in, all smiles. 'Good morning, Amy. We missed you last night,' she said, taking off her new full-length suede coat.

'I *so* wanted to go but I had some things to do,' Amy replied, upbeat.

'What a shame. You missed a super evening. Absolutely everyone was there. I left at eleven but it was still going strong. We all got to meet Miranda. She's absolutely lovely. Such a sweetie.'

'Oh, I can imagine,' said Amy, through gritted teeth.

'She's delightful.'

'I'm sure.'

'And they're so in love.'

'How wonderful.'

'I think they'll be deliriously happy together. They're so well suited,' enthused Beth.

'Two peas in a pod,' said Amy, her sarcasm too subtle for Beth to detect.

'You know who her father is?'

Amy shook her head.

'Sir James Rancorn-Burch,' Beth said excitedly.

Amy stared at her blankly.

'I thought everyone knew who Sir James Rancorn-Burch was,' Beth demurred.

'Everyone but me.'

'Multi-millionaire is an understatement. Multi-billionaire is more like it. In my copy of *Who's Who*, it says he has property portfolios around the world – owns half of New York, apparently. Plus he has interests in numerous companies, everything from gold to gas, entertainment to manufacturing. You name it, he owns it,' Beth gushed. 'However, apparently Sir James is quite a pious and authoritarian sort of man. Greg will have to prove himself before he gets a slice of the action. I heard it on good authority that Sir James is going to watch his career for the next two years, see what he achieves off his own bat. Then he'll be invited into the family business. If all goes to plan Greg could be running the whole damn corporation. He's certainly fallen on his feet.'

Amy turned her face to the wall and grimaced.

William popped his head in. 'Good morning, ladies.'

'Morning, William,' said Amy.

'Delightful morning, isn't it?' said Beth, swirling round to face him.

William nodded. 'Could we have a chat, Amy?'

'Of course.'

'Now, if you're free.'

Amy got up and followed him down the corridor and into his spacious office. It had full-length glass windows on both external sides, and a view of Piccadilly Circus. He sat down at his metallic, oval desk and Amy took the seat opposite.

'Great news about the TGA contract. Even Pablo's

happy. And he's *never* happy,' he said, with a smile that made the wrinkles show up around his eyes.

He was a slender man in his early fifties, but he appeared younger, with a friendly, open face and a seemingly relaxed manner. But Amy knew he was no one's fool. He was on the ball and commanded a lot of respect, but he was fair and open-minded, laying his cards on the table instead of having a million hidden agendas. By all accounts he was a family man with two young sons from his marriage to a beautiful Polish ex-model, and an older daughter with his first wife.

'Hopefully he's off your back for a while,' she said.

'Probably not, but that's life in today's market. Anyway, I wanted to thank you for your own contribution to winning the TGA contract. I thought afterwards that I should have mentioned you and Sally yesterday.'

'It's not a problem,' she said.

'Greg tells me Mark Greenshawe is most impressed by you.'

Instantly suspicious, Amy tensed inside, yet on the outside she maintained her confident, professional demeanour. 'Did he?'

'Yes. That, along with your experience, is why I want to discuss a temporary change and addition to your job role. I'd like you to be involved in the implementation of the airline's relaunch. We may have won the contract but the hard work starts here.'

'What did you have in mind?' she asked.

'We need someone to be the main liaison between TGA's marketing department, their chosen advertising and PR agencies, and our own operations team. The appointed person will have to sit in on numerous meetings, and they'll have creative input. It'll be down to them to ensure that all the various agencies and departments are briefed and pulling in the same direction.'

'That's a lot of work,' she said. 'Although I've come up with strategies on how to handle it, I thought someone from Sales and Marketing would implement them. Why me?'

'This is a huge project. With your experience of PR, marketing and high-level management negotiation, you're ideal. I wouldn't feel happy with a less senior person involved, and Mark Greenshawe wouldn't appreciate it either. He wants to talk to senior managers only. Greg was going to assume this role but his promotion makes it impossible. I anticipate it'll account for about thirty per cent of your time.'

This worried Amy. 'Probably more, if handled right, and it would detract from my main role of implementing growth strategies and winning new business. Long-term, isn't it best if I continue fully focused on my original aim? Pablo wants results.'

'I appreciate that,' said William. 'And of course I have considered the long-term picture. However, this change would only be for three or four months, the length of the project. I believe the benefits of having you on the TGA team will outweigh any short-term setbacks. Greg's having a team meeting at eleven, which you can attend. He'll oversee the project and will brief you on the requirements of your role better than I can. He's drawn up a job spec.'

'I have a job spec?' she said, trying to control the curtness in her voice.

'Of course. As I said, this is just a temporary change. Half of your time at the most.'

'Reporting to Greg?'

William looked puzzled. 'It depends on how you

choose to see it. With regard to this project, then yes, he's overseeing it so you'd submit your ideas to him.' He passed a blue file across to her.

'But I was brought in to report directly to you.'

'You'll continue to report to me with regard to the rest of your work.'

'This wasn't the job I applied for. With respect, William, you're changing my role without consulting me.'

William sat back in his chair and tapped his lip with his index finger, deep in thought. Eventually, in a calm, friendly manner, he said, 'Amy, I'm sure I don't need to tell you that in a changing market we all have to be flexible.'

'It's not that I'm inflexible. However, I believed my position was on par with the Sales and Marketing director. I don't want to compromise that now by reporting to him.'

'You *are* on par with the sales and marketing director. I'm merely asking you to take on an extra role and that extra role just happens to have Greg as the senior figure. I don't understand your reluctance. This is an exciting project for CEM, for the whole industry. I thought you'd want to be involved.'

Amy couldn't believe this was happening, but she could see that William was unimpressed by her less than enthusiastic reaction. She smiled. 'It's just that I don't want it to detract from my main role of increasing the profitability of the company. I am totally committed to that.'

'Handled right, we could win numerous new clients on the back of this. Greg's already submitted an excellent report on how we should capitalize on such a high-prestige account. He believes we can use it to get CEM's name across the whole of Europe.'

Amy's lips thinned and she clenched her fists, yet she kept her smile – just about. 'I'd like to read it.'

'Ask him for a copy.'

'Oh, I will.'

At that moment William's telephone rang. He apologized for the interruption, answered it and began an in-depth discussion. Amy took the opportunity to open the blue file, which contained details of the TGA project team and the relevant job specs. First she came across Sally's. She would head the operations side, directly managing a team of thirteen, who would organize the logistics of moving the road show between venues in the UK and Europe. Her team would be responsible for booking and supervising the venues, hotels, caterers, transport and the production company. A team of fourteen roadies would tour with them, rigging and de-rigging the set, including the dummy aeroplane fuselage. Sally's staff would also manage the invitation process, which involved designing and creating a database to hold the details of the airlines most valued clients and frequent flyers. These people, along with representatives of the travel industry and the main corporate travel bookers, would be sent invitations and asked to reply by telephone to another separate team of four who would man a live booking service. In all, Sally would be responsible for over a hundred staff.

Next, Amy found Daniel's job specification. His title had become senior business development manager. Ben should have got that promotion, she thought. On this project Daniel would act as a liaison between the TGA sales teams and Sally, monitoring invitation responses.

Then Amy came to her own job specification. It was pretty much what William had said: she would be CEM's representative in all publicity, advertising and

PR matters, sitting in on numerous meetings. The trouble was, over the next few months there would be hundreds of them and she could see this turning into a full-time job. Plus the man she detested most in the world was in charge. *How could they work together?* It was a nightmare, yet she was powerless to change anything.

William put down the phone and Amy closed the file.

'So, are you OK with this move?' he asked.

Amy knew that if she refused she might lose William's support and now, more than ever, she needed it. 'I'd like my reservations noted,' she said, 'but I'll give it my best shot.'

He looked relieved. 'I did want to attend Greg's meeting at eleven myself, but unfortunately I have other commitments. Good luck with it all. I'm sure it's going to be a great success.' He brought his hands together and nodded, a sign that he considered the meeting closed.

'What about my proposals for the internal changes?' she asked.

'I think we should postpone that for a couple of weeks. Greg needs to get the TGA project team up and running.'

'I think it imperative that we still push ahead with all other business,' she said, politely but firmly.

'Of course, but not for two or three weeks' Amy.'

'I've put a lot of work into firming up my proposals.'

'Drop me a copy, however a step at a time. Now if you'll excuse me, I have other matters to attend to.'

Amy stood outside the boardroom. It was as if she had X-ray vision and could see through it to the enemy who awaited her.

It was gone eleven, yet she couldn't propel herself inside. Her fists were clenched, her stomach tight, her lips pinched. Her eyes betrayed the hatred that pumped through her. Yet she knew that if she was going to get her own back, she had to keep her head.

Breathing in deeply, she exhaled slowly, several times, deliberately calming herself, and then with a defiant and anarchistic air about her, she pushed open the door and marched in.

As expected, three unfriendly faces looked up. Sally glanced at her, then turned away, Daniel appeared to be suppressing a childish smirk, and, of course, there was Greg. He was sitting in the middle of them at the head of the table, ridiculously presidential. He smiled broadly, yet there was no warmth in it: it was a symbol of gloating triumph. He lay back in his chair, clasping his hands behind his head; a man so totally at ease with himself. Unlike the other two, he kept his eyes on her as she approached and sat down next to Sally.

Eventually, in his velvety smooth and, in Amy's view, infuriatingly smug voice, he said, 'Welcome to *my* team, Amy.'

'Thank you, Greg. I feel *very* welcome.'

His eyes narrowed. 'I'm sure you'll get used to reporting to me.'

'It's for such a short time that I won't need to.'

'The future may hold things that we are not yet aware of.'

'My sentiments exactly.'

He seemed amused, then added curtly, 'For now just take on board the need for punctuality. If a meeting is called for eleven, it means eleven. Inefficiency won't be tolerated.'

She made no acknowledgement and continued to stare at him without expression.

He sat up straight and addressed all three, in a serious and focused manner. 'Right. Sitting around this table is the management team for the Trans-Global Airlines relaunch. If anything doesn't go to plan, it'll be one of your three arses I'll be kicking.'

The other two tittered but Amy's insides stewed and simmered in hatred. How can he feel no shame? she wondered. What sort of man is he?

'I want to take a moment to discuss your roles in more detail,' he said. 'I hope you've all read the team breakdown. I don't want anyone turning round halfway through and saying they didn't know a particular area was their responsibility.'

He spoke for at least ten minutes about what he expected of each of them. Daniel and Sally nodded continuously like obedient drones. Finally he came to Amy. She sat perched forward, legs crossed, pen in hand.

Greg started off by repeating what William had said to her. However, with each minute that passed he added additional responsibilities. Apparently he expected Amy to be the on-site CEM representative at the filming of the TGA television adverts. The trouble was, there were several weeks of shooting involved and some of it was in America. He also wanted her to fly round Europe to meet with the TGA manager of each country and brief them personally on the progress of the relaunch.

'I'm not running around like some glorified messenger,' she snapped. 'If I suffered from paranoia I might think you were trying to keep me out of the way.'

'It's a compliment, Amy. We need someone of your experience,' he replied. 'William also wants you to attend, with me, the main management meetings with TGA.'

'This is only supposed to account for thirty per cent of my time. Your specification is a full-time job.'

'Surely that's a case of your own time management.'

'It's impossible. I need to concentrate on my role in strategic planning.'

'Now that I'm sales and marketing director, I expect there'll be less call for that. It feels like a duplication of roles.'

Her eyes narrowed. Her face tightened. 'I disagree. William does too.'

'I'll talk to him.'

'So will I.'

'Wasn't it you who suggested cutting overheads,' he added with a smile.

For a few seconds there was silence. Amy saw Daniel and Sally exchange an amused glance. She stared pointedly at each one of them in turn. No way would those two intimidate her. Looking back at Greg she said resolutely, 'We can both discuss this in front of William, if you so wish. I'll attend some of the filming of the adverts but I'm not going to flit round Europe. That's a complete waste of my time, and I know William will agree with me. I have other more important business to attend to. I suggest you appoint someone from Operations.'

His eyes seemed to darken several shades. 'I'll give

it some thought.' Then he addressed all three. 'Attending TGA's management meetings and having constant update meetings with yourselves will be my only involvement – twenty per cent of my time max. If it's any more, it'll mean that one of you isn't doing your job right. Now that I'm sales and marketing director, my energies need to be fully focused on growing all areas of business at CEM. That is the prime role of a sales and marketing director.' A moment later he flung each of them a lengthy report. 'Familiarize yourselves with that. It gives you your TGA contacts. I want you all to make initial contact with the relevant people, produce your own report and schedules on how you intend to tackle your areas. I'd like it on my desk by Thursday. Daniel and I will be off skiing for a week and I want to read them while I'm away. In summary, for the next four months I expect you all to eat, breathe and sleep TGA. I won't tolerate anything less.'

Again the drones nodded while Amy seethed inside.

'In my absence, Sally's in charge.'

Both women glanced at each other then away. No way am I reporting to her, thought Amy. How was this happening? A million thoughts rampaged through her mind.

'Is everyone happy?' asked Greg, businesslike.

'Lots to do. But I like it that way,' said Sally.

'Very happy,' said Daniel.

Greg smiled, then looked at Amy. 'Any queries?'

Out of nowhere she beamed at him. 'Nothing I can't rectify. I know exactly what I have to do to address this situation.'

He appeared to hesitate and then, as if challenging her, said, 'I shall look forward to it. Life's a drag without surprises.' He gathered together his papers. 'Meeting concluded. Go forth and kick arse.'

The other two laughed, but Amy picked up her things and left.

Amy opened her front door and gasped.

'Hello, Amy. Thought I'd surprise you.'

Her mouth fell open. What the hell was he doing here?

'Hope you don't mind me calling round?'

Dumbfounded, she shook her head. Is it only my life that's in some out-of-control vortex? she thought.

'Can I come in?'

With a lacklustre nod, she stepped aside, and he walked casually across her living room to the balcony doors and peered outside. 'Plants are doing well.'

'Yes,' she said, still at the other end of the room, unsure what else to say.

Then he turned back to her. 'It's great to see you.'

Amy hesitated. 'It's good to see you too.'

With his smile remaining he sat down on one of the sofas and gazed around the large room. Amy went and sat down tentatively on the opposite one, crossing her legs and arms. What was he doing here – her ex – Simon Delaney! Successful IT Analyst with a string of qualifications and letters after his name. Amy would like to add a few more letters. CP. EJ. EN. Commitment Phobe, Error of Judgement and Emotional Neanderthal.

'So,' he said, 'I expect you're surprised to see me.'

'You could say that,' she said.

He laughed, a hearty belly laugh – the way you laugh when you really fancy someone and everything they say seems hilariously funny. 'How's the new job?'

'Er . . . Good. I'm really enjoying it. They're a

brilliant bunch of people. Great team. Best thing I did was to move on.'

'Sounds it.'

'Yeah, I've been lucky.'

'You look great.'

Amy knew she didn't. Expecting a lazy evening, she'd taken off her makeup, her hair was pulled off her face with an old hairband, and she was wearing her extra-baggy-round-the-bum, slime-green jogging pants and a holey purple jumper. I look crap, she thought. His remark irritated her because throughout their year-long relationship he had showered her with subtle criticisms about her appearance, always hidden under suggestions on hairstyles and outfits that he thought might suit her. Like a fool she'd even worn his disingenuous presents of dresses, tops and, of course, underwear. As he was ex-Merchant Navy, turnout was of immense importance to him. He was a perfectionist and had expected no less of Amy.

It had been a relief when they finished. She had been able to return to her glorious shortcomings. It wasn't even as if he was some oil painting. He wasn't bad-looking but he wasn't exactly good-looking either. He had grey-blue eyes, short mousy hair, a pale face, thin lips, and was tall and thin. It was easy to guess that he worked with computers: he looked very conservative – a grown-up Boy Scout.

It suddenly occurred to her that Simon would be well suited to a CEM type. They could strive together for perfection. But deep down the CEM types wanted the husband and the kids, and Simon, God bless him, would bail out long before that plane landed.

'We've missed you at Protea,' he said. 'Management meetings just aren't the same. No more ructions. Everyone agrees on everything – boringly tame.'

'Thanks. You make me sound like trouble.'

'Not at all. Passionate and motivated. Admirable qualities.'

She eyed him suspiciously.

'I'm sure it will please you to know that since you left the sales figures are down fourteen per cent.'

A smile shot across her face.

'Tom says the sales team are all feeling a bit deserted and wonder why you haven't been in touch.'

'I've been meaning to pop along one night,' Amy told him, feeling guilty, 'but it's been such long hours at the new job. I'll give him a call tomorrow. It's nice to know I've not been forgotten.'

Simon looked directly at her then lowered his eyelids. 'I suppose I've missed you too. Daft, isn't it? We don't appreciate what we've got until it's gone.'

Amy's eyes were on the floorboards and she wondered where this conversation was going.

'So you've been OK?' he said.

'Really good.' She thought she saw a glimmer of disappointment in his eyes. 'How have you been?' she asked.

'Actually, I haven't been great.'

'Oh?'

'I've missed you.'

She frowned and said defiantly, 'Really. I thought you were seeing the new receptionist.'

'Oh, Kim – she was just a temp.'

'As the receptionist or your girlfriend?'

Again he laughed. 'That's one of the things I miss about you, your sense of humour.'

But it wasn't a joke, Amy thought. If she were a smoker, it would have been a good moment to light up – something to do with her hands, something to focus on.

'Don't I get a cup of tea?' Simon asked jovially.

There was a noticeable delay before Amy stood up, went to the kitchen area and flicked on the kettle. As she took two mugs from the cupboard, she turned to find that Simon was at her side. She walked round him, put the mugs on the work surface and placed a teabag in each. They stood together, like a couple of lemons, waiting for the metallic kettle to boil.

'You sit down. I'll bring them over,' he said.

This was her kitchen. 'How about *you* sit down?' she said.

'OK,' he murmured, gazing into her face with such admiration as if she'd just singlehandedly tackled a crocodile or something.

Amy was rattled. Simon was the past. Life moves on. She had drawn a line well and truly under their relationship. *What* was he doing here? She sighed quietly, imagining a heavy, tense scene between them. But they'd had that scene. For the briefest of moments she considered another possibility. Maybe he did love her, after all. Perhaps he had been for counselling, found an inner awareness and solved his numerous issues. Yeah, right!

After she had made the tea she tried to remember if Simon took sugar. How dreadful – they'd practically lived together! His details had been filed away with all the other ex's details.

She picked up the sugar bowl and his mug, put them both on the table in front of him and went back for her own. Then she sat down opposite him again.

'Why are you here, Simon?' she asked.

He sat forward, shoulders hunched. 'I know I shut you out.'

Amy noticed that George Clooney was sitting on the

windowsill, staring at her warily with his big green eyes.

'I'm not sure why,' he went on.

'Maybe you should look into why.'

'It's just at times you—'

'Whoa, stop!' She lifted her hand. 'I didn't say I wanted to know the answer or be blamed.'

'I thought you'd want to talk about it. You were always going on about wanting to talk more.'

'That was when we were going out. We're not any more.'

'You were really good for me,' he said.

'Too good.'

'I won't deny that. It's just . . . people have to learn, don't they? I've learnt a lot about myself. I just wanted to see you again and say . . .'

Amy braced herself.

'. . . sorry!'

'Oh,' was her only response.

Simon smiled at her. Eventually Amy smiled back. This was good, she thought. Closure! He'd come round to say sorry. Maybe the vortex was dissipating.

'Do you want to go for a drink?' he asked.

'I'm a bit tired,' she said.

'Just a quick one.'

'It's getting late.'

'It's not even nine.'

'Maybe it's not such a good idea.'

'Why not?' he asked.

'Simon, until fifteen minutes ago I didn't expect to see you again.'

'That's kind of another reason why I called round. The thing is, we may run into each other now and again.'

Her whole body stiffened.

'It was you who gave me the idea, really. I felt I needed a change so I looked through the internal job vacancies within the group. Anyway, I saw Lazlo Manco were looking for a group IT manager.'

The colour was draining from her face.

'The board want to bring all the subsidiary companies into line, in terms of systems, software and equipment. The new IT manager will be based at the head office overseeing a team of ten who'll visit the smaller companies within the group, taking care of their IT requirements. It'll save a packet on consultants' fees, plus there'll be continuity in terms of approach. Anyway,' he said, with a jubilant smile, 'I got the job and I start next week.'

'Congratulations.' She could hardly get the word out of her mouth.

'Thanks. I thought I better let you know. Probably die of shock if you saw me walking down the corridor at CEM. Funny how things work out.'

'Yes . . .' The vortex was back.

'In fact, I understand CEM needs a new *ad hoc* database designed for a large project you've won. Trans-Global Airlines.'

Stunned, she said nothing.

'One of my team will do the programming but I'm going to act as consultant on it. It'll just be a few visits from me. I've got to contact a Sally Roberts and a guy called Greg Hamilton-Lawrence. Do you know them?'

The vortex was out of control.

22

'Wow! Things aren't exactly working out for you,' said Tessa.

Amy glared at her. 'A slight understatement, don't you think? It's not enough that psychopath Greg is sales and marketing director. Worse! *I* have to report to him.' She prodded her chest. 'Now screwed-up ex-boyfriend has walked back into my life, risen from the dead like Lazarus.' She gulped down her wine and quipped, 'Oh, yes, and my secretary has turned into Tara Palmer-Tomkinson. No, things aren't exactly working out for me, Tessa.'

As soon as Simon had left her apartment Amy had changed into a pair of jeans and a blue T-shirt, grabbed two bottles of wine and run down to Tessa's, where she'd spent the last hour telling her friend about her awful day.

Over the last three years Tessa had sat through the retelling of many episodes of Amy's life, including broken relationships, exciting flings, parental torment and three promotions, but she had never seen her quite so worked up. Amy was normally controlled and cool – ice cool – especially when it came to work.

Now she grabbed the second bottle of wine and opened it. For the next hour she ranted about the awful situation, eventually however, too exhausted for anger and nicely numbed by the wine, she made an announcement that CEM, Greg and Simon would not be mentioned any more that night. 'In the words of Scarlet O'Hara, I'll think about it tomorrow.' She leant back in her chair and looked instantly more relaxed, Jaffa cake in one hand and glass of wine in the other.

The top button of her jeans was undone and she had kicked off her shoes; her hair was loose and messy. 'Let's talk about something more interesting . . . I know! How shall we get you and John Smith together?'

Tessa shrugged. 'Let's face it, it's just not going to happen.'

'Of course it will.' Amy put down her glass. 'In fact, as your personal strategic planner, I shall come up with some failproof strategies. We can't let this opportunity pass you by.' She closed her eyes. The next minute she opened them wide, revealing a mischievous glint, and leapt up.

'What?' asked Tessa, looking worried.

'Strike while the iron's hot!' Amy headed for the door.

'*What?* Where are you going?'

'To invite him for a drink – if he's in.'

'*Now?*'

'Yes.'

'*No!*'

But Amy was already in the hall, quickly followed by a panicked Tessa. '*Don't you dare.*'

'Don't worry. It'll be *my* invite. He won't know it's anything to do with you.'

'Don't. *Please!*'

But Amy opened the door and crossed to John's door. Tessa darted back to her flat.

With a silly grin, Amy knocked loudly and a couple of seconds later he was standing in front of her. The first thing that struck her was that he'd shaved his beard off, then that he was wearing a stylishly cut, dark navy suit with a light blue shirt that was open at the collar. He looked so much younger, probably mid-thirties at the most.

'Good evening, John.'

'Hello, Amy.'

She saw him glance at her feet and she suddenly realised that her jeans were undone, revealing her lacy black knickers. She grinned at him and did them up. 'Tessa and I are drinking our woes away, and we wondered if you had any woes that you'd like to drink away.'

He was looking at her as if *she* was the oddball, instead of it being the other way round.

'And besides,' she added, 'you still haven't been tested on the house rules and refuse collection.'

He continued to stare at her, both wary and amused. Finally he replied, 'I've been revising, I'll just get my keys.'

A short while later he followed Amy into Tessa's apartment.

'Red wine OK?' asked Amy.

He nodded and sat down on the sofa while she went out to the kitchen. She expected to see Tessa there but the room was empty. Unperturbed, she grabbed a clean glass and poured John some wine, returned to the living room and handed it to him. 'You've some catching up to do.'

'I can see that.'

She fell into the opposite armchair, tucked her legs beneath her, picked up her own glass and sipped. For at least a minute they just sat there, occasionally glancing at each other, seemingly both curious and suspicious.

Eventually Amy decided to open a conversation. 'You look different today.'

'An important meeting.'

She didn't pursue it. Again the silence ensued, yet neither seemed uncomfortable, or mentioned Tessa's absence. Eventually with an obvious sarcastic tone he said, 'I thought the girl who had everything wouldn't have any woes.'

'Oh, you know, how to have my hair, what colour nail varnish to use, what credit card to put my holidays on, things like that.'

'I can see why you'd get drunk to escape such burdens.'

'Hmm,' she said, in a long, contemplative tone. 'What about you? Do you have any woes?'

'Who doesn't?'

'Care to share them with us? Our advice is free and Freud has nothing on Tessa.'

'Thank you, but no.'

At that moment Tessa appeared at the door, eyes on the floor like a self-conscious teenager. She managed a brief smile at John before she went over to the armchair in the corner and sat down, legs crossed, hands in lap, looking unnaturally attentive, as if she was attending a job interview. Amy noted the newly applied lipstick and combed hair.

'How are you, Tessa?' asked John.

Without meeting his eyes, Tessa nodded. 'Fine . . . yes, fine. Fine, thanks . . . yes.'

Amy decided to take control until Tessa calmed down. 'I hope you're spending my taxes carefully,' she said to John.

He rolled his eyes. 'Your compassion for your fellow man moves me to tears.'

'Practical, that's all. Have you always worked at the dole office?'

'Only two years.'

'Really? What did you do before? Don't tell me you worked with Mother Teresa in Calcutta. Or maybe you started an orphanage in Bogotá?'

He gave her a ghost of a smile. 'Actually I was a dealer in the City.'

Amy gasped. '*No way.*'

'Afraid so. Futures market. Nine years.'

'My God.' She sat up straight, eyes gleaming. 'How come you ended up in the dole office? Not another Nick Leeson, are you? Have you millions stashed away?'

He shook his head. 'It might surprise you but I enjoy working at the unemployment office. It doesn't have the prestige or the salary of working in the City, but at least it's real.'

'What's so real about it?'

He put down his glass. 'The people are real. They money they need is real. The anger they feel, and sometimes show, that's real too. The frustration, sometimes embarrassment, the whole spectrum of emotions. Their lives are real lives. And what I do, and how I conduct myself, affects their lives. Unlike in the City. Then I sat in front of a computer screen playing with huge numbers that I gambled on at the touch of a button. That's not real. I got to a point where I didn't want to do it any more. It felt pointless, all of it, the clients, the meetings, stress, targets, money, socializing, drinking, cocaine, arse-licking, even the goddamn corporate hospitality.' He cast a hostile glance at Amy and his voice grew louder. 'It was empty. The people were empty. Lost in the corporate illusion. It was all *bollocks*.' The word rang out across the room, echoing off the walls. Then, calm as can be, he picked up his wine, sipped it and relaxed into his chair.

Silence descended. Amy frowned at his outburst, but Tessa was wide-eyed and awestruck, obviously impressed by his passion.

'So you left your job to help people?' said Tessa, with a radiant smile.

'Not quite. I needed to escape for a while so I took a year off and went travelling. When I came back, I signed on and they said they were looking for staff. I thought I'd do it for a while but I enjoyed it and the hours are easy. I'm home by five so I can concentrate on my writing.'

'*You write!* As in a book?' gushed Tessa, pupils dilating.

'Yes.'

'Fiction?'

'No. It's partly a travelogue, based on my time in Asia and Africa, partly a sort of personal-growth journey. A journey round the world and a journey to find myself.' For the first time he looked slightly embarrassed, especially when he saw that Amy was suppressing laughter.

'That sounds amazing,' said Tessa. 'What's it called?'

He cleared his throat. 'Its working title is *From Prozac to Phuket*.'

'And did you find yourself?' asked Amy, with a half smile.

His eyes rested on her. 'Hopefully. But a journey like that never ends.'

'You should get together with Tessa. No doubt you'd both write the best psychology book going. You could be the Sonny and Cher of the self-help world, travelling the globe on your old motorbike, helping us corporate types find ourselves.' She raised her hands to the ceiling. 'Alleluya! It's John and Tessa to the rescue. You could set up a successful business, what with merchandising and everything. I can just see the John and Tessa dolls. Maybe a halo around yours, John, to emphasize your missionary zeal.'

Tessa looked horrified but John smiled. 'If I'm ever looking to sell out my integrity and embrace tackiness, I'll know who to call,' he said.

'I'm only joking. It's refreshing to meet a man of such sensitivity and insight. Especially a straight man. You are—'

He nodded.

'Just checking,' said Amy. 'Can't be too sure these days.'

Tessa looked even more horrified.

'Anyway, good luck with the book,' said Amy.

'Actually, I met a literary agent today. He's read a few chapters and likes it.'

'You were incredibly brave to make those changes in your life. Most people would be too scared,' said Tessa, sitting forward on her chair.

'I was scared too. But one should befriend one's fear, embrace it with open arms. Then, strangely, it dissipates. Running from demons only empowers them. That's the third chapter of my book.'

Tessa's whole exterior practically melted: a man who understood fear was the biggest aphrodisiac possible, in her eyes. It was *definitely* fate that he'd moved in across the hall. 'I'd love to read it.'

'Not sure if you're mad or brave just to jack everything in,' said Amy.

'I felt I had to. I gave notice at work, let my house in Islington and—'

'You own a house in *Islington*?' said Amy. 'You must have been a successful trader, then.'

'I headed the futures desk for Chase Peraguine International Bank. But . . .' he paused '. . . I wasn't happy.'

'Sod happiness when you have a salary like that.'

'Amy, you have a lot to learn.'

At Tessa's request John went on to tell them a bit about his travels and the unusual people he'd met along the way. In Thailand he'd been elephant-trekking in the jungle; in India he'd lived on a remote beach, catching fish for his dinner; he'd lived with a tribe in a small village in Ethiopia, helping tend the land.

Then, after only half an hour he said he had to go. 'Thank you for the wine,' he said. 'I hope your woes have departed.'

Amy was lying on the sofa, her feet propped on the arm. 'You're so different from how you initially came across.'

He shot her a look that she couldn't work out. 'As you said the other evening, no one is ever who you think they are. Good night – I'll see myself out.'

As the front door slammed Amy swung her legs down and sat up. 'Well, he's a turn-up for the books, no pun intended.'

Tessa was gazing at the door. 'I think I'm in love.'

23

Suddenly Amy heard footsteps in the corridor outside and her heart leapt into her mouth. She slammed the file shut and stuffed it back into the drawer, probably out of place. She stood, as casually as she could, next to the filing cabinet, pretending to fill out her expenses form. That was her excuse for being in the accounts office. It was seven forty-five in the morning and although some of the girls from Operations were in, the accounts staff didn't usually arrive until nearer nine.

Amy's legs felt wobbly and her head was thumping from last night's wine. She held her breath and waited, expecting the door to open at any minute, but whoever it was continued past, and she breathed a sigh of relief. What am I doing? she thought. I've really lost it this time.

She waited another minute, then put down the expenses form and opened the filing cabinet again. She glanced at the door, and flicked through numerous files before she found it: 'Henson Insurance – Burbage Manor House'.

Like all the other files it was filled with all the invoices from the subcontractors who had supplied equipment or services for that day's activities. A file was kept in Accounts on every event that CEM organized. She looked at a copy of the CEM budget, which was broken down into man-hours, sub-contractor totals and CEM profit mark-up. There was also a copy of the final invoice that had been sent to Henson Insurance. Then she saw the two-page invoice from Benchmark Catering. Her heart raced. Amy darted across the room, shoved it into the photocopier and pressed the button. All the while she prayed no one would come in. This was the riskiest bit. Thankfully it was done in seconds and she ran back to the file, shoved the invoice inside it and closed the drawer. It was done.

Now she folded the incriminating evidence and placed it in her file with all the other photocopies she'd taken that morning. Then, picking up her expenses form, she left the room and went back along the corridor to her office.

24

'That should do,' said John, and patted the ground once more.

Tessa let go of the conifer tree, which she'd been steadying while John had filled in the earth around the root.

'Thank you, everyone. A job well done,' said Hilda. 'That's it, I believe.'

Tessa's heart sank. She turned her face to the tree so they wouldn't see her disappointment. It was only in the last fifteen minutes that she'd got to work with John. Until then, she'd spent the day with Hilda, painting the black railings at the front of the house while the three men had done the digging and clearing at the back. What an anticlimax. She'd been building herself up all week for this. Unlike everyone else she was delighted they hadn't already finished the garden: it had been another opportunity to see John.

Despondently she followed John and Hilda to the shed at the rear of the garden.

'Thanks, everyone. Many hands make light work,' said Thomas, chirpily, taking their garden tools from them. Steve was sitting on the grass having a cigarette in the warm afternoon sunshine – the complete opposite to last week's weather.

'Good to be outside on a day like this,' said John, sitting down next to him.

'That's the spirit,' said Thomas. 'Amy doesn't know what she's missed.'

'Cornwall, wasn't it?' John said to Tessa.

'Her friend owns a farm down there. They spend the weekend horse-riding and windsurfing.'

'Sounds great.'

Within fifteen minutes everyone had said goodbye and gone back to their apartments. Tessa sank into a chair, and gave a long, weary irritated sigh. For what seemed like ages, she just sat there, gazing at the floor through detached and remote eyes. The silence of her flat echoed in her ears. She looked around its four walls, which today felt like the bars of a cage. She glanced at the television, then at the bookshelves and finally the music system, but none appealed to her or held her attention. It wasn't even four o'clock and the evening ahead felt oppressively long.

Living like this was safe, but it was also boring, bleak and suffocating. At times she hated herself. Of course she would have liked to go horse-riding and wind-surfing like Amy, but she couldn't. All those *people* down there. She wouldn't be able to run away and shut her door on them. With nowhere safe to hide the fear would well up in her, terrorizing and paralysing her. It was as frightening as jumping from a plane thirty thousand feet up with a tablecloth as a parachute.

Why couldn't she be like everyone else? What would John ever see in her? What would *anyone* see in her? She was too scared to do the things normal people did. She felt deflated and exhausted with the burden of thinking that this was it: a poky flat with the occasional visitor.

I hate myself. I totally hate myself.

Her dreams of long, intimate discussions with John were fading. She'd probably be too nervous even to speak.

'No! No!' she screamed. The desire to cry was unbearably strong, yet she knew it would solve nothing. It never had in the past.

The doorbell rang. She sat motionless, shocked, then

stood up and went out to the hall. She peered through the spyhole, and jerked backwards when she saw who it was. Her heartbeat quickened. She took a moment to gather herself, then opened the door.

'Hi, Tessa,' said John. 'Steve and I are popping out to the Coach and Horses for a quick drink. Thought you might like to join us.'

She stood like a statue. She hadn't been inside a pub for over two years.

When no answer was forthcoming he said casually, 'It was just if you were free. Hilda and Thomas can't come.'

She swallowed loudly. *Tell him you're busy, feeling unwell, expecting a visitor – anything!*

'OK,' she said. 'But can I meet you in there? A few things to do.' That gave her the option not to go. She could weigh up the numerous awful eventualities that might happen, then make a decision.

'See you shortly.'

She closed the door, fell back against her wall and let out a little cry. *Oh, my God!* A pub. They were always packed with *people*! Worse, they were all enjoying themselves: totally content in life; in their skins; on this planet. A social situation like that was impossible. Would she be able to escape if she had to? Would they all stare at her, knowing how she felt inside, that she was the *nutty one*?

Then again, she thought, it was just down the road. She could always leave, say she felt unwell. After all, what else was there? Another night alone, in her cell. John had called for her. *My God, maybe he likes me! I can do this. I can go to a pub! John and I can fall in love.*

Goddamn it, I'm going!

*

Nearly an hour later Tessa was standing outside the Coach and Horses. She was wearing jeans, a tight V-necked T-shirt and a large amount of makeup, red lips, blue eye-shadow and black mascara – she hadn't worn as much since her twenties. Her reddish hair was sleeker-looking – she'd put on some hair wax. Feeling extra brave she had abandoned her kitchen-sink bag and instead held a small black clutch bag, which contained only money, her door keys, glucose tablets, plasters and a tampon – just in case.

Her breathing was short and her stomach was knotted. She knew it was stupid to feel like this. It was only a pub. But it was what was inside. *People!* Lots of them. And one was John. She almost laughed as she imagined telling Amy that she had gone for a drink with John in a pub – she wouldn't believe her. Tessa didn't believe it herself.

With an almost irresistible urge to run home, dry mouth, pounding heart and legs like jelly, Tessa pushed open the door and walked in.

Faces stared at her. Eyes clung to her. Mouths chattered about her. A group of mean-looking men laughed at her.

Don't be stupid. No one's looking at you! In fact, she saw now, it wasn't that busy. A few people sat at the bar and others were dotted about the room.

'Tessa, over here.'

She looked to her left and saw John at a table to the side. Her heart did a little dance – was it a flutter of excitement or the palpitations of a panic-attack? Unsure, she pasted on a brave smile and walked over.

'What are you having?' he said.

In an almost inaudible whisper she said, 'Gin and tonic, thanks.'

He nodded and went over to the bar, leaving Tessa

sitting erect and motionless, staring at the wall. She wondered where Steve was: there was only one beer glass on the table. *I am relaxed around people. There is nothing to fear about people.*

A couple of minutes later John returned, placed her drink on the table and sat down with a fresh pint for himself. 'Cheers.'

She nodded, and with a noticeably shaky hand reached for her glass.

'Steve had to dash off. I nearly went myself – Wasn't sure if you were coming,' he said. *Oh, God, it was just the two of them.* Again, her heart did strange things. She fixed her eyes on a beer mat.

A silence ensued. The background din of all the other occupants chatting away pounded in Tessa's ears. Her heart was beating so fast that she was sure she'd have a heart-attack. I shouldn't have come, she thought.

'It's good we've got the garden done,' he said.

Unable to look at him, she nodded.

'I'm looking forward to sitting out there in summer.' He waited for her response. When none came, he continued, 'I love being outside. That's what I liked about my travels so much. Just being outdoors. Do you get to travel much?'

She shook her head.

'I hope to go travelling again. At times I find London too busy and crowded. Don't you?'

'Yes, crowded,' she said, and glanced anxiously at the door.

'Are you OK?'

He's already spotted that I'm nutty. It's so obvious. 'A headache,' she quipped.

'Oh, I'm sorry. Is it bad? Do you want to head off?'

For the first time she looked at him directly. There's

just your cell, she told herself. 'I'll wait awhile. See how I feel.'

He smiled and she did too. She took a gulp of her drink, let her shoulders relax and forced herself to ask, 'How's the book?'

'Good. That agent I mentioned wants to sign me.'

'That's wonderful. I'd love to write,' she said quietly.

'Why don't you?'

Tessa blushed.

'I think if you want to do something, you should at least give it a go. You might be surprised.'

She shrugged and glanced away.

A little later he asked, 'Do you work?'

'Not at the moment. Not since my divorce.'

'Sorry to hear that.'

'Don't be. He wasn't very nice.'

He didn't probe her. Instead he changed the subject. 'Amy seems an interesting character,' he said. 'Have you known her long?'

'About three years, since she moved in. She's a good friend . . . Do anything for you. I really admire her energy and courage.'

'Energy and courage,' repeated John, with a grin.

Tessa thought he was gorgeous when he smiled. His whole face lit up. She guessed he was a few years younger than her, but what did that matter? He had the maturity of a man twice his age. He was wonderful, she thought. And he was living opposite her. How perfect was that? And here she was having a drink with him! In a pub! *My God! I'm actually in a pub. I can do this! I'm normal!*

With a touch of euphoria, Tessa looked at the bar. Maybe when they'd finished these drinks, she might even be able to go up and order another round. The idea agitated her and she had to check that the twenty-pound note was still in her bag – the third time since she'd put it there. But when she tried to open it she couldn't. One of the two studs was stuck. A wave of fear shot through her; her front door keys were in it. She tried to force the stud open.

'Need some help?' said John, putting down his glass.

'It's stuck,' said Tessa, fretfully. She held out the bag in front of her and tugged with all her strength, determined to get at her keys. It flew apart and her glucose tablets fell out. Flushed with embarrassment, she clumsily bent down on all fours, crawled under the opposite table and put them away. Then she sat down again. Her money was there, after all, but she felt less confident about approaching the bar. She decided to finish her drink and leave. Quit while she was ahead! This was just the first, hopefully, of many visits. And it had been a good start, a new beginning. Then she looked at John.

He was staring, aghast, at his beer.

Tessa followed his eyes.

It was then that the world, her breathing and her heart stopped. Armageddon had hit the Coach and Horses in Crystal Palace. Floating in the middle of John's drink was her tampon.

She let out a whine, like an injured dog.

Oh, God! This isn't happening. Everything in the background faded into a fuzzy haze. All she could see was his beer with her tampon floating in the middle.

At that moment her 'out of body' experience happened. Maybe it was God's way of protecting her from the awful event, because it felt, as she would later retell the story to Amy, as if she floated upwards. In the gap between reality and surrealism, she was on the ceiling looking down at herself and John as they sat, stunned, horrified, speechless, staring at the tampon.

Time stood still, until she found herself slipping back into her body, back into the pub, back into the maelstrom of horror.

John was the first to move. With his right hand he fished out the tampon and put it into Tessa's palm. As his fingers touched hers, she shuddered. Then she stuffed it into her bag.

John laughed. 'Well, it's a new one on "There's a fly in my soup".'

Tessa leapt up. 'Have to go,' she cried. 'Bad headache.'

'Tessa, wait! It's OK, really. It's funny.'

But she darted at full speed across the pub and out of the door.

25

'Ready?'

Amy looked up from her desk to see an aloof-looking Greg standing in her doorway. He was wearing a stylishly cut dark grey suit and was lightly tanned from his skiing trip. 'I'll be in my car,' he said and walked away. Amy sneered. An afternoon with Greg – how awful. She dropped her head into her hands and groaned. Thirty seconds later she breathed in deeply and adopted a defiant expression.

Soon she was walking confidently across the underground car-park, carrying her handbag and briefcase. Greg had already started his BMW. His elbow was resting through the open window and a Simply Red CD – a band Amy hated – was blaring. She climbed into the front passenger seat, crossed her legs, folded her arms, and Greg drove off, heading south through London. His driving was erratic and rushed: one minute he accelerated sharply to overtake another car, the next he braked abruptly, squeezing back into the long line of slow-moving traffic. The music did its best to fill the void.

They were on their way to Gatwick Airport, which was where TGA were holding a senior management meeting to discuss the relaunch. Amy couldn't see why her presence was needed but William had requested that she attend every fortnight with Greg.

An hour into the tense journey they reached the start of the M23 and Greg put his foot down, hitting a hundred miles an hour along the motorway. His window was still open and the wind was playing havoc with Amy's hair, but she said nothing. Usually before an important meeting she'd be all fired up, but today she would rather have been anywhere else.

Eventually, turning off the motorway, Greg reached across and switched off the CD player. As if it was too much effort to speak to her, he said, 'I suppose we best discuss our plan of action.'

'Which "plan of action" is that?' she said guardedly.

He changed down a gear and accelerated, overtaking a couple of cars, cutting one up. The driver blasted his horn. 'The meeting, of course. A united, professional front.'

'Goes without saying.'

'What had you planned?' he asked.

'Apart from a brief update, which will take all of five minutes, I'm confused as to the necessity of my presence.'

'Ditto. But smile and play the game.'

'I don't care for games.'

He glanced at her, then let out a burst of contrived laughter.

'What's funny?'

'Women like you. You want to be treated as equals yet you can't handle it.'

'Handle what?' she said sharply.

He sighed, exasperated. 'We're both adults. Why are you acting like a lovelorn teenager?'

'*What!* Am I missing something?'

'Me getting engaged to Miranda, it's obviously put your nose out of joint.'

Her face distorted with rage. 'Fuck you! That's not it and you know it! You treated me like a fool. "Some women are for marrying and some just for screwing", remember? What game was that?'

'Jesus, it's just sex, Amy. Women are so bloody emotional.' He seemed amused. 'Most men think that.

They just haven't got the guts to say it. Like it or not, you're not the marrying kind – not that there's anything wrong with that. The world needs women like you, Amy. You're the type men have passionate affairs with. In fact, I'm not averse to taking up where we left off in Florence. It was an enjoyable dalliance.'

She gasped. 'I am averse to that. *Fucking averse.* You are more deranged than I thought.'

'That may be, but now I'm your boss.'

'For this project only.'

'Amy, don't be naïve. This is just the start. Things will work out my way. They always do.'

A surge of anger swept through her, so she took a few deep breaths. Then, she said quietly, 'Time will tell Greg.'

He was doing seventy miles an hour in the outside lane down a dual-carriageway, but he turned his head to stare at her with the strangest expression – part disdain, part bemusement. Amy glanced at him, then back at the road. They were coming up fast behind a Ford Focus and the dual-carriageway was reverting to one lane, yet Greg continued to stare at her. 'Rock the boat, Amy, and it'll be you who gets wet.'

'Rock it? I'm going to fucking torpedo it.'

The Ford Focus braked suddenly and Amy gasped as Greg finally saw it and overtook it on the inside as the road narrowed to a single lane. Again they were hooted at but he seemed oblivious to it.

For the next few minutes he drove at speed, humming. At last the TGA building appeared up ahead and he parked beside the entrance. As he got out he said, 'I'm glad we've had this talk – cleared the air a bit.' He slammed the door and walked away.

*

In TGA's boardroom, Mark Greenshawe welcomed Amy warmly and she spent some time chatting with him before everyone sat down at a huge table, about twenty in all. He beckoned her to sit next to him.

Barty and Withington, TGA's advertising agency, kicked off the meeting with a presentation on the planned advertising campaign. Giles Barty, flash, trendy and like a lot of advertising types – head stuck up his own arse, enthused eloquently about the concept of the adverts. Apparently they had hired the *Star Trek* actors who had played Captain Jean Luc Picard and Captain Janeway to appear in them. They would be energized straight into the executive-club section on one of the TGA refurbished 747s. Supposedly bowled over by the service, quality of food and comfort, they would decide to abandon their twenty-third-century technologically advanced and warp-speed-driven spaceships in favour of travel by TGA. The slogan was 'TGA – A futuristic service in the present day'.

Amy thought the idea tacky and ludicrous, especially in view of the millions they were spending on it. However, Giles was convincing, and once Mark Greenshawe had indicated his approval, the drones and minions beamed support for the campaign. Amy was the only one who questioned the image in relation to TGA's future positioning within the market. But it was no good. The advert was commissioned and, no doubt, Giles Barty got to buy another Porsche on the back of it. The rest of the meeting was routine. Amy delivered her update and showed them the final artwork for the invitations.

The drive back with Greg was silent. Amy gazed out of the window as he flitted in and out of the traffic at speed, overtaking any car in his way. However, at Purley he headed for Croydon.

Amy said nothing until he took another turn into a large trading estate.

'Where are you going?' she asked.

'I have to call in somewhere.'

After another couple of turnings he pulled into the car-park of a three-storey office block with a large warehouse attached to it. On the front of the building in large green letters was 'Benchmark Catering'. This could be interesting, she thought.

'Ten minutes,' he said, as he parked.

'Are you meeting Harry?'

He nodded.

'I'll come in with you,' she said. 'It would be good to look round.'

'Another time.'

'Nonsense,' she said, opening her door. 'Harry did say if I was ever in the area . . .' She got out and grabbed her handbag. Greg got out too, and walked towards the entrance, Amy striding determinedly behind him.

'I didn't expect you today,' said Harry Jackson, shaking her hand as she and Greg were shown into his office on the third floor.

'You did say that if I was ever in the area I should call in and you'd give me a tour.'

Harry nodded slowly, then shook Greg's hand.

'Impressive offices,' said Amy.

'Thank you.' He gestured to a couple of sofas, and the three sat down.

'Business must be going well,' she said.

'Well enough. Can I get you both some coffee?'

'Not for me,' said Amy. 'I believe time is short and I'd really like to have that tour. It's important for me to get a feel for our suppliers.'

Harry looked questioningly at Greg.

Unmoved, Greg nodded, 'Maybe you could get one of your team to walk Amy around while we discuss business.'

'Of course. Would you like to come with me, Amy?' he said.

She got up and followed Harry into an office where she was introduced to an enthusiastic young sales executive called Anthony. When he heard she was from CEM he jumped to attention. Harry went back into his office and Anthony led her down a large rear staircase towards the warehouse, giving her the spiel on the background and history of Benchmark Catering. Apparently it had been founded in 1952 by the Illsley family then bought by Harry Jackson in 1995.

'So it's a private company?' asked Amy.

'He's the main stakeholder along with a couple of private investors.'

'Who are?'

He was opening the door to the warehouse. 'I'm not sure of their names. They're sleeping partners. We all see it as Harry's company. He's built it up into what it is today.' He smiled. 'Hope it's not too cold in here.'

She followed him in and the temperature dropped by several degrees.

'This warehouse is two thousand feet square,' he said proudly, and led her down a long aisle with crates stacked up to the ceiling. He explained that they contained glasses, plates, cutlery – enough to feed thousands at any one time, plus uniforms, tables, chairs, portable ovens and cold-storage containers.

'Obviously food is perishable so a lot is sent directly to each venue. However, some is kept in these refrigeration and freezer units overnight.' He opened a door: inside, an assortment of boxes and packets contained everything from vegetables to meat.

They continued walking to the other side of the warehouse, where Amy saw hundreds of cases of wine.

Anthony took out a few bottles. 'Sometimes we buy to order but in most cases we buy bulk from the growers. That's how we can be so competitive.'

She smiled. 'I realize you're excellent on quality, that's why CEM uses you, but I would have to challenge that comment on price competitiveness.'

He looked both hurt and stunned, as if she'd just told him he was crap in bed. 'But we're one of the largest catering companies in the UK. We have incredible purchasing power, and although we would never sell on price alone – because service and quality are of equal importance – we can match or beat all of our competitors.'

Amy raised an eyebrow. 'That hasn't been the case with CEM. I've been carrying out a cost-comparison exercise and Benchmark hasn't come out favourably.'

He looked worried. 'You'll have to speak to Harry. He and Julie, his secretary, prepare your quotations.'

'Is that usual? Doesn't he do that for other clients?'

'Sometimes, but you're a major client so he likes to keep control of the account.'

She followed him as he walked on, describing the contents of each aisle they passed. Then Anthony led her back into the office block, giving her a little talk on all of the company's different departments.

'This is where we do all our staff training,' he said, showing her a large room filled with about twenty waiting staff who were listening to a lecture on customer service. He explained that no employee could work on any event without having successfully completed a training programme – even the part-time casuals.

Next he walked her through the accounts office introducing her to several staff, who were all polite and friendly, obviously used to visitors. He even took her into the staff canteen. On one wall there was a large noticeboard, with details of competitions for the most knowledgeable wine waiter, the best turned-out member of staff, and numerous social events. Vacancies were advertised here too: they were looking for more waiting staff, accounts and data-input clerks – Benchmark was obviously expanding.

The tour ended, and Amy thanked him for his time. She caught up with Greg in Reception and they walked back to his car together. 'I hope you found the tour interesting,' he said.

'Oh, yes,' she replied. 'Very interesting indeed.'

'Do I need to invest in a life-jacket?'

'You tell me.'

His eyes narrowed and he frowned. 'Just be careful you don't drown yourself in the process.' He started his car and they drove away.

26

'*My God!* Would I be right in thinking that you just put a plastic recyclable bottle in your *black* bin?'

Amy jumped. John Smith was sitting on the ledge outside his window, which overlooked the rear garden on the ground floor. He was wearing jeans and a black T-shirt and was drinking from a bottle of Budweiser in the last of the evening sun. 'Surely an item for the green bin!' he said, with mock-concern.

She pulled a face, then turned back to the bins, removed the bottle from the black one and placed it a few feet away in the green. 'You'll be parking in the wrong space next. It really won't do. This house has rules, you know,' he said with a wry smile.

She walked over to him. 'Well, aren't we the control freak?'

'Can't think where I got that from.' He swallowed some beer. 'So, how's the world of high-flying, fast-moving, adrenaline-packed business?'

'Thrilling,' she said caustically. 'How's life at the dole office?'

'Exhilarating.'

'I suspect not.'

He put his hand on his heart pulling an aggrieved, wounded look before holding up his bottle. 'Fancy one?'

She surprised herself by saying, 'I suppose it's more appealing than doing my washing.'

He climbed back in through his window. Two minutes later a large red cushion flew out, missing her head by inches, followed by John with a fresh bottle of beer. He handed it to her and pointed to the cushion, then settled himself on the stone ledge. She picked up the cushion and sat down with her back against the wall of the house a few feet from him. They toasted each other.

'I suppose you heard about the incident with Tessa,' he said.

She grinned.

'Is she OK? I've knocked on her door a couple of times since, but she must have been out.'

Amy glanced at Tessa's bedroom window, which was shut. In a quiet voice she said, 'She's embarrassed but she'll be OK. Just give her a bit of time.'

'There's no need for her to be embarrassed.'

'*A tampon in your beer!* Even I, thick-skinned and bolshy, would be embarrassed by that. And she is neither of those things. She's very sensitive and extremely shy at times. But she's really nice too. Unusual but interesting. You should get to know her. She's open-minded, intelligent, with a great sense of humour. As I said, she can be very shy so you'd have to take the lead.'

He seemed slightly puzzled. He began to say something but stopped. Amy sipped her beer, enjoying the warm evening, hopefully a taste of summer to come.

'How's *From Prozac to Phuket* coming along?' she asked.

'Frustratingly slow. I'm stuck on chapter seventeen.'

'What's it about?'

He took a swig of his beer. 'Love.'

'Oh, yes, and what exactly are you stuck on?'

He hesitated, then shrugged. 'It's a complex subject. I haven't quite captured it.'

'You and eighty per cent of the population.'

'I meant on the page. Not in life.'

'Oh, I see. And what are you trying to capture?'

'The particular section I'm stuck on is about what I've labelled matchstick love.'

'What's that?'

'A momentary flame that extinguishes quickly. There's no substance to it. Yet many confuse it for the real thing until it fizzles out. Then they move on looking for the next experience, the next little matchstick that lights up their life only to burn out.'

'And what makes you the expert?'

'I'm no expert,' he said calmly, 'just another person searching for the answers.'

'How tiresome to search for answers all the time.'

'Bloody tiresome. That's why I resorted to drinking beer in the garden.' He flashed a mischievous look. 'Beautiful evening,' he said, gazing out across the garden. The apple trees were in full blossom, and the pansies and marigolds were in flower.

The sweet smell of the blossom did its best to hide the exhaust fumes from the evening rush-hour. Amy took out her hair clip and shook her head so that the tresses fell loosely around her face. She put out her arms and had a good stretch, then rubbed the back of her neck.

Soon John started to talk about life at the dole office, which sounded like it had its fair share of excitement. There were angry claimants threatening to wreck the place, people trying to make fraudulent claims, private investigators and debt collectors posing as policemen. 'It's anything but boring,' he said.

'But the *wages*! And I don't suppose you get a company car, share options or an expense account?'

'Life can exist without them.'

'Not my life. Surely you must have seen a huge drop in your income.'

'The rental from my house tops it up.'

'So it's not even mortgaged?'

'Paid it off.'

'You hypocrite.'

'Why?'

'You look at me sometimes like I'm some anally retentive nerd for working in the corporate sector when you've already sorted out your finances. I doubt your work colleagues own houses in Islington. You're bloody typical of a champagne socialist. Lip service, nothing more.'

He laughed. 'A *champagne socialist*! I developed beliefs, which I pursued.'

'But by then you were in a position to pursue them. You made sure you had something to fall back on.'

'A cynical translation. You can look for a hidden agenda in anyone's actions.'

They fell into a heated debate about politics and personal beliefs, and disagreed on everything. At times they both raised their voices, but before they knew it, the evening sun had vanished and they were sitting in the dark.

'It's getting cold,' she said, 'and after talking with you I've decided my washing appeals after all.'

'Want a coffee?' he asked.

'Thanks, but I really should go.'

'Don't be so bloody boring and conservative.' He climbed through his window, and held out his hand for her to follow.

'I'm neither of those things, thank you.' Scowling, she took his hand and scrambled over the sill to find herself in his bedroom. She walked out quickly into the living room. He went into the kitchen, and Amy couldn't help having a look round. On the walls hung a set of eight large black and white photographs of African scenes, people and animals. They were powerful images and she wondered if he'd taken them himself. Next she walked over to a glass-fronted cabinet and studied the hand-carved wooden boats inside it. Then she went to the book shelves, which covered two walls. *Transcendental Meditation, Buddhist Philosophy, Inner Child Awakenings* – there was a whole section on ecology and world politics including, the complete writings of Karl Marx and Mao Tse Tung.

'Do you read?' he asked, appearing with two mugs.

'Occasionally, but usually romances, full of glorious, pulsating matchstick love.'

He raised an eyebrow and handed her a mug and she sat down in an armchair. He took the one opposite. They both stared at each other then glanced away. Amy sipped her coffee and continued to gaze round the room.

'Do you always see yourself in corporate hospitality?' he asked.

'If I survive another six months in it, I'll be surprised.'

'Why?'

'Office politics.'

'Do tell. It'll remind me of the cut-throat, back-stabbing world I've escaped from.'

Amy eyed him pensively. She was interested to hear what he'd make of her suspicions. And it wasn't as if he'd run into anyone from CEM, so she didn't have to worry about them finding out. 'There's this guy at work, Greg. He's a real shit – and I mean a real shit. Unfortunately no one else seems to think so. But, then, he treats them differently from how he treats me.'

'Why? What's he done?'

'Various things that I don't want to go into. However, what I can say is that I suspect he's getting backhanders from one of our suppliers.' She went on to tell him of how Benchmark had been awarded nearly ninety per cent of CEM's catering requirements, even though they were uncompetitive on price.

'It could just be sloppiness on CEM's part in monitoring the account and getting the best deal.'

'In another company maybe, but CEM is the most efficient company I've ever worked at. The women are like the Stepford wives. Too perfect!'

He smiled. 'But why do you think this guy's involved?'

'Because he and Harry, the Benchmark MD, are practically best mates. There's definitely a reason why the company's awarded so much of our business. It's just the sort of thing Greg would be involved with. He has no limits, no boundaries. He lives for risks.' Amy sat forward, intense and focused. 'Sally would have to be in on it too. She controls the budgets.'

John sighed. 'That's not much to go on. And backhanders are accepted in the business world. Some people see them as unofficial commission. And the difficulty is in proving it. Most transactions would be carried out in cash.'

'I know. That's the trouble. Any advice?'

'Unfortunately some companies deliberately turn a blind eye to it. If this guy is good at his job then no one may care.'

'We're owned by a European finance house, Lazlo Manco. Believe me, they'd care. We're under pressure to make more profit. If I could find proof that Greg is on backhanders from Benchmark then he'd be sacked on the spot.'

'Wow, you must really hate him,' said John.

'He's a total bastard.'

'The world is full of bastards, and sometimes avoidance is better than fighting them.'

Amy screwed her face up in dismay. 'That sounds like the comment of a man tired of life.'

John scowled. 'Rubbish. There are just better things on which to expend one's energies.'

'He made a fool of me.'

'Revenge, then?'

'Possibly.'

He eyed her pensively. Amy looked away and after a few seconds stood up.

'Thanks for the beer but I have to go.'

'Be careful,' he said, as she left.

There he was, right on time, ten past eight in the morning. Her heart fluttered and her legs went to jelly; it was like being sixteen all over again. Tessa watched John Smith walk slowly – sexily – across the car-park. Today he was wearing tight-fitting tan trousers tucked into black biker boots and a light blue shirt under a black leather jacket – he always wore that when he was riding his bike. But she hadn't seen those trousers before. They suited him, she thought.

He stopped at his motorbike and glanced behind him. Tessa leapt back from the window. Then she stepped forward again to peer through the gap between the curtains. John ran a hand through his blond curls, then put on his helmet. Next he swung his leg over the saddle and tried to start the bike. Tessa knew it would be the fourth or fifth attempt before he got it going. Today, however, it took six. He'd have to get it fixed, especially if she was going to ride on the back of it. She didn't want it breaking down.

Then he was off, out of the car-park and down the road. He was like Clint Eastwood riding off into the horizon, ready to take on the world, kill the baddies and, of course, win the girl.

I'm in the early stages of stalking, Tessa thought. She had even taken to watching him from her bedroom window while he hung out his washing. When he went inside she stood for ages staring at his boxer shorts, deciding which ones she liked best. A couple of evenings ago he had sat in a deck-chair with the paper for seventeen minutes. He had turned the pages so carefully and read with such concentration. She had tried to go outside – she had some sunflower seeds to plant – but she just couldn't do it. Not after the tampon episode. The memory of it made her shiver.

However, all was not lost: she had a plan. Fuelled by the determination to become 'normal', Tessa had decided that courageous steps were called for and had enrolled on a reflexology course at the local holistic centre. The thought of touching other people's feet was distressing but Derek, who was running this course, said the human body contact would cure her of her fear of people. It gave her renewed hope and it was only another two hundred pounds plus there were just six people on the course, four of whom she'd met before. Like her, they were course junkies and full of fears, phobias and compulsive-behaviour patterns, so Tessa felt reasonably relaxed with them. Odd people never judged other odd people.

If it's the last thing I do, I'll become normal, Tessa vowed. I'll do it for John.

28

'I believe you know Simon Delaney,' Sally said curtly.

Amy tensed. 'Yes, we used to work together.'

'Ah, yes – Simon,' said Greg, with a broad smile. 'What a coincidence that he of all people should end up designing the TGA database. I look forward to meeting him. Does he play golf or is his spare time confined to playing cards?'

They were having their weekly internal management meeting in the boardroom, at which each person was required to talk about the coming week's objectives. Daniel, in his new position as senior business-development manager, was also there, along with Carol, the financial controller and, of course, William.

Sally had just finished, and had mentioned that she would be meeting Simon that afternoon.

Inside Amy flinched at the thought of Simon meeting Greg and Sally. Thankfully she was out with clients for the rest of the day. Never again would she get involved with someone at work – and this time she meant it.

Daniel spoke next and mentioned a number of tenders he was working on and a couple of new clients he'd signed up.

After Daniel Greg, oozing confidence, spoke about new sales targets and the addition to the team of Ralph Middleton. He was joining CEM next week as a new business-development manager. 'Ralph will be an asset to the team. He's ultra-professional, focused and ambitious. He should make a strong impact.'

Of course he'd say that, thought Amy. Ralph was another of his mates from school.

Then Greg told them that there was another vacancy: Ben had given notice.

Amy was saddened to hear this, but the others merely nodded and Greg changed the subject.

Then it was Amy's turn. Usually she gave a quick run-down on her plans, but, after last night, after deliberating for a couple of hours on how best to deal with her suspicions over Greg, she decided that this morning would be as good an opportunity as any to open the can of worms discreetly. It was risky but she figured that the only other option was to hack into Greg's personal bank accounts, which was a little extreme, not to say illegal.

She informed the meeting that the new website would be up and running by next week. She had also persuaded *Event Monthly*, the trade magazine of the industry, to do an in-depth feature on CEM in their next issue. She mentioned the time she had spent on the TGA project, then opened the file in front of her. With a deliberate relaxed smile she said in an easy going manner, initially addressing William, 'I had some time this week and so, as per my suggestion, I carried out a minor cost-comparison exercise.'

Sally exchanged a glance with Greg.

'An in-depth exercise still needs to be undertaken. I merely looked at our catering suppliers and examined three major events that we'd organized in the last two months, Henson Insurance, Marsh Media and the News Land Group. I compared Benchmark's prices with Duchess Catering's and Hallmark International's, both quality caterers. Although I realize Benchmark Catering offers an excellent service, it concerned me that the company came out ten to twelve per cent more expensive.' At that point she shut up. No accusations, she told herself. Just basic facts to gauge Greg's response.

Surprisingly there was silence for what felt like eternity, but was probably about thirty seconds.

Greg shook his head dismissively. 'Maybe we should just give our clients McDonald's? That would be cheaper still.'

Daniel and Sally laughed obligingly.

'That's a higher percentage than I would have thought, Sally. Is this true?' asked William.

Sally's lips twisted. 'I'd have to check Amy's comparison. We're all aware Benchmark are slightly more expensive than their competitors, but they offer quality and our two companies work together excellently. It's a relationship that has been built up over the last three years. We can rely on them a hundred per cent, which counts for a lot.'

'And Benchmark have passed across *numerous* leads, Bank of Utah, Nutron Electronics. Those accounts have netted us a few hundred thousand,' added Greg.

William nodded. 'That's true. The trading relationship has been mutually beneficial.'

'Of course,' said Amy. 'And one could understand if they were two or three per cent more expensive, but ten to twelve per cent is questionable. Translate those percentages into the TGA contract and that's a lot of money CEM is losing, several hundred thousand, in fact. I visited Benchmark recently, and one of their sales reps told me they were very competitive on price. I'm puzzled as to how this can have happened and why we give ninety per cent of our catering requirements to a company that isn't even competitive. Can you think of a reason for that, Greg?'

Greg was leaning back in his chair, eyeing her with amused detachment.

'You did ask three catering companies to quote on the TGA contract, didn't you, Sally?' asked William.

'Of course I did. And I want to state that I don't agree with the percentages Amy has mentioned. I'll look into this myself. Second, if she has such concerns, she should have aired them to me, instead of carrying out this exercise herself. You can't judge prices on three deals alone. Overall the percentage might be completely different. Third,' her cold eyes cut into Amy, 'is it Amy's job to get involved with the suppliers and event budgets? I thought she was supposed to increase profitability through external growth and turnover.'

'Increase profit by any means,' said Amy.

'Hold up, ladies,' interrupted William, diplomatically. 'We're all supposed to be pulling in the same direction.'

'I find her accusation of my inefficiency insulting,' seethed Sally.

'I wouldn't dream of saying such a thing.'

William tapped his pen on the table. 'Sally, I'm sure Amy didn't mean to give that impression. However, I'd like you to look into this matter as a matter of urgency and report back to me next week. If we're losing money I want to know about it.' Sally nodded. 'Have you finished, Amy?' he asked.

Amy looked at Greg who was unruffled. 'Actually, as we're talking about prices, there was another query I might as well mention.' She picked up her copy of the Benchmark invoice for the Henson event. 'We're being invoiced for five hundred bottles of Pouilly Fuissé, when in fact, the clients were served Pouilly Fumé. There's two pounds difference in the price, which accounts for a thousand pounds. It's not a huge amount but if a mistake can happen once, maybe it happens more often and we're paying for products we've never had.'

If looks could kill then Amy would just have been

machine gunned against the office wall by Sally, who took the invoice from her and examined it. 'This is just a photocopy. On the back of the original invoice you would see in red the letters CR followed by a number. This confirms that a credit note has been raised against any pricing errors. As usual the budget was cut on this event at the last minute. Occasionally our suppliers invoice us from the original budget, but we always pick it up.'

Carol, who had been quiet until then, agreed with Sally and explained the process the accounts department went through before they paid any invoice.

Amy's heartbeat increased its pace. A knot formed in her stomach. In a less-assured voice she said, 'Do you know for sure that a credit note's been raised?'

Carol offered to find it and left the room.

Everyone was staring at Amy, who looked down at her papers. *Please, God, don't let there be a credit note.*

Suddenly she started to question whether anything underhand was going on, after all? Had her hatred of Greg made her imagine things?

Less than five minutes later, Carol walked in with two pieces of paper and handed them to Amy: a copy of the original invoice for Henson Insurance and a copy of the credit note. Benchmark had credited them thirteen hundred pounds, having offered the wine at a competitive rate.

'Our payment procedure is watertight,' said Carol, and sat down.

'I take it everything is OK?' said William, now looking slightly irked.

'A misunderstanding,' said Amy.

'I expect the percentage price differences will be a misunderstanding too. I'll get back to you, William, with a detailed report,' said Sally.

William blew his nose. 'Now, if we can move on, there's a couple of issues I want to go over.' He started to speak about Lazlo Manco. Amy listened and, on the outside, appeared calm. Inside she felt as if her internal organs had been transplanted in all the wrong places. *Fool, Amy.* She glanced at Greg, who was staring directly at her. He raised both eyebrows, smiled and winked.

William was explaining that the parent company had just published the third quarter's profit results. They were eight per cent under the forecast the City had been expecting and the group's share price had fallen to £7.95. Pablo was not a happy man. In view of this, there was now even more pressure on all the companies to produce profit not just turnover. A number of the proposals Amy had suggested in her initial report would be implemented.

Thank God something was going her way, Amy thought.

'I have had a separate meeting with Sally and Greg and we have agreed that Operations will be restructured. Some of Sally's team will move over to become account managers, taking over existing accounts and reporting through the sales and marketing route, under Greg. The business-development managers will concentrate solely on winning new business. Sally and Greg will work out an appropriate transition plan.'

Within a couple of minutes William had brought the meeting to a close.

As Greg was preparing to leave he whispered into Amy's ear, 'You'll have to do better than that.'

When she stood up to leave William said, 'Could you stay for a moment, Amy?'

She sat down again.

Once everyone else had left he smiled, but she knew something was wrong.

'I've given a lot of consideration to the points in your initial report,' he said, 'and there were some very interesting ideas.'

'Thank you. I've now updated it, with more research and firmer details on each area.'

'I'd like to see it as soon as it's ready.'

'I'll give you a copy this afternoon. I was holding on to it, waiting for the next specific meeting with everyone,' she said.

William looked away. 'It's probably more effective if you submit your ideas directly to me. I'll consider them, give you feedback and then inform the relevant sections.'

'I'd prefer it that way too. Otherwise you can end up discussing things indefinitely, never agreeing or moving forward.'

William was silent for a moment with a strange expression on his face that Amy couldn't read. 'In periods of change it's important to have everyone moving forward together. A disunited team never wins.' He leant forward. 'You have just successfully alienated Sally. She's a very important player in this company. Her co-operation would have helped you considerably.'

Amy remained cool. 'It's within my remit to submit strategies on every area of this company's practices. You warned me yourself that my position would put people's backs up.'

'Initially, yes. However, I expected you'd win everyone over in time, but the opposite may be occurring. You should have carried out the cost-comparison exercise in co-operation with Sally. She might have helped you. Although I backed you, I can understand why she's annoyed. After all, it is a criticism of her work.'

'I had important queries, William, that I felt should be looked into.'

'I agree and, believe me, I'll look into them. But it's the way you handled it. I don't wish to patronize you but there is such a thing as diplomacy. I'm not naïve as to the goings-on and personalities within offices. And I doubt you are. But I feel you're tackling some of these issues as if you've got some agenda. I don't know why. I don't want to know why. I just want you to work as part of a team,' he said.

Maybe she had been a bit unprofessional but what else could she have done? thought Amy. There was no way she could tell him of her suspicions at this point. He'd think she'd really lost it. And she had no proof. Maybe there wasn't any. Maybe John Smith was right and it was just sloppiness and inefficiency.

'You're right, William,' she said, with a smile. 'Maybe my diplomacy needs some work. Although no offence was intended, I'll apologize to her.'

'I know you don't want to, but I think you should.' He gathered up his papers. 'For the next month or two, concentrate on your role with TGA, plus media and PR for CEM and external growth strategies. Give the internal practices of CEM a break. Drop me your report, which I'll look into. If need be we'll talk, but let me be the one to instruct the others on any changes.'

She inclined her head in agreement.

'I'll get Sally to report back to me on those prices and, if necessary, I'll have a meeting with Benchmark myself. You put some effort into winning over some of the team. Believe me, it'll help in the long run.' William stood up, and before he left, he patted her shoulder.

'Don't get me wrong, Amy, I think you're an asset to the company.' With that he left.

Amy sat at her desk, and in her mind's eye all she could see was Greg's smug expression in the meeting. At that moment her terminal bleeped with an incoming email and she opened it half-heartedly. Then she stiffened.

```
Amy,
I concur that something isn't quite right
but you won't find any proof at CEM. The
proof will be found in the records at
Benchmark.
Yours,
Interested Party.
```

Quickly Amy checked the sender ID – *Interestedparty@hotmail438*. She wondered what to do, then made up her mind.

```
Interested Party,
Who are you and what do you know? Why the
anonymity? I can be trusted if you can.
Yours,
Amy.
```

By the end of the day there was no reply.

29

What's that guy doing with John's motorbike? thought Tessa. Things were getting more peculiar by the moment. She was already worried because John hadn't come home last night. He had left for work yesterday on his bike and now some stranger was pushing it into his bay.

Tessa hoped he was all right. Where could he be? Last night she had convinced herself that he must have a new girlfriend. But there hadn't been any women in his apartment, just that blonde tarty one who was going out with his mate Paul. Her T-shirts were so low-cut that she was practically topless. Goodness knows what John thought of that. She wouldn't be his type.

Tessa wondered what was going on. She had an eerie feeling that something bad had happened. She had felt this way just before her ex-husband had told her he was leaving her for Suzie, the woman who ran their dog-obedience class. He had even taken Pepper, their Jack Russell, with him.

And now that same feeling had descended. *Something bad had definitely happened*. Standing back up she stared outside at his motorbike. It didn't look damaged but he never went anywhere without it, so what was it doing here? Maybe he'd gone missing. Maybe he'd just had enough of everything and done something silly. He was a sensitive soul who must have trouble dealing with this insane world.

Don't be stupid, she told herself. Fate had brought John Smith to live opposite her, so why would fate tear him away now?

*

Two hours later Tessa was walking back to the house. She was feeling sick and a little shaky. She had just attended her reflexology course where she'd had to practise on Henry Flute's feet. They were large and hairy, with bunions. Yuck! He was seven stone overweight, stank of garlic and sprayed you with spit when he talked. Throughout the half-hour ordeal she had felt ill and was now desperate to get home and wash her hands – her whole body, even – with disinfectant.

Although Derek had told her how proud of her he was that she had got through the class, Tessa had admitted to herself that she wasn't really cut out for such intimate contact with people. She felt almost as though she'd just had sex with Henry Flute – with everyone watching.

When she got to the lamp-post, the two-hundred-yard marker from the house, she looked up to cross the road and stopped in her tracks. An ambulance was pulling out of their car-park. Her heart leapt into a manic sprint and her legs felt even shakier than before.

The next instant she darted across the road and towards home. It was a dull, grey day and a light was on in John's apartment.

Be alive, John Smith. Please be alive.

She ran into the hall, stopped and stood outside his door for several moments, unsure what to do. After all, she hadn't seen him since the tampon episode. But she felt compelled to check he was alive and well. She lifted her hand to knock but it froze in mid-air, refusing to move. *Why did life have to be so hard?* The next minute she heard voices inside: Hilda and Thomas. The door opened and Thomas was standing there. 'Hello, Tessa. You've come to check on the invalid, too, have you?'

Tessa was aghast. *Invalid?*

'It was just a matter of time before this crime wave

Matchstick Love

affected someone in the house. Unfortunately it was John. Go on in. I'm just off to collect some shopping for him. At least good neighbours will hopefully revive his trust in the human race. We don't want him getting paranoid,' he said.

Tessa swallowed, wondering what sight was about to greet her. 'Hello,' she called, and tiptoed through John's hall.

'That you, Tessa?' cried Hilda.

Tessa walked into the living room. John was lying on a sofa. His right calf was heavily bandaged and two crutches lay beside him on the floor. He looked tired, with dark circles under his eyes, his short blond hair was sticking up and he had two days' growth of stubble. 'Hello, Tessa,' he said.

'*My God!* What happened?'

Hilda, who had been trying to light the fire, tutted loudly. 'Poor chap was attacked.'

Tessa gasped and covered her mouth with her hands.

'It wasn't that bad – I'm fine,' he said. 'A claimant was demanding his Giro, which he knew wasn't due for another couple of days. He was giving one of my team some grief and when I went over to intervene he picked up a computer and threw it at me. It cut and bruised my lower leg.'

'That's awful. You must be shaken up badly.'

'It was a bit of a shock, all right, but I'm fine now. I've been signed off for two weeks so I figured I'd get down to some serious writing.'

Her shock gave way to admiration. 'You're so brave.'

He shrugged awkwardly.

'He can only hobble a few feet,' bellowed Hilda, 'so it's down to the rest of us to look after him.'

'Thank you, Hilda, but I'm fine.'

'Nonsense. Thomas and I will check on you in the morning and Tessa can pop in every afternoon. Around three? Is that OK with you?' she said to Tessa.

Tessa nodded enthusiastically. Fate had dealt her another ace. It was scary but exciting.

'That really won't be necessary,' protested John.

'We insist, don't we, Tessa? It's our duty as good neighbours. We can fetch your shopping and do any chores you can't manage. Anyway, I'm sure you'll appreciate a chat over a cup of tea. You'll die of loneliness otherwise.'

'We'll just come in for a few minutes so as not to disturb your writing,' added Tessa, tactfully.

Hilda brushed some coal dust off her hands. 'The kettle has just boiled, Tessa. You can make John a nice cup of tea while I fetch some firelighters. Damn thing won't light.' With that she walked out, leaving them alone. The slam of the front door echoed through the flat, leaving a heavy silence in its path.

Tessa stared fearfully at the floor. The ticking of the carriage clock on the mantelpiece seemed to triple in volume, banging against the inside of her head. Act normal, she told herself, and braved a look at him.

'I knocked a couple of times since the pub,' John said. 'I was—'

'I'll make the tea,' she interrupted.

In the kitchen she put down her bag. She was actually in his kitchen. *Wow!* She couldn't wait to tell Amy what had happened. Who knew what it might lead to? Two weeks of deep, thought-provoking conversation with John Smith. *Thank you, God!*

She opened a cupboard above her and took out a mug, then opened more cupboards looking for teabags, which gave her an opportunity to see what was in them:

Matchstick Love

pasta, rice, kidney beans, pulses. He obviously looked after himself. John Smith was perfect. Eventually she located the teabags in a jar on the sideboard, made the tea and returned to him. He thanked her and sipped, then pulled a face. 'No sugar,' he said.

She frowned. 'You take sugar?'

'Two. There's a packet in the bottom left-hand cupboard by the sink. There should be some biscuits there too. Ignore the other cupboards – Helen left all that stuff.'

She stared at him blankly.

'I'll get it if you like,' he said.

'Oh, no, sorry. I'll go. You shouldn't move.' She took the mug from him and went back into the kitchen. She opened the bottom cupboard, which contained numerous packets of biscuits, several bags of crisps, five tins of beans and six cans of beer. But, worse than that, there were four cartons of *Pot Noodles*. Oh, no, she thought, pulling a fraught expression. John Smith eats *Pot Noodle*!

It took her a few minutes to compose herself. Then she put two exceptionally level teaspoons of sugar into his tea, went back in to him and handed him the mug with a packet of Jammie Dodgers.

'Thank you. Aren't you having some tea?' he asked.

'I only have three cups a day. The last one's not due until six, after my dinner.'

He eyed her quizzically.

'Too much is bad for you,' she added, perching on the armchair. The ticking of the clock began to increase in volume again. She considered what globally crucial or psychologically enhancing topic she could bring up that they would enjoy discussing.

John reached for a biscuit.

Tessa blurted out, 'Did you realize that by the year

2050 the world's population will be over nine billion, one hundred and four million people?'

He stopped chewing. 'No, I didn't.'

Tessa glanced at the door. Could that be all he had to say on the subject? No comment on the human and environmental impact? The ticking of the clock grew louder again.

'I've just read the latest figures on testicular cancer. Yet again there's been a rise,' she said.

Silence.

She realized what she'd said. Oh, God! Her face began to flush. It was too late to retract it. Act calm. 'Screening programmes are important,' she added quietly.

John nodded. 'It's kind of you to call in every day, but you don't have to. I'm fine. You must be busy.'

'Not really.'

'You said you don't work.'

'Not at the moment.'

'Are you looking for something?'

She swallowed and said timidly, 'I'm not on benefits, if that's what you mean.'

He smiled. 'I wasn't asking as a representative of the unemployment office, I was just . . . interested.'

That was a good word, she thought, and she considered her reply. It probably wasn't the best time to tell him that she hadn't worked for two years because of her social phobia. She needed a bit more time to get back to normal, so that she could talk about it as a past complaint. Past complaints always sounded glamorous, especially if you'd managed to overcome them; it was positively trendy for actors and pop stars to sell their stories of past addictions and phobias. Whereas ongoing problems that were discussed in the present tense merely unsettled people, bringing on looks of pity or discomfort. No, the timing wasn't right to tell him yet, thought Tessa.

'I used to be an accounts clerk for Tesco but with my divorce settlement and an inheritance I didn't need to work for a while.' She sighed. 'I took some time out. That was two years ago.'

'Really? What did you do?'

'A bit of this and a bit of that.'

'Did you travel?'

Her mind wandered briefly to all the sugar he was putting into his body – when the time was right she'd have a word with him about that. And those *Pot Noodles* would have to go. 'I just took some time out. I read and did various courses.'

'You retrained?'

Her shoulders felt heavier with every question he asked. She was sure she was boring him. 'In a sense I retrained . . . I did various courses – meditation, self-hypnosis and Tai Chi. Right now I'm studying for a qualification in reflexology.'

'I've had reflexology several times and find it so relaxing. If you're ever looking for a guinea pig let me know. Any afternoon I'd be more than willing – in fact, I'd be grateful.'

Tessa stitched on a smile in the hope that it might hide her alarm. *Touching John Smith's feet! Impossible!* He might as well have asked her to have sex with him in the middle of a supermarket. But she found herself saying, 'Sure, any time.'

'How about next week?'

'OK.'

'Glass of champagne, ladies?' said Greg. He took the bottle from the ice-bucket.

Tink, Issy and Beth thanked him enthusiastically and sat down at the table in Kudos wine bar, where Daniel and Greg were already seated.

'It feels like ages, Greg, since we've been out with you. You've been neglecting us recently,' said Issy, flirtatiously.

'We were beginning to think that you were too important for us now,' added Tink.

'Forgive me, what with work and my engagement, life is hectic. However, this evening you have my undivided attention.' Greg raised his glass and toasted each of them in turn.

'What about Ben? You'll have to give him some of your attention. It's his leaving do, after all,' said Tink.

Greg glanced to the other side of the room where Ben was sitting with William and several girls from Operations. 'Ben has chosen to leave the family. A quick goodbye will suffice.' Then, as if the subject was laid to rest, he leant forward. 'Actually I understand it's *Issy* who's too important to be drinking with us commoners. I hear you're an item with Charles Davenport, the heir to De Montford Hall. Haven't you done well?'

'We're quite besotted with each other.'

'Beth and I are terribly jealous. The only males we've met recently were a couple of electricians,' said Tink.

'How does an IT consultant sound?' said Greg.

Tink pouted. 'It would depend on the individual. Are they handsome and successful?'

'You can judge for yourself. He'll be here shortly

with Sally.' He cast a sympathetic look at Beth. 'I hear you've reverted to single status.'

She nodded, pouted like Tink and said nonchalantly, 'My Ex wouldn't have been suitable in the long term.'

'He worked at a local building society and holidayed in the Costa del Sol,' said Tink, in tones of horror.

'It's only right, then, that Beth gets first refusal on the IT consultant,' said Greg.

Tink frowned, then caught Greg's eye and smiled.

'Is he nice?' asked Beth.

'I've only met him twice, but I get the feeling you'll like him.'

'How exciting,' said Issy. 'Greg wouldn't recommend anyone who wasn't nice.'

Daniel burst out laughing, but a pointed look from Greg made him stop.

'How are the wedding plans?' asked Issy.

Greg leant back in his chair, and glanced at a group of women coming into the wine-bar. 'Miranda and her mother are taking care of all that. I shall just turn up on the day.'

'You're such a rotter,' scoffed Tink, giving him a devilish wink. All of them laughed loudly.

At half past seven Amy walked into Kudos, which was packed and bustling. Practically the whole of CEM was there, standing in little groups or seated at tables, chatting, drinking and laughing. Electronic dance music was playing in the background but the raucous din of conversation drowned it. She glimpsed Ben in the opposite corner, and began to make her way over to him, saying hello to various colleagues as she squeezed past them. Half-way across she spotted Greg and Daniel at a table, then frowned when she saw Beth was with them. That was all she needed – her secretary extra-friendly with Greg. She no longer trusted Beth and was having to keep things hidden from her. She carried on towards Ben.

'Amy, so glad you could make it,' he said, and attempted to stand up.

'Sit down. What are you having?'

William, who was sitting next to Ben and chatting with Carol, stood up. 'I'll get these.'

'I've already got two lined up,' said Ben. 'If I drink much more you'll be carrying me out.'

Amy laughed. 'I'll have a vodka and orange juice, William, thanks.' She sat down. 'You've got a good turnout,' she said.

'I wasn't sure who'd show. I'm not exactly flavour of the month, am I?' he said resentfully. He poured another glass of wine down his throat. His shirt was undone and his tie was hanging out of his trouser pocket.

'Have I missed something?' asked Amy, perplexed.

'Ignore me, I'm drunk. I've been in this posers' paradise of a wine bar since lunchtime drinking their overpriced plonk.'

She had difficulty hearing him over the noise but got the picture. 'Are you going to miss CEM?'

'Not really.'

'Well, I'll miss you. You were one of the few who welcomed me.'

Ben gazed at the floor with what could only be described as an expression of remorse. She was about to question it, but William appeared with her drink and pulled up a chair.

At eight o'clock Sally arrived, accompanied by a tall, slim, brown-haired man, who wore a pristine dark grey suit. They made their way over to Greg, who stood up and kissed Sally's cheek, then pulled over a couple of empty chairs. 'Everyone,' he said, 'I'd like you to meet Simon Delaney.' All three women smiled broadly and shook his hand in turn. 'And you've met Daniel over there.'

'Yes, hi.'

'Simon is senior IT consultant for the Lazlo Manco group. He's designed the TGA invitation and booking database,' said Greg.

'Pleasure to meet you all,' said Simon, as he sat down between Beth and Sally.

Another bottle of champagne arrived.

'Are you celebrating?' asked Simon.

'At CEM we're always celebrating. You'll have to get used to that,' said Greg.

'I probably won't be around that much. Peter, one of my team, is your programmer. I'll just oversee it.'

'Nonsense, you'll have to call in and check his work. We're very particular at CEM. You can join us here for drinks afterwards,' said Greg. 'I have a feeling you're going to fit in well.'

'Have you been with the group long?' asked Tink, turning sideways to view Simon better.

'Five years. I used to work at Protea.'

'That's where Amy worked. Do you know her – Amy Lambert?' said Issy excitedly.

'She was the sales and marketing manager.'

'What a coincidence. She's sitting over there with Ben.'

He turned his head to where Issy was pointing. 'I'll pop over shortly and say hello.'

'I'm her secretary,' said Beth.

'She's a bit of a workhorse,' Simon told her. 'I bet she has you doing long hours.'

'Everyone at CEM is a workhorse,' said Daniel. 'It's part of the job spec. You'll get used to it.'

'She's certainly delightfully feisty,' said Greg. 'Did you find that?'

'She's full of character,' said Simon. 'Management meetings just haven't been the same without her.'

Sally and Daniel exchanged a resentful glance.

On the other side of the room Amy was on her third vodka and orange juice and was enjoying chatting to Ben, William and the Operations girls. She was laughing at a joke William had told when her eyes fell on Simon sitting with Greg. Shit!

At that moment William stood up and smiled. 'Do excuse me. As MD I'd better circulate.' He patted Amy's shoulder and moved on to the next table.

'Are you all right?' asked Ben.

She visibly cringed. 'See that guy in the grey suit with Greg?'

'The IT guy?'

'That's my ex-boyfriend.'

'I see. Do I take it that it ended badly?'

'Not really. And I knew he was joining us, but I hadn't expected to see him tonight – least of all chatting with Greg.'

Ben pulled a face, which surprised Amy. 'I thought you and Greg were friends,' she said.

'We got on well for a time but he turned against me. He upped my target twenty-five per cent and reorganized all the accounts, giving me the crap ones. That's why I decided to look for another job. In a sense I had no choice.'

'I didn't know that. But why did he do it?'

'Doesn't matter.'

'Tell me what happened, Ben.'

He finished another glass of wine and rubbed his right eye. 'It was when he found me in your bedroom in Florence, trying to warn you off. Greg never forgives or forgets. He said he couldn't trust me any more and that meant I was an outsider – someone for him to get rid of. He'd already lined up another of his cronies to take over my job.'

'What a little shit he is! He's unbelievable,' muttered Amy. 'Anyway, thanks for trying to warn me off. You obviously knew he was still with Miranda. I've met my share of bastards but he really takes the biscuit. He's giving me a hard time too. He'd love it if I left, but he can dream on.' An idea struck her. 'You haven't sent me an email, have you?'

'About what?'

'Interested Party.'

He looked blank.

She nodded and gazed into space. 'The thing I don't understand is why Greg was so hostile to me at the beginning then went out of his way to charm me, and then became even more hostile. What was the point? He gets on fine with the other women. Has he slept with them all?'

'CEM girls are usually off limits.'

'Then why go after me?'

Suddenly Ben looked guilty and shuffled in his seat.

'What?'

He seemed to be wrestling with himself. Eventually he pulled his chair closer to her and said, agitated, 'Amy, what I'm about to tell you will make you furious. You may even hate me for not warning you properly – but I thought it was a joke. I didn't think it was for real. I swear I didn't. Even so, I should have told you that night.' His head hung heavy over curved shoulders.

'Told me what?'

'You have a right to know this, Amy – I'm afraid I don't have the balls, the know-how or the inclination to tackle Greg. I'm sorry.'

'Sorry for what?'

'It was a bet, Amy,' he said. 'A goddamn bet.'

'What was a bet?'

'To sleep with you.'

Her face didn't flicker – it was as if his words hadn't registered – but gradually all colour seeped out of it, leaving her complexion grey and lifeless.

Ben cradled his head in his hands. 'Daniel bet Greg that he couldn't get you into bed within three weeks. The loser paid for the other's skiing trip. I'm sorry, Amy, I honestly thought it was a joke. They're sick, the pair of them.'

Amy was frozen. She couldn't even blink. Then the colour returned to her face. Within thirty seconds the paleness transformed into a blotchy redness.

'Are you OK?' Ben asked.

Almost in slow motion she stood up.

'What are you going to do?' asked Ben. He sounded panicked.

At that moment Greg walked across to the gents'.

Two seconds later she took off after him, storming through the bar, thrusting people aside. She reached the gents' and, without thinking, burst in.

He was standing at one of the urinals. On seeing her he jumped and quickly zipped up his trousers. Apart from one other man, who was leaving, the place was empty.

Slowly, she advanced towards him and stopped a few feet away. 'You fucking bastard,' she spat out. 'So it was a bet.'

Totally unruffled, he merely shook his head and

rolled his eyes, saying calmly, 'Ben! I might have known. He never could keep a secret.'

Amy's whole body was shaking with rage. Her fists were clenched. She felt as if someone had run a razor blade through her insides, ripping every organ to shreds. 'Is that all you've got to say?' she cried, tears glazing her eyes.

He shrugged. 'What can I say? I do hate a sore loser.'

'You bastard!' she screamed. 'I'll go to the police! I'll go to Pablo! Your career at CEM is over – William will hear about this.'

'It's your word against mine.'

'And Ben's.'

'Ben will be seen as a disgruntled ex-employee who wanted to make trouble. Daniel and I will deny it, of course. William won't know what to do. He won't sack me. You wouldn't win a litigation case. You were a willing party.' He smiled. 'Very willing as I recall.'

'You'll pay for this!' she yelled.

'I doubt it.'

'You'll pay.'

'Pure fantasy.'

'You'll regret it, I swear.'

'Unlikely.'

'I'll do whatever I have to.'

'So will I.'

'I'll discredit your name.'

'You'll discredit your name in the process. Your past will be dragged up. How many ex-partners have you had, Amy? How many of those did you work with? Believe me, I'll find them all. Don't start acting like you're some sweet little virgin.'

'Why did you do it?' she cried.

He raised an eyebrow. 'Because I could.' He stood completely still, hands on hips and smiled.

The smile was the final straw. It said he didn't give a shit. Yet in that moment when she could have lost all control, something clicked within her. She had travelled beyond anger to revulsion. Even the air she breathed felt laced with hatred.

Her silence seemed to unsettle him.

'I suggest that the easiest way to conclude this is for you to leave CEM. I'll even give you a glowing reference,' he said.

She didn't hear him because she was lost in her own thoughts. Then, calmly, she said, 'I'm going to ruin your life, Greg Hamilton-Lawrence, as God is my judge and however long it takes.'

She opened the door and walked straight into William. 'I think one of us has made a mistake here,' he joked.

Without any emotion she said, 'It's me, William. I made the mistake. But I intend to rectify it.' She went back to where she'd been sitting and grabbed her handbag.

'What happened?' asked Ben, but she ignored him and marched out.

31

Tessa had just finished brushing her teeth and was climbing into bed when she heard a loud banging on her front door. She put on her red dressing-gown, went out into the hall and was about to peer through the spyhole when she heard, 'Tessa, it's Amy. Let me in! It's an emergency!'

Tessa unlocked the six bolts on her door and an agitated Amy burst in.

'What's happened?' cried Tessa.

Amy was pacing up and down the living room, muttering to herself.

'*Amy, what's happened?*'

Amy continued pacing and said, in a weird, autocratic voice. 'I have a plan. I was thinking about it all the way back in the cab. It involves you.'

'What plan? What—'

'Just listen. You'll think it's crazy and it's going to scare the hell out of you. You're going to say no but—' She stopped and stared directly at her friend. There was a manic, reckless expression in her eyes. 'You have to do this.'

Tessa perched on the arm of the chair. 'Do what? What the hell's going on?'

Amy was still pacing the room, gesticulating dramatically. Then, as if she was giving instructions on how to solve a mathematical equation, she said, 'I now have an explanation for Greg's behaviour. Daniel bet Greg that he couldn't sleep with me within three weeks. The loser was to pay for their skiing trip.'

Tessa gasped. 'Sick bastards!' she cried. 'I can't believe it! How did you find out?'

'Ben told me.'

'I'm so sorry, Amy. This is just too awful. Those pigs!'

'Histrionics won't solve anything,' said Amy. 'This is a time for careful planning. Any emotion is a hindrance to what's got to be done. Take on board what I've said but then put it to one side. We need to think ahead, not back.'

'*Amy!*' squeaked Tessa. 'You sound weird. What's happened is awful. Please tell me you're planning to tell William—'

'Greg would deny it. And I don't want my dirty washing aired in public.'

'You don't have any dirty washing. He's the one who has things to hide. He's the one in the wrong.'

Amy stood still and glared into space. To Tessa she looked like a stranger.

'What plan? What will I say no to?' Tessa asked quietly.

Amy bit her thumbnail. 'It came to me in the cab. I'm still convinced Greg's taking some shady backhanders from Benchmark.'

'You don't know anything for sure.'

'I just know.' Amy sat down on the edge of the sofa. 'The Interested Party email was right. I won't find conclusive proof at CEM because Greg would obviously be getting cash. It's nothing to do with CEM's books. However, to get the cash out of Benchmark there would have to be some record in their accounts. Probably false invoices – but there would have to be something to authorize a withdrawal.'

Tessa stared at her.

'When I was there I noticed that they were looking for accounts and data input—'

'No way,' Tessa blurted out. 'Don't even think it.'

'Hear me out.'

'No.'

'It would just be for a week, maybe even a day. Then you could leave. They're in—'

'Forget it.'

'Croydon. I'd pay for a taxi there and back. You've worked in accounts before, you'd know—'

'You're losing it, Amy.'

'You'd know exactly where to look for the evidence. A quick—'

'And I thought I was mad.'

'Photocopy. That's all.'

Tessa was completely petrified. 'I'd get locked up for stealing! I'd be in prison!'

'Don't be ridiculous.'

'Ridiculous, she says!' Now Tessa was pacing up and down. 'Look I know how much you must hate this guy and you're right to hate him. It's criminal what he's done to you, but this isn't the way.'

'*This is the only way!*' shrieked Amy. 'I've done a million favours for you, driven you here, there and everywhere. Gone with you when you were too nervous to go alone. This is the only thing I've ever asked of you.'

'*And it's bloody huge!*'

'You have to do it.'

'Even if I wanted to, I couldn't. I haven't been inside an office for over two years, let alone attended an interview. It's too much for me. I'd freak out.' Tears were running down her face. 'I'm too scared to walk into a supermarket, let alone turn into a corporate spy. It's insane. *You're* insane.'

'*I need you to do it.* You said you wanted to overcome your fears. You've been in a pub recently. You have tea with John. You're changing, Tessa. You can do this. You have to do it. *Please.* I need you.'

'Amy, you're not thinking straight. Sleep on it. Tell William – I bet he'll be horrified and back you. Get your head together.'

'My frame of mind is perfect, thank you,' Amy flared. 'You're the one with issues. Unless you start resolving them you'll never get it together with John. It'll just be another fantasy, along with all your other dreams.'

Stunned, Tessa bit her lip. 'That was very cruel,' she said.

Amy exhaled loudly and marched to the door. There were tears in her eyes as she said, 'I'm sorry. I don't know what else to do. I'm desperate, Tessa. I'm at the point where I'll do anything. All I know is that he has to pay.'

32

Amy topped up her wine for the second time, ignoring his half-empty glass. His eyes were locked on to her. She looked at him, stony-faced, and he leant back in his chair, hands resting on the table.

The busy restaurant seemed to disappear into the background, the din of conversation and the exotic smells faded. The attentive waiters fell out of focus. All she saw was him. All she felt was hate. And here she was, having dinner with him.

Amy examined every contour of Greg's face and, for the first time, noticed a faint scar across his forehead. Apart from that his skin was clear and lightly tanned, with a darker tint around the jaw. His dark-hazel eyes, framed under strong black eyebrows, rarely blinked. The next moment he clasped his hands and rested his chin on them, appearing amused by the situation in which they found themselves.

'Where the hell are they?' she snapped. 'I want to get this over and done with.'

'Hardly a professional attitude. They're our biggest client right now.'

'Having to spend an evening in *your* company is not how I wish to occupy my personal time.'

'At CEM staff don't have personal time and, quite frankly, most women would love to spend an evening with me.'

Amy refused to rise to the bait. Short-term arguments were irrelevant. Revenge was her priority. She couldn't believe she was actually sitting here, about to have dinner with him, as if everything was OK. But he would not win. She folded her arms and gazed around the exclusive Mandarin restaurant, just off Kensington High Street. It had been Mark Greenshawe's choice. He and Janis Halloran were nearly half an hour late.

'I had a very enjoyable time the other night,' said Greg nonchalantly.

She ignored him, picked up the menu and studied it for something to do.

'He's quite a guy. In fact, romance might be blossoming.'

She continued reading.

'Good old Simon Delaney. We had dinner.'

At that she looked up. 'I always suspected there was something behind your dislike of women.'

'For all their flaws, women satisfy me in that department. Well, most of them. However, I was talking about Beth. She and Simon hit it off. I believe he asked her out. I hope that doesn't bother you?'

Her eyes penetrated deep within him. Then in a smooth, velvety tone of voice, more in keeping with his manner than her own, she asked, 'What *exactly* is it about women that you don't like?'

He gave a bored sigh.

'It must be incredibly irritating to you,' she continued, 'to feel the need to screw something you can't stand. Ironic, really. Is it something to do with your mother? At a guess, I'd say you hated her.'

He glared at her.

So he isn't untouchable, she thought.

'What exactly did your mother do to you?' she persisted. 'Did she fuck up Greg's little head?'

He leant so far forward his face was barely two inches from hers. His hazel eyes grew so dark and intense like pools of burning tar. 'You're more venomous than I thought.'

'Yes,' she said with a smile. 'I am.'

'Goddamn traffic in this capital city of yours,' complained Mark Greenshawe in his Texan drawl. He had arrived at the table, with Janis by his side. 'They need more helicopter routes.'

Greg and Amy jumped up and welcomed them, with handshakes and polite kisses. Immediately a waiter poured Janis a glass of wine.

'I'll start with a Scotch on the rocks,' said Mark. Then his eyes ran over Amy. 'You look lovely.'

'Thank you.' She was wearing a low-cut scarlet silk shift dress and her blonde hair was loose and curled at the ends.

'Unfortunately we've had to come straight from the office. However, work is now well and truly over for the day, and it's time to play. Work hard, play hard,' he said.

'My sentiments exactly,' said Greg, helping Janis take off her jacket.

'I'll drink to that,' Janis said, exuberantly. Amy was surprised: she was usually so restrained and serious.

Mark pressed Amy's hand. 'Don't hold it against me if I let my hair down tonight.'

She nodded and smiled, but inside she wished that she was anywhere else in the world.

After some polite conversation, they looked over the menu. Mark was a regular at the restaurant and ordered a selection of dishes for everyone. Soon they were eating ginger duck, sautéed coconut beef, lemon chilli crab, and several vegetable dishes.

While Greg asked Janis about her two children, Mark started to tell Amy about his ranch in Texas. 'Five thousand acres, three thousand head of cattle and sixty horses. Charlene, that's my first wife, breeds them.'

'Sounds amazing. Don't you miss all that space?'

'Sure I do, but I go back every month for a few days. Two of my kids live there, Daisy and Bud. Felicity, my other daughter, is four and lives with her mother in Switzerland. I go there every month as well.'

'Sounds like a lot of travelling.'

'I like moving around. And I miss my kids. Every Christmas we all get together. Last year we hired a condo in Colorado.'

Amy looked intrigued. 'Both wives?'

'Sure. Charlene and Bizante get along just fine. I insisted. I wouldn't have it any other way.'

'How can you insist?'

His eyes danced with mischief. 'We're all adults, Amy. The three of us get a lot of pleasure from each other. Some people let their emotions run away with them. They're so restricted. I embrace open-mindedness, Amy.' The next moment he grinned. 'Do you see yourself having children one day?'

'Maybe.'

'Forgive me, but you're not getting any younger. Don't let that boat sail without you.'

She laughed at his cheek.

'Isn't that right, Greg?'

'What's that?' said Greg, breaking off from his conversation with Janis.

'A person has to plan ahead. Amy would like children one day, so I've told her to hurry up.'

Greg raised an eyebrow. 'I'm not sure if there's a man on the planet good enough for Amy.'

'Decent men are hard to find,' she riposted.

'Well, if Janis can manage it, and she's a complete workaholic and, if I might say so, damn moody in the mornings,' said Mark, 'then a beautiful intelligent woman like you should have no trouble. For the record I state my formal offer of assistance.'

The other three laughed, but Amy just sipped her wine.

Soon Greg resumed his conversation with Janis, who at one point whispered something in his ear, which sent them both into fits of giggles. Mark continued to talk about Texas and his considerable assets there; he had obviously made his money before joining TGA.

The waiters continually topped up their glasses. Amy lost track of how much she'd drunk, not that she cared: tonight she needed it.

Mark was an interesting guy but in a way he was like an older Greg: he viewed the world as his playground, which at that moment she found arrogant and shallow. But TGA was a major client; Mark and Janis had to enjoy their evening.

'Do you shoot?' asked Mark.

'Only clay pigeons,' Amy said.

'What about grouse in Scotland? Ever done that?'

She shook her head and continued eating.

'It's fantastic up on the moors. A friend of mine owns this sixteenth-century castle, which a group of us stay in. It's beyond words,' he said. 'And there's thousands of grouse. Even the worst shots can usually bag a few. I'd love to fly you up there one weekend.'

'Oh, I couldn't shoot a living bird. Only clays.'

Mark laughed. 'So, Amy Lambert is sentimental. A woman's flaw, yet the male finds it endearing.'

'I've been up there,' said Janis. 'There's thousands of the birds. It's not as if you're making them extinct. It's what they're bred for – for us to shoot them.' She giggled. 'It's the purpose of their existence.'

'Man's purpose, not theirs,' said Amy firmly.

'You could wait in the castle until we get back,' said Mark, rather patronizingly. 'That's what fair maidens used to do.'

'I'm not the fair-maiden type.'

'Amy is rather headstrong,' said Greg. 'I've told her it will be her downfall. In earlier times she'd probably have been burned at the stake, suspected of witchcraft. I can't figure out why the practice was ever stopped. It's a wonderful way of keeping troublesome women in line.'

Janis and Mark laughed.

'He's dreadful, isn't he, Amy?' said Janis, giggling away. She exchanged a smile with Mark, then pretended to frown at him.

Oh, God, thought Amy. Janis was an older Sally, besotted with her boss. What was going on? She felt as if she was in some strange twilight zone filled with Greg and Sally doubles. 'Thankfully a woman having a brain and an opinion doesn't mean she has to die any more. At least, not in the West,' she said.

While the conversation wandered off into new markets for economic growth Amy felt increasingly frustrated. She loved commerce and industry, so why did she feel out of place, resentful? Generating wealth was a good goal, but these people made her want to scream. Everything and everyone was just a game, a gamble, a commodity to be bought or sold.

The evening seemed a blur of conversation, laughter, wine and a constant supply of strange dishes that Amy wasn't sure she liked. Yet she ate, drank and laughed. They were *the client*. They had to enjoy themselves. She listened intently to every story that Mark told, raising eyebrows to show interest, gasping to show shock, and laughing to compliment his wonderful sense of humour. Somewhere in the gap between her integrity and her duty to perform, she rode the social wave like the expert she was, occasionally looking daggers at Greg, who fed her lines to develop in conversation, all in pursuit of the clients' enjoyment.

She finished another glass of wine and realized that in some way they were all Gregs and Sallys: no one was without an agenda.

When the dessert had been cleared away and the coffee was served, Amy continued to drink wine.

'We'll have to have a round of golf again, Greg. I'm off to Australia for five days next week so it'll have to be after that,' said Mark.

'Definitely. Come to my club this time.'

'You ladies really ought to take up such a wonderful sport,' said Mark.

'No, let's keep it a male refuge,' said Greg. 'Men need somewhere to claim hormonal asylum.'

Again Janis burst into a peal of laughter, but Amy remained aloof.

Later Mark invited them back to his London apartment for drinks, which was conveniently around the corner. Amy said she had to go home, but Mark insisted so she reluctantly accepted. She walked beside him down Kensington High Street, while Greg and Janis walked behind, arm in arm.

'Beautiful evening,' said Mark.

'I hope we get a good summer.'

'Somewhere on the planet there'll be a good summer, and I'll just go there. If the mountain won't go to Muhammad . . .'

'Can everything be attained so easily?' she asked.

'What do you mean?'

'You seem to get whatever you want – you buy it, charm it, even the weather.'

Suddenly his eyes were serious. 'Everything is within reach. Why wait for God in the twenty-first century? Be your own God.'

He took her arm, led her down a side-street and stopped at the entrance to a Victorian mansion just behind Harrods. The door was opened by a uniformed doorman. 'Good evening, Mr Greenshawe.'

'Evening, George.'

The four went up in the lift to the top floor, and walked out on to a spacious landing, with only one door. It was Mark's apartment, and they followed him inside, down a plush corridor and finally into a vast drawing room. It had wall-to-wall white carpet and four gold-embroidered sofas faced each other in the middle. Huge chandeliers hung from the ceiling and large abstract paintings covered two walls. Dead animal heads – deer, mouse, bear and even a tiger – stared out from the third, and on the fourth, stone sculptures of naked women stood in little alcoves surrounded by large circular basins of water. Too much money but too little taste, thought Amy.

In one corner there was a metallic black drinks bar. Janis excused herself and went to the bathroom. 'Right, what's everybody having?' said Mark.

'Mineral water, please,' said Amy, and sat on a stool.

'Copping out on us already,' he said, pouring three large Scotches.

'I think I've had enough.'

He frowned, but disappeared to fetch it, leaving Amy and Greg alone. 'Top-level clients should be entertained as they wish,' hissed Greg. She glanced sideways, staring at him oddly, but he just looked at her and nodded.

Mark returned, with a bottle of mineral water, then

Janis came back from the loo. Mark had finished his Scotch already and refilled his glass.

'It's an impressive apartment,' said Amy.

'Compared to my place in Texas it's like a broom cupboard. That's the thing about London, everything's so damn small. My apartment in New York is on the twenty-seventh floor and has the most fantastic view of Central Park. The only view I have here is of the back of Harrods.'

'That's much sought-after,' said Janis.

'But I want space and height, not some fancy supermarket.' For the next half-hour he dominated the conversation with a long story about his father's escapades in the Second World War; evidently Mark Greenshawe senior had won the war single-handedly for the Allies.

Bored, Amy turned discreetly to Janis. 'Is the loo through that door?'

'Along the corridor and it's the last door on the left.'

Amy went out into a long, dark green corridor. *Broom cupboard?* The apartment was huge.

She walked down it, passing several doors on either side, and right at the end opened one to find herself in a bathroom. She turned on the gold tap, splashed her face with cold water and decided to leave as soon as she could.

When she emerged from the toilet into the corridor she was surprised to see Mark sitting in a chair half-way down it.

'Everything OK?' he asked.

'Fine.'

'I wanted to show you something.' He waited for her to reach him, then opened another door and led her into a dimly lit room. The dark wooden walls were covered in bizarre masks. Others hung from metal display stands that lined the sides of a red-carpeted walkway; it was like a little museum of haunted faces.

'It's my hobby. I've got African tribal masks, Inca wedding masks, Egyptian funeral masks, Peruvian stone masks. I have one of the largest private collections in the world. A hundred and fifty-two in all.'

The room was eerie and was full of shadows. 'An unusual hobby,' Amy said calmly. 'Whatever happened to train spotting or fishing?'

'I'm an unusual guy. Here, let me show you.' He took her hand and led her deeper into the darkened room. The only light came from several tiny bulbs that had been set into the ceiling.

'This one is an Olmec ancient American mosaic mask – And here's an early African witch doctor's mask. They say those who wear it can converse with the spirits of the dead.'

'Why would anyone want to?'

He didn't answer and continued to walk her around and explain the origin, purpose and material used in making several of the masks. After a while, she realized her hand was still in his and tried to pull free, but he clasped it tighter. When they came across what appeared to be a small, brown, mud-like face, with feathers at the back, he took it off the wall. 'Here, put this on.'

'I'll give it a miss, thanks.'

'But it's a fertility mask. You're supposed to wear it while making love and the gods will bless you with a healthy son.'

'But today we have fertility drugs – less cumbersome than wearing that!'

'It's not cumbersome at all.'

Matchstick Love

'How were you supposed to kiss?'

'There's a place for your lips. Put it on – I'll show you.' He tried to place it over her face but she stepped back. 'No. It's spooky – this whole room is spooky. Let's go back to the others.'

Mark Greenshawe was obviously disappointed. 'I like it. Don't you think it's sensual?'

'Not in the slightest.'

'Let's sit down.' He pointed to a long green sofa at the other end of the room. Four suits of medieval armour stood beside it, with swords and shields, and metal chains.

'I think I'll join the others,' she said.

'They've left.'

'*Left?*'

'Janis was tired and Greg said he'd hail her a cab.' Suddenly feeling nervous she glanced at the door, then back at him. 'Let's go back to your bar. It's probably time for another drink.'

'There's plenty in here.'

'I'd prefer to go back to the drawing room.' She turned and moved back along the narrow walkway towards the door. When she tried to turn the handle he grabbed her and turned her to face him.

'Mark,' she said, with a forced smile, 'I'd like to leave.'

His pupils were dilated and his eyes had a manic quality, which frightened her. He was a tall, strongly built man, towering above her. He ran his fingers down the side of her face as he said, 'I told you, I embrace open-mindedness, Amy. I thought you did too.'

Her instinct was to push him away, with force if necessary, yet something told her to play it cool. 'Why don't we go over to the sofa and you can pour me a Scotch?' He took her hand again and drew her back through the maze of empty, haunted eyes. On reaching the sofa, she sat down and he went over to a large wooden chest built into the wall. He opened it, took out two glasses and opened a bottle of Scotch.

Amy jumped up. 'Just popping to the loo,' she cried, marching towards the door.

'Again?'

'Must be all the wine.' This time she got out of the room and ran down the corridor, past several doors, unsure which led back into the drawing room. Her heart was in her mouth. She burst through a door and found herself in a bedroom. There was movement on the bed – two people in a naked embrace.

'Sorry,' she said instinctively.

They disentangled themselves and sat up. Amy's jaw dropped and she was momentarily glued to the spot. *It was Greg and Janis!*

A door slammed in the corridor behind her. Amy darted out and ran to the next door. She pushed it open and, thankfully, found herself in the drawing room. Not that she stopped. She sprinted across it, heading for the door – out of this crazy place and away from these crazy people.

In the hallway she tugged at the bolts on the front door and, once outside, lunged for the lift button.

'Amy, darling, why the hurry?' Mark Greenshawe was standing at his front door, with what appeared to be a warm, concerned smile. 'Is anything wrong?' he asked.

She was breathing heavily. 'I needed some air.'

'You seem a bit jittery. Did my masks scare you?'

At that moment the doors to the lift opened behind her, but she stood still and nodded.

'As you English say, I suppose it isn't everyone's cup of tea.'

Matchstick Love

'No,' she stated firmly. 'It wouldn't be my cup of tea.'

'Well, I'm glad we've cleared that up.' With that he went back inside and shut the door.

33

Walking across the car-park, Amy heard a car pull up sharply behind her. She was momentarily blinded by its headlights and tensed. It was half past one in the morning.

A rear door opened and she heard, 'On the razzle again, Amy?' The next minute two crutches popped out, followed by a dishevelled John, wearing a blue T-shirt and jeans. 'Thanks for the lift,' he said, and waved as the car pulled away. Then he turned back to her. 'You OK?' he asked.

She fumbled in her handbag for her keys.

'What's happened?'

'Just a horrible evening,' she said.

'I don't suppose you fancy a night-cap?'

She hesitated. 'I wouldn't mind a cup of coffee.'

They walked together into the main hall.

'I hope your leg isn't too painful,' she said, as he put his key into the lock. 'Tessa told me what happened.'

'Just do me a favour and don't offer me any sympathy. I know people mean well but I'm up to my eyes in it.'

'Don't worry. Any that I can muster will be directed at myself.'

'That bad?'

'Worse.'

He stood back to let her walk in first.

Within a few minutes they were sitting at opposite ends of the same sofa, sipping coffee. Amy was lost in thought.

'What was so horrible about the evening? The caviar not to your liking?' he asked.

Matchstick Love

It was a minute or two before she replied. 'People are so fucked up. I've had the strangest evening. I'm not sure what to make of it.'

'Go on?'

'The guy I hate most in this world, Greg Hamilton-Lawrence, and I took two important clients out to dinner.' She told him about the dinner, how Mark Greenshawe was just an older version of Greg, and then how they had gone back to his penthouse apartment.

'And?'

'I think Mark wanted to have sex with me while I wore a creepy mask in this dungeon-like room.'

'*What?*'

'I know it sounds crazy but it's true . . . I think.' She told him about the mask room, how Mark had behaved, her running off and walking in on Greg and Janis.

'Did you do anything that might make him think you'd be up for something like that?' he asked.

'*No, I bloody did not,*' she cried.

'It was a question, not an accusation.'

'Well, I didn't. There was a little flirting, but that's par for the course. Clients sometimes try it on, but that's not what worried me. A polite brush-off, and the matter is usually dropped. But this was different. Mark's eyes were scary. I just knew I had to play it cool and get out of there fast. He's another guy with no boundaries.'

'He sounds like a deranged pervert.'

'Just another wealthy businessman who's used to getting his own way. They act like they're gods. And I can't *believe* Greg and Janis. I'm no innocent, but he's engaged! *And Janis of all people!* She looks like a librarian.'

He half smiled. 'It's been known for librarians to

participate in sex.' Looking more serious he added, 'And from what you've told me of Greg, his engagement won't mean anything to him. I don't know why you're shocked. Maybe you're more virtuous than you think.'

'I don't screw clients, if that's what you mean.' She pondered for a moment. 'Well, there's been one or two, but that was because I liked them, and not recently . . . Why aren't you more shocked?'

'I've been there, remember? Seen a lot worse. The best thing is to avoid certain people, or if that's not possible, always be on your guard.'

She sipped her coffee.

'Are you OK?' John asked, sounding concerned. 'It must have scared you.'

'You don't know the half of it.'

'Why? What else happened?'

'I must be suffering from your disease.'

'And what's that?'

'A sudden aversion to corporate types. I can't stand the shallowness and the arrogance. It's weird to think like this, especially as every man I've ever dated was a Mr Corporate, working his way up the lick-arse ladder of success and promotion. *In fact*,' she groaned, 'I'm guilty of that myself – not the lick-arse bit but I've put so much energy into climbing those bloody rungs. I wouldn't have bothered to date anyone on a lower rung than me. I was a willing slave to the corporate caste system. Can you believe that?'

John refrained from answering.

'Tessa was right,' she was thinking aloud now.

'About what?'

'She said that men are my Achilles' heel and that I don't give decent ones a look-in.'

'What a pity.'

Matchstick Love

'The nice ones must be invisible to me.'

'Shame.'

'Can't spot them. Put me in a room with ninety-nine decent men and one bastard and I'll end up chatting to the bastard.'

'What if one of the decent guys approached you?'

She shook her head. 'It must be a two-way thing. Decent guys aren't attracted to me.'

'I doubt that.'

'True.'

'Seriously, Amy, you're wrong,' he said firmly.

She glanced at him, then away. She ruffled her hair and the shoulder strap of her dress slipped. Unconsciously, she stroked her arm, gazing at a spot on the floor just beyond him. Then her eyes focused on his. 'I thought of you tonight,' she said.

He looked puzzled.

'Suddenly I could relate to you packing it all in. It's all such a load of bollocks.'

'Why don't you, then?'

'Unfinished business.' The next instant she smiled. 'Maybe I'll read that book of yours after all.'

'I'm touched,' he said ironically.

'Oh, get off your high horse and have a night off from saving the world.'

'Is *that* what you think I'm trying to do?'

'Aren't you?'

'I have enough difficulty saving myself!'

'From what?'

'Myself.'

'How profound. Got a little monster inside you?'

'Hasn't everyone?'

'You see, that's the difference between you and the Mr Corporates. They don't admit to things like that. It's unacceptable to be anything less than super-human.'

'How deep Amy has turned out to be,' he said wryly.
'Oh, I'm so deep I nearly drown myself. I have to wear armbands just to keep afloat.'
'Well, I'm so deep you'll need a diving chamber to reach me. At my level the water pressure is intense . . . painfully so.' He smiled in a mysterious sort of way. Her eyes narrowed and she was biting her bottom lip. She ran her hand through her hair again. 'Yes I suspect you are intense.'

His eyes were on hers, unwavering, unblinking, crystal blue. Those eyes could strip you bare, she thought. They were the eyes of a passionate man, she realized, not of the psychopath or druggie she had first taken him for. She put down her mug. 'I once asked you who you were, John Smith,' she said.

'Do you really want to know?'

For at least a minute they neither moved nor spoke. It was now two in the morning and the house was silent. There wasn't even any traffic passing outside.

Using his hands to support his weight, John moved awkwardly along the sofa, dragging his leg behind him, until he was sitting close to Amy. He gazed straight into her eyes. 'John Smith is a man who doesn't fool around. He needs more than that.' Then he leant forward, pressed his lips to hers and kissed her. When he released her Amy tried to speak but no words came. He smiled and kissed her again, for longer this time, his arms around her. His lips were moist and firm, and she felt the tip of his tongue in her mouth. Suddenly she pulled away.

'What's wrong?' he whispered.

'This.'

'Why?'

'After recent events I can't imagine sleeping with another man for some time.'

'Who said anything about sex? Can't a man and a woman get to know each other without having sex right away?'

She bit her lip and sighed. 'There's another reason.'

'What?'

'I can't say.'

'Why not?'

'I just can't say, OK?'

He looked confused. 'Do you like me, Amy?'

Her head sank into her hands. 'Why is everything so complicated?'

'*What*'s so complicated?'

She got to her feet abruptly. 'You're a nice guy, John, but I have to go.'

'Maybe we could go out some time?'

Amy was tempted, but she shook her head. 'I'm sorry, but it's impossible.' She went out slowly, closing the door quietly behind her.

34

'I'm doing it! It's all arranged!' cried Tessa. She had hurled herself into Amy's apartment, and was now wringing her hands. 'But you have to help. You can't go to work. You have to drive me.'

Amy closed her front door as Tessa paced up and down the room, one moment grinning the next looking scared. 'I rang them yesterday. I've been trying to get hold of you ever since. Didn't you get my phone messages? *I left three!*'

Amy glanced at her answering-machine, which was flashing. 'I didn't check. Got in late.'

'That explains why you look so exhausted and hung-over.'

'What's going on?'

It was seven in the morning and Amy had just stepped out of the shower when she'd heard someone banging on her door. Now, wrapped in a large towel, she was mystified by Tessa's behaviour.

'I haven't slept a wink!' shrieked Tessa. 'I almost came up in the middle of the night to tell you. You'll have to phone in sick. I've got to be there at ten to have a chat with a really nice woman called Toni. I can't believe it! I'm not promising how long I'll stay. I won't do anything risky, but I'll go and see.'

Amy's eyes widened.

'Yes, Benchmark!' cried Tessa. 'I've got an interview at ten – accounts clerk on a three-month temporary contract.'

Amy was stunned. 'I never thought you'd do it.'

'Neither did I, but I so want to be able to do the things other people can. I told Toni about my eight years in the accounts department of Tesco. She said I could probably do Benchmark's work blindfolded as it wasn't very complicated. And now that I've met John, I have an incentive to push myself. When your day's filled with so much fear you have to have a reason to face it.' She smiled broadly. 'John's the reason. I have to be able to go places with him, meet his friends. This is an opportunity for me to start setting my life back on track. It's all thanks to John. And you, of course. You're a great friend and I want to help you out.'

Amy didn't know what to say.

'I'm terrified, Amy, but I've really psyched myself up. And the woman I spoke to sounded so nice. I even told her I was nervous at interviews. She said that as it was a temporary position it was just a case of filling in a form and having an informal chat. She's the supervisor in the section I'd be working in. But I can't go unless you drive me and wait outside in case I panic. If I get through this I'll get a taxi there and back every day. You said you'd pay. I couldn't catch a bus, not with other people on it!'

'Don't do it,' Amy mumbled.

'*What?*'

'You don't have to do this. And definitely don't put yourself through it for me.'

'Look, you were a bit heavy-handed the other night but really it's OK. You were right. You've done me loads of favours. I'm not saying I can help but I want to try. Not just for you. For me, for John.'

'You're fine the way you are, Tessa.'

'I'm full of phobias and fears. That's not fine and you know it. You're just feeling guilty, aren't you?'

Amy frowned.

'It's OK, Amy, really.'

'Why should I feel guilty?'

'For going on at me the other night, but it's OK. Maybe we're both crazy.' Tessa giggled. 'I'm actually spying – double-oh Tessa to the rescue! John will be so impressed, dating a real-life spy.'

While Tessa continued at the rate of a hundred words a second, Amy went into the kitchen and put the kettle on. Soon they were sitting at the table drinking tea and discussing the interview. Some time later Amy was shocked to see that it was eight o'clock. She should have left for work half an hour ago. It was then that she remembered the meeting with William that morning that Greg had mentioned. He had said it was something about sales forecasts, but they were constantly discussing sales forecasts. However, she should go, if only to protect her position. But Tessa was volunteering to work at Benchmark. This was huge! There was even a possibility that she might find something that would incriminate Greg. She had to drive her there. They agreed that Amy would collect Tessa at half past nine.

Ninety minutes later Amy was driving her neurotic friend towards the offices of Benchmark in Croydon. Although Tessa was professionally dressed in a turquoise suit, her earlier buoyancy and elation had vanished. 'What shall I tell them about the last two years, why I haven't worked?' she asked, biting her nails.

'Tell them you were looking after a sick relative, travelled the world, anything they can't easily check. It's only a temporary job so they won't grill you.'

Tessa nodded, unconvinced. Two minutes later, what was left of her composure deserted her. 'How in the world can I go through with this? What if I have a panic-attack? What if I feel sick? What if I need the loo? What if you're not there when I come out?' Initially Amy attempted to answer her, but the questions were never-ending. In the end she just listened. In Tessa's head anything was possible – an earthquake, a tornado or a military uprising.

'Say the word and I'll turn the car round,' she said.

'But I *have* to do this. I want to be normal again.'

'There's no such thing as normal. No one's bloody normal. We're all crazy. You're more sane than most of us.'

Eventually they entered the trading estate and Amy drove past the Benchmark offices and parked in a side-road behind a biscuit factory. She switched off the engine and looked sideways at Tessa.

'No one really understands this fear,' said Tessa, wiping a tear from her eye.

'I know how difficult it is for you.'

'No one does. Right now it feels like I'm going to face a firing squad.'

'There's no firing squad, Tessa.'

'*I know*, I was just using an example to show you what I'm having to overcome.' She opened the car door and got out. Then she poked her head back in. 'You promise not to move? You will be here?'

'I promise. Remember, you can leave at any time. I'll be here, I promise.'

Tessa nodded, turned slowly, then walked anxiously off to face her firing squad.

At ten a.m. Greg walked into William's office, and found him sitting at the oval table next to his desk, surrounded by files and paperwork. He sat down opposite him.

'Morning, Greg. Isn't Amy with you?'

'Beth's just told me that Amy rang in sick.'

William looked vexed. 'What's wrong with her?'

'A bad stomach, I believe.'

'Doesn't she know how important this morning's meeting is? We've got to prepare some figures for Pablo. He's on the warpath again.'

'I can only imagine that she must be very sick not to be here.'

'Was she all right last night? How did that go?'

'It was a good evening. Both Mark and Janis seemed to enjoy themselves.'

'And Amy?'

Greg looked uncomfortable. 'She did drink rather a lot.'

William pinched his lips together.

'I was quite surprised,' added Greg. 'Thankfully Mark and Janis just laughed it off. I don't think any offence was caused. I rang them this morning and they seem fine about things.'

'What happened?'

'Oh, nothing, really. Amy was just a bit too friendly with Mark, if you know what I mean, but it's fine. As I said, Mark laughed it off.'

William went to his desk and pressed the intercom system. 'Get Amy on the phone immediately, please. She's at home.'

Amy was sitting in her car, her head against the window. She yawned and noticed in the wing mirror how pale and drawn she looked. She couldn't believe how tired she'd felt recently. Hating someone and constantly thinking of ways to get revenge obviously used a lot of energy because lately in the evenings she

Matchstick Love

had collapsed on her sofa, exhausted. She hadn't been to the gym for ages – it felt too much like hard work. Last night she'd hardly slept at all, replaying the events of the evening in her mind, Mark and the mask room, Greg and Janis – kissing John! She prayed that Tessa would never find out.

Just as she was drifting into a light sleep, her mobile rang. She took it out and saw the caller was the office. Sound sick, she thought.

'Hello,' she said, in a weak, lacklustre voice.

'Amy, this is William. I understand you're ill.'

'Yes. Dreadful stomach. Possible food-poisoning.'

'Charlotte has been telephoning your home.'

'I'm at the doctor's. I'll be in later.'

There was a pause – Amy hated it when William paused. It meant disapproval.

'It was a very important meeting this morning, Amy.'

'I do apologize, William, but I was in no fit state to come in. I'll be there as soon as I can.'

Another pause. 'Food poisoning, you say.'

'I believe so. We did have some very strange dishes last night. I wondered if Greg was suffering too.'

'No. He's sitting here with various reports.'

Amy sneered but quickly added in a friendly voice, 'I'll be there as soon as I can.'

'Goodbye,' said William, and hung up.

Amy stared at the phone. William had seemed really off with her, which wasn't like him. But he was under a lot of pressure. Of all the mornings not to go in! No doubt Greg would make the most of it – she couldn't let William's support slip away: without it, she had no chance.

Suddenly there was a loud banging on her window. 'I start Monday!' screeched Tessa. Her face showed that she was bursting with pride. She ran round to the passenger side, jumped in and hugged Amy. She couldn't stop grinning. 'She was so nice. And I was fine. I'll just be in the accounts-payable section, inputting invoices on to the computer. That's a doddle. Plus it's just me and one other girl in a small office. I really think I might be able to do it.'

'That's fantastic,' said Amy, eyes sparkling. 'Look for anything suspicious, false invoices. Check their whole computer system.'

'Stop!' Tessa raised her hand up. 'I'm going to settle in first. Then I'll look.'

For the whole of the journey back, Tessa relayed the details of the interview. 'I can't wait to tell John this afternoon. He'll think it so exciting and brave of me.'

'He'll think we're both crazy,' said Amy.

'Yes, but not insane-crazy, adventurous-crazy, wild and untamed. Which, of course, we are.' She was overcome with joy. 'It's just a question of time before John Smith and Tessa Bradshaw are an item . . . an inseparable item.'

35

'*Warning*' from '*Interested Party@Hotmail438*' greeted Amy when she logged on to her computer.

```
Amy,
Watch your back. Your name is being
discredited. Have you found any proof yet?
Look harder.
Interested Party
```

Amy scrutinized it several times. Who the hell was it? She typed back:

```
Dear Interested Party,
Who are you? Why don't you reveal yourself?
Let's work together. Tell me what you know.
Amy
```

She sent it but didn't expect a reply. Was Interested Party really on her side?

Leaning back in her chair she gazed into space, biting her thumbnail, deep in thought. So her name was being discredited. She didn't need Sherlock Holmes to tell her who was doing that.

She had arrived at work at half past twelve to find that Greg and William had gone for an early working lunch. Expecting an invitation to join them, she telephoned William on his mobile and informed him that she was now at the office. He asked how she was feeling, then told her he'd catch up with her later that afternoon.

Amy felt sidelined, which she knew was partly her

own fault. She closed the door to her office and sank down at her desk. No doubt William would be invited to play golf with Greg and Mark Greenshawe next week. The three of them would bond even more. How was a woman supposed to compete with that?

She read Interested Party's email again and, for the first time, felt concerned about her position in the company. The tide of opinion was moving against her. She prayed Tessa would find something incriminating against Greg at Benchmark next week, but nothing was guaranteed. And there was a good chance that, come Monday, Tessa wouldn't go in. Her nerves might get the better of her.

Amy sat up straight and shook herself. Get some bloody work done and impress William, she told herself. I'm an ideas person. Her obsession with exposing Greg had affected her concentration on her work. She pulled out an A4 pad and wrote across the top. 'Ideas for winning new accounts'. It was time Amy Lambert showed how dynamic she could be.

She was just coming to the end of a page of jottings when there was a knock on her door. Before she could say anything, it opened and Simon was standing there.

He seemed surprised to see her. 'Oh, sorry. I thought you were ill today.'

'I recovered.'

He didn't move. 'Just wanted to say hi.'

Amy rolled her eyes. 'Beth's at lunch, she'll be back at two.'

He looked a little embarrassed. 'I suppose this could be a bit weird.'

'Of all the women in the world, you have to get involved with my secretary. Has the world run out of receptionists?'

'It wasn't planned. I just got introduced to her . . .

She's nice. You don't mind, do you?'

'Just don't say a word to her about me.'

'Why would I?'

'Because I know the most intimate details of your ex-girlfriends, how they misunderstood and mistreated you. In the first two months of our relationship you were actually quite vocal. Just make sure I'm not lumped in with them.'

He looked offended – but, then, Simon always looked offended. 'If it's a problem I won't see her again. Nothing's happened yet.'

Amy tossed her head. 'That should depend on how much you like her. If she's just another temp, then I would appreciate you finding someone else. However, if you think she's The One, who am I to stand in the way of true love?'

Simon sighed. 'OK, I won't go out with her again.'

'Sorry. I'm probably being extra-sensitive – but it's this place. It's a bloody twilight zone of underhand psychos.'

'I thought everything was going great – best thing you did.'

'Well, I lied. People do, occasionally.'

'Are you OK?'

'I can't go into it all now. Maybe another time.'

He came into the room now and sat down opposite her. 'You look tired, Amy.'

'I *am* tired, and I haven't been feeling great recently, never mind today.'

'Can I do anything?'

She studied him briefly. 'There is a technical query you could help me with.'

'Not what I had in mind but go ahead.'

She tapped the desk with the end of her pen. 'Someone's been sending me anonymous emails. The sender ID is Interested Party at Hotmail438. Is it possible to find out who it is?'

'What sort of emails?'

'Nothing important. I just need to know who's sending them. It has to be possible to find out.'

'Difficult, though. If they're coming into the building from outside I'd have to trace the server. You'd have to give me your password, and even if I do trace them, the sender may have registered under a false name,' he said.

'But I thought you could track it down to the exact terminal in a building.'

'I'm not the FBI.'

'But you could give it a go.'

'I have a friend who does that sort of thing. I'll ask him.'

Her eyes lit up with excitement.

'What's going on? If you want me to help I'll have to see the emails.'

She leant forward and lowered her voice: 'Simon, you have to keep this quiet. You have to promise. It's serious.'

He eyed her cautiously but nodded, so Amy printed him off copies of the two emails and told him that she suspected there might be some financial irregularities and that someone was receiving backhanders.

'You should take this to Lazlo Manco immediately,' he said.

'I have no proof, and I could lose my job for bringing false allegations against someone. I just need you to trace the emails.'

'I'm not promising anything. It could take me a little while. Let me know if you get another – I might have to put a tracking program on your system. It depends how badly Interested Party wants to keep hidden.' He shook his head. 'This is all very cloak and dagger. I hope you know what you're doing.'

'I know something isn't right. I just need proof.'

'Against who?'

'Can't say.'

'Or won't say?'

'I just need your help, Simon.'

'Drama seems to follow you around,' he remarked despairingly.

'I don't invite it.'

'Just be careful. This is serious stuff.'

'I know that.'

He stood up. 'I have to go. We're checking the new database this afternoon.' He moved to the door, and stopped. 'By the way, I've got tired of temps.' He saluted her, and went out.

Amy returned to her ideas. Less than five minutes later there was another knock but before she could say anything the door flew open and standing there was Greg. He stood like a silhouette framed in the doorway, holding a white envelope. He closed the door, walked over to her desk and sat down opposite her.

'Hello, Greg,' she said formally. 'How are you today?'

'I'm exceptionally well. How are you?'

'A lot better now, thanks.'

'You missed an important meeting, but William and I managed without you. Pablo is coming in next week. I'm doing a presentation to him.'

'I expect I'll have to do one too.'

'Unnecessary,' he said smugly. He put the envelope carefully on the desk before her. Her name was typed across the front. She glanced at it, then back at him. 'Aren't you going to open it?' he asked.

She wondered if it was her P45, but dismissed the idea: William wouldn't sack her – not yet anyway. She ripped it and took out a large ivory-coloured card. An invitation to Greg and Miranda's wedding reception.

'Everyone else from work is invited so it would look odd if you were left out. However, I expect you to have another stomach upset on the day.'

He picked a loose hair off his trousers and dropped it ceremoniously on to the floor. 'By the way, Mark is most disappointed in you. Modern-day Cinderellas who dash away from the ball are rather tiresome.'

'His expectations were too high. At least Janis didn't go home disappointed.'

'Like Mark, I embrace open-mindedness.'

'It's never-ending, Greg, isn't it? The crap! The hostility! The games! I'm sick of them.'

'Dear me, Amy. I thought you had more balls. My little run-ins with you and your attempts to torpedo my boat have been most amusing. In fact, they brighten up an otherwise dull day. Don't tell me you've given up already. Why, the boat hasn't even rocked yet, merely swayed gently in the breezes.' He lifted his hand and emulated a sail in the wind. 'Amy Lambert, what an anti-climax you've turned out to be. You looked like you had such potential, but you're just like the rest of them. Pretty little fillies who fall at the first fence.'

Amy was still examining the wedding invitation. Slowly a smile began to curve her lips. 'I realize there's very little you care about, so it's difficult to hurt you. If you don't care, how can you be hurt?' Her face was serene. 'However, you truly want to marry Miranda. Not because you love her, but because you want to get in with her wealthy family. It's an important strategic step in your long-term goal.'

He eyed her warily.

'We all have an Achilles heel, Greg, and I believe I've

Matchstick Love

just discovered yours.'

He did not react: in fact, he appeared to be in a trance. Then he reached and took from her the card. He stood up and tore it in half. Then he walked out, laughing. But there was something different about his laugh that made Amy smile.

36

Tessa finished her third large brandy and dropped some Rescue Remedy under her tongue.

John had got home half an hour ago and she was trying to pluck up courage to go over and administer the reflexology she had agreed to do for him. I can't go through with this, she fretted. But today she had gone for an interview, so anything was possible.

Half an hour later, after three more drops of Rescue Remedy, Tessa left her apartment with a large bag. It contained her forms, cleansing wipes, a towel and her notes. Under her arm she held a folding plinth. She knocked loudly on John's door.

'Evening, Tessa,' he said, as he opened it.

'I've brought my things,' she said, with a nervous smile.

His brows knitted.

'The reflexology.'

'Oh, right. I forgot you were doing it today.'

Relief swept over her. 'We'll leave it for another time, if you like.'

'No, it'll be good. If it suits you, of course.'

Tessa followed him slowly into his living room. Her heart was banging against the walls of her chest. She didn't know how her legs carried her in but she soon found herself standing in a corner of the room.

The TV was on and John switched it off. 'Cup of tea?'

She shook her head. The room was silent, apart from the ticking of his damned carriage clock. Over the last two weeks, Tessa had come to hate it: it symbolized long, tense silences.

'How are you?' he asked.
'Good... and you?'
'Yes, good.'
Again the ticking invaded the room. Tessa was still holding her bag and the plinth, which was heavy and cumbersome. She let it slip to the floor.

'I'll just go and wash my feet,' he said, and disappeared.

Tessa considered making an excuse and running home. She could hear the taps running. How could she touch John Smith's feet? Feet were so personal. Her hands were shaking and tears were gathering in her eyes.

No! What about my new life? Be exciting and wild, she told herself. Men like that. *I can do this. I just need a strategy.* Chapter four of *Manifesting your Dreams* tells you to act like someone you identify with and admire. Mimic their qualities, and those same qualities will become yours. Who did she admire? Joan of Arc and Joan Collins, of course. Joan of Arc was strong and courageous, fighting for what she believed in. But Joan Collins was also courageous, plus she usually got her man.

Tonight, Tessa Bradshaw, you're going to be Joan Collins!

With a sudden surge of confidence she unfolded the plinth, set it up in the middle of the room and put cushions and a towel over it. Then John walked barefoot into the room. He had changed out of his jeans and was now wearing a pair of blue jogging pants and a white T-shirt that clung to his chest. A tingle rushed through her. She hadn't felt like that in years, and for a split second she considered feigning sickness, but then she reminded herself that she wasn't Tessa now, she was Joan Collins!

In that moment Tessa's head tilted flirtatiously. Next her chest started to protrude outwards and her right hip swung sideways, which she rested her hand on. Taking a deep breath she pulled a smouldering expression; eyelids half lowered, lips pouting. There wasn't enough smouldering, these days, she thought, just blatant eroticism. Well, she and Joan would be ambassadors for its rebirth.

John seemed rather uneasy. 'Shall I get on?' he said, pointing to the table.

Tessa nodded, then winked at him. After a moment's hesitation he climbed on to the plinth and sat upright with his back against the cushions and his legs outstretched before him. Tessa bent down seductively and pulled a towel from her bag, which she placed over his feet, carefully tucking the edges underneath them. 'We don't want them getting cold, do we?' she whispered huskily.

Next she pulled up a wooden chair beside John and sat down. 'A few questions about your background. It's part of the session and it's important for me to know my clients,' she said. 'Name?'

'John Smith,' he said.

'Age?'

'Thirty-three.'

Seven years younger than me! Huh, that was nothing. Joan would date him if he was thirty-seven years younger.

'Occupation?'

'Benefits supervisor and part-time writer.'

'Impressive.' Keeping her Joan-like, cool yet flirtatious composure she continued down her list of questions, asking them in an odd breathy voice, 'Do you have, or have you had in the past, any medical problems?'

'None.'

'Perfectly healthy. Impressive. So you're not on any medication?'

'None.'

'I expect you're like me, I hate taking tablets. *Au naturel* is how I live my life. A very full and exciting life.' She flashed him a wicked grin. 'You'd never guess what Amy's got me doing – I'm spying for her at a company called Benchmark.'

'*What? The caterers?*'

'You know about that?'

'The suspected backhanders, yes. She's mad, that one. Crazy and unpredictable – Amy's determined, I'll give her that. She doesn't take things lying down.'

'I'm the one doing the spying.'

'Then you're as mad as she is.'

'Yes, I am, wild and mad. Great qualities, don't you think?'

'Sometimes. Be careful, though, it's no joke stealing information from a company. What if you're caught? Have you considered that?'

As Tessa, she would have shrivelled up like a dead leaf, but as Joan she just sighed and said, 'Isn't that half the fun, the threat of being caught? A girl needs some excitement in life.'

'Do you have a sore throat?'

She swallowed hard and shook her head.

'You sound a bit croaky, like you're coming down with something. Sure you don't want that tea?'

Tessa's Joan Collins exterior started to crack. A fretful expression was trying to get back on to her face, but she fought it. 'What brings you pleasure in life?' she asked, sounding more like himself.

'Writing, travelling, good food, good wine and,' he smiled, 'being in love.'

The word sent a shiver down her spine.

'What makes you stressed?'

'Being in love.'

A few minutes later the form was complete and it was time for the physical part. The Rescue Remedy deserted her. So did the brandy. And so did Joan Collins.

Trembling inside Tessa stood up and moved her chair to the foot of the plinth so she was at eye level with his feet. *This was it!* She began to lift off the towel. She felt so embarrassed, as if she was unzipping his fly, and instinctively closed her eyes. It just didn't feel right. Toes were so personal. Tessa dropped the towel to the floor, and sat there with her eyes closed, trying desperately to summon up Joan Collins again. But it was no good. She was on her own. She counted to five, opened her eyes and shuddered. There they were. His feet! His perfect feet attached to his perfect body. A couple of minutes passed without her doing anything.

'Ready when you are,' said John.

Brace yourself, Tessa, she told herself. They're only feet. She tried to begin the treatment but her arms wouldn't move. It was as if they were filled with lead.

Move, goddamn it! But they wouldn't. Memories came flooding back of when she was eight and her mother had entered her in an Irish dancing competition. Up there on stage, in front of the judges and the audience, she had been frozen to the spot. Her mother had been in the wings frantically waving her arms, encouraging her, then finally shouting at her to move. But Tessa couldn't. Her mother had dragged her off the stage.

'Is everything OK, Tessa?'

She gazed up at him but no words came.

Dear God, rescue me.

And, like some divine intervention, the doorbell rang. She still couldn't move.
'Tessa?'
The doorbell rang again.
'I'll go,' he said, got up and disappeared through the door.

Amy stood outside John's door and rang the bell again. She was just about to go when the door opened and there he was. 'Can we talk?' she asked.

'I was just having a reflexology session with Tessa and—'

'*Tessa? Reflexology?*' gasped Amy. She rushed past him into his living room, and there was Tessa, sitting motionless beside the plinth. Tessa had surprised her with the interview at Benchmark – but doing reflexology on John was amazing! Then she registered her friend's fearful face and went to her. 'Are you OK?' She touched her shoulder.

Tessa looked up at her pleadingly.

Instantly Amy knew it had all got too much for her. She took Tessa's hand and pulled her to her feet. 'Tessa doesn't feel well,' she said to John, as she passed him in the doorway. 'I'll be back soon for that chat.'

John scratched his head. He looked completely flummoxed.

Within the safety of her flat, Tessa let out a groan. She fell back on her sofa, cradling herself.

'He must think I'm mad,' she said. 'And he'd be right. I was a fool to think I could go through with it. Now he'll never be interested in me.'

'You don't know that,' said Amy. 'It was so brave of

you to try. A few weeks ago you wouldn't have gone into his flat on your own, let alone tried to touch his feet. Just think what you've done recently – been to a pub, attended an interview. Hell! Next week you're starting a job.'

Tessa shrivelled in size with the thought of the job.

'Don't give up now,' Amy begged her. 'You've come so far in the last few days.'

'Tell John I got an instant migraine. Tell him I'd had a stressful day with the interview.'

Amy was just leaving the room when Tessa said, 'What did you want him for?'

Amy stopped in her tracks. 'I think he's been using my bin. It's always full when I go to use it.'

'Oh. It's probably a mistake.'

'I expect so. I just wanted to mention it to him.'

A moment later Amy was ringing John's bell again. Almost immediately the door opened. 'Is everything OK?' he asked.

'Depends how you look at it.'

'You'd better come in.' He opened his door wider. She walked into the living room and took up a position by the fireplace, twisting her hands. John seemed somewhat troubled. 'I had far too much to drink last night,' Amy said. 'I know it was only a kiss but I would appreciate you forgetting it happened.'

John didn't speak, so she added, 'You're a nice guy but we're worlds apart.'

Silence followed. 'There is another reason,' Amy said.

He raised an eyebrow. 'I don't drive a BMW? I don't earn a hundred thousand a year? I don't socialize in the right places?'

'No!' She paused. 'Tessa likes you. In fact, she thinks she's in love with you.'

John's jaw dropped. 'I had no idea.'

'Tessa is a good friend. You must never mention that kiss to her. I would hate to hurt her and, believe, she would be hurt. And please don't tell her that I told you she likes you. Not even if you get it together. Not that you will . . . so just forget it happened.'

'She's a really nice person,' he murmured. 'Slightly unusual, but that's OK.'

'I just wanted to explain – clear the air. Besides, you think I'm an uncaring fascist, and you hate my world.'

'I thought you were tiring of it too.'

'It gets to me at times, but it's my life. It's all I know. You just caught me at a vulnerable moment last night, otherwise I would never have let you kiss me.'

He must have taken that as an insult because he glared at her. 'Maybe you should ring up that Mark Greenshawe guy and become wife number three. There'd be a nice house thrown in – and what's a mask between friends?'

She shot him a filthy look and walked out, slamming the door.

'I said to him, "There's no way you're coming near me stinking of booze." I sent him packing to the spare room. Blimey, some men would have it night and day if you let them, but who wants to kiss a barrel of beer?' said Sharon, who was eating a Mars Bar and sipping coffee. 'I mean, he's cute, my Phil, but a girl needs a bit more enticement than that. We're not built like them, are we? We need *caressing*.'

Tessa nodded uncomfortably.

'The only caressing Phil does is when he waxes his Mazda,' laughed Sharon, rolling her eyes. 'You not married, then?'

'Divorced,' said Tessa, quietly.

'I keep threatening Phil with that. Got a boyfriend?'

'Not at the moment.'

Sharon grinned mischievously. 'We'll have to fix you up with someone. Gary from Marketing is about your age. Everyone thinks he's gay, but I think he's just gentle. It's difficult to tell nowadays. I read somewhere that it's got something to do with the pill residue in the water supply.'

'Oh,' was all that Tessa could say.

Sharon continued chatting about sex, her husband Phil and stories she'd heard on the grapevine about people at work. Eventually she put her coffee mug to the side and resumed tapping away at her computer. Every now and then she'd make another comment about Phil, often an intimate detail about him. Tessa had forgotten what office conversations were like. Sitting in the small, cluttered office that she and Sharon shared, she couldn't quite believe she was there. Then the fear descended on her and she was tempted to run out, but instead she picked up an invoice anxiously. Think of John, she told herself.

After a sleepless night with several trips to the bathroom, she had decided to pull out of the Benchmark job; being stuck with people all day was just too much. She had been just about the cancel the cab she'd ordered when John knocked at her door: 'Just wanted to wish you luck on your spying mission. Let's hope you're not shot at dawn,' he said.

'Actually, I'm rather nervous.'

'I don't blame you. I didn't realize you were so brave – or so crazy! Good luck,' he said.

That was it. Tessa *had* to go through with it. She couldn't tell him she'd pulled out.

At exactly five to nine her cab had pulled up outside the offices of Benchmark Catering. Tessa managed to open the cab door and pay the driver, then walked slowly towards the entrance. Her heart was in her mouth and she felt queasy.

Toni, the Accounts manager, had greeted her in Reception and led her up the stairs to the first floor where she was shown to her desk in the little office. Thankfully it was just herself and Sharon working in it and Sharon had been more than helpful in teaching Tessa how to input the huge pile of invoices into the system. She was a bright, bubbly person in a pink miniskirt, white low-cut T-shirt and pink high-heeled sandals.

Toni had been right about the work, thought Tessa. It wasn't difficult, just invoices from Benchmark's suppliers, everything from wines they'd bought direct from vineyards, to champagne, caviar, prawns, bread and meat. One invoice was for fifteen thousand cocktail sausages.

Yes, the work was a doddle – it was being around people that scared her. At regular intervals throughout the morning, the fear rose up in her. In those moments she nearly ran off, worried in case she cried, fainted, vomited; in her head anything was possible. The telephone number of the cab company was written on a yellow Post-it note, which she'd stuck to her telephone. It gave her a sense of security during wobbly moments. Once she'd even dialled it, then hung up before anyone answered. Thankfully, each attack subsided and Tessa got on with her work – until the next one. But it was exhausting and she felt quite nauseous; she knew that if she could get through this, she could get through anything.

At lunchtime Toni came in to check on her and seemed happy with the amount of invoices she had processed, which gave her a huge boost of confidence. She might actually get through the day.

The whole building seemed to empty at lunchtime and most of the accounts team went to the pub across the road. Tessa remained at her desk, eating her sandwich, drinking her water and staring at the Post-it note.

At five o'clock, exhausted but thrilled with her achievement, she walked out to her cab for the twenty-minute journey home. *She had done it!* Tears of pride, elation and damn right relief filled her eyes.

My God I'm actually normal – daring, crazy but normal!

As expected Amy appeared in her apartment that evening eager to hear about Tessa's findings, but after a cup of tea and learning that she had nothing to report, went despondently back up to her own apartment.

On Tuesday Sharon took Tessa into the main accounts room and showed her where to file the supplier invoices. It was a huge open-plan area with nine people in it, but Tessa was hidden behind filing cabinets so no one paid her any attention.

Each invoice had to be matched up against the corresponding purchase order raised by Benchmark and stapled to it; it was an efficient and standard set-up. Like the previous day, she became fearful, but less frequently. She began to relax a little and enjoyed listening to Sharon chatting away about randy Phil.

'See that guy over there?' whispered Sharon, boobs bursting out of another low-cut T-shirt and pointing to a greasy-haired, skinny man in his forties crouched over his desk.

'What about him?' whispered Tessa.

'That's Reg, he's the office pervert. Never looks you in the eye, always ogles your chest. He does it deliberately.'

Unlike Sharon, Tessa didn't really have any boobs so she guessed she'd be safe.

'Jeff caught him surfing the Net one lunchtime looking at porn. He was given a verbal warning. He's Harry's cousin, otherwise he'd probably have been sacked. Watch yourself with him – he likes the shy ones.'

I'm not shy, thought Tessa, I'm a social phobic. There's a difference. Then she corrected herself: I *was* a social phobic.

That evening Amy sighed downheartedly with Tessa's latest lack of feedback. Tessa on the other hand had a skip in her step, feeling totally proud of herself.

On Wednesday Tessa was asked to help out with credit control and found herself telephoning various clients to chase up payment. She had done that when she worked for Tesco and was surprised by how fast the patter came back to her. Although she was still nervous, it was a huge improvement on all-consuming fear.

She forgot about backhanders and spying mission. Benchmark seemed an efficient and pleasant company to work for and she even went into the canteen with Sharon and Dave, the other temp, for her morning and afternoon coffee breaks. However, at lunchtime she still ate her sandwiches alone at her desk while they all headed for the pub. That was still a step too far – and she was haunted by the nightmare of the tampon.

By Thursday night Amy had become anxious. 'Have you searched the computer system yet? Checked all the files?'

'Not yet.'

'Why not?'

'Well, the system is security-coded. My code is just basic, letting me input invoices and view certain tables.'

'And have you viewed all those tables?'

'I will do. Sharon and I have been very busy. Everyone works hard, and I don't want to let the side down.'

'*What?*' cried Amy. 'You're supposed to be getting information, not going for promotion! I need something on Greg and I need it fast. I can feel William's support drifting away.'

Tessa eyed her with an air of motherly disapproval. 'To be honest I don't think there's anything going on. Everything seems normal for an accounts office.'

'But have you looked hard enough? If Greg is getting backhanders, there has to be some sort of record, an invoice, a debit, something that would ensure the books balance on cash withdrawals. An auditor would pick it up otherwise.'

Reluctantly Tessa promised to dig deeper, take a few more risks. Amy thanked her and left immediately.

She was just relaxing on her living-room floor when there was another knock at the door.

It was John. 'I wondered how the secret mission was going,' he said.

Overflowing with new confidence she invited him in for a glass of wine. He sat opposite her and asked numerous questions about Benchmark. She told him what she'd just told Amy.

'I suppose some of the invoices could be false,' he suggested.

'It's possible but there's a whole team of people who check everything. I can't imagine they're all in on some shady plot. They're just normal people with normal lives. Actually, I think Amy hates this guy Greg so much that she's allowed her imagination to run wild. She's not been herself recently. She used to be so cool – nothing ruffled her. Now she's driven by revenge and she's not thinking straight. That'll harm her career much more than this Greg could.'

'What do they check the incoming invoices against?'

'The purchase orders, usually. To raise one you have to get either Toni, the accounts manager, Harry, the MD, or Sarah Rawlings, the financial director, to sign it.'

'Just the one signature.'

She nodded.

John sipped his wine, staring into the distance. 'Why not run your eyes over the purchase orders approved by Harry? Look for things that appear unusual or necessary – and regular invoices. Amy might be right. It sounds as if she could do with some help in fighting

Greg. It's worth looking into, and if you're going to be a spy you might as well be a top-class one.'

'I'll try my best. You've just missed her, actually. She was here earlier, trying to debrief me. Would you like some more wine?'

He was gazing at her with an expression she couldn't read.

'Just half a glass?' she added, uncharacteristically assertive.

'Why not?' he said, with a broad smile and relaxed into his chair.

Amy collapsed on to the sofa and closed her eyes. It was only nine o'clock but she felt exhausted, drained and nauseous. Her face was even paler than normal and she had no desire to dress up and hit the town. Hatred and revenge were obviously not good for her health. She needed a holiday but there was no way she would take any time off at present: with her out of the way anything could happen. She opened her eyes and reached for her vodka and orange. She knew she had been drinking too much recently but it helped her switch off.

Then she hauled herself to her feet and went over to the full-length mirror. She frowned at her reflection. There were large grey circles under her eyes and her lips were colourless. Maybe I need an iron tonic.

Her annual medical was due shortly: she'd ask to be tested for any deficiencies. They might prescribe multi-vitamins. She needed something to give her a boost.

And as soon as she had the evidence against Greg she would take a week's holiday in the sun.

38

On Friday morning, drained yet pleased with her week's achievement, Tessa was inputting a new batch of supplier invoices on to the system. Her eyes ached from staring at a computer screen and she was glad it would soon be the weekend.

Sharon was at the dentist and Tessa, alone, found her mind wandering off into the things she'd like to do with her life: work for a charity, become a counsellor. Out in the world again, she had realized how much was possible. She also wanted John Smith, and was surprised by her own determination to win him. She had a feeling that things were going to work out. Last night she'd felt so relaxed in his company and he had stayed for over an hour. She knew he liked her, but he'd made no move. Probably shy! The first kiss was always awkward. Poor men, she thought. It was still up to them to instigate it. But John was into equality. He'd probably be thrilled if she did.

While she was waiting for the next batch of invoices, she found herself with fifteen minutes to spare and, for the first time that week, thought about possible financial irregularities. Reluctantly she decided to take a quick look at the purchase orders on screen. She started with the most recent, clicking on the 'Next' icon as she looked over each in turn. They were mostly for food, drinks, equipment and additional waiting staff. Everything a large catering company needed. A box in the bottom right-hand corner of the screen displayed the initials of who had approved the purchase, TD for Toni, SR for Sarah Rawlings, or HJ for Harry Jackson. Toni seemed to approve most, and Tessa only stopped to study the HJ ones. She checked the whole of last month but nothing stood out. Harry had approved management-consultancy fees, advertising, and artwork for a new company brochure. It all looked fairly standard.

After she had checked another month's purchase orders, Tessa saw that Harry had approved more consultancy fees from the same company – Dalcon Trading. But that wasn't unusual: maybe Benchmark was restructuring or branching out into a new market.

In the third month Dalcon Trading came up three more times. That's a lot of consultancy fees, thought Tessa.

Intrigued she went back another three months. Over the last six months, eleven purchase orders had been raised against Dalcon Trading, totalling a hundred and thirty-one thousand pounds! It might not be anything, she told herself, but it was worth looking into. Nothing else stood out.

Tessa scribbled down the purchase-order numbers and dates, then put the list into her bag. When she got a moment she would check the manual files to see if there was more of a breakdown on the actual invoices to show what the consultancy fees were for.

That lunchtime everyone went to the pub for lunch. As it was a Friday the office was deserted. Sharon, who had only been back half an hour from the dentist, begged Tessa to go with her but she declined, feigning a headache and an allergy to smoke.

After she had eaten her sandwiches, she decided that this was as good a time as any to look at the Dalcon invoices. She armed herself with a pile of papers that needed filing, her excuse to be in the area, and hid her list of purchase orders in her trouser pocket. Laughter rose within her when she thought about what she was doing. Fearful Tessa, about to investigate possible underhand dealings!

Butterflies in her stomach, she walked tentatively into the accounts office. Thankfully no one was around, so she tiptoed over to the filing cabinets. She put down her filing and looked at the first purchase-order number on her list. Deliberately casual, she picked up the relevant lever-arch file and flicked through it. The hard-copy Benchmark purchase order stated thirty-two thousand pounds for consultancy fees for the month of April and stapled to the back was the corresponding invoice from Dalcon Trading. It gave no further breakdown as to the consultants' services.

She checked the other invoices against her list, but not one included a breakdown. Her only hope was to check the debtor ledger to see what expense account the invoices had been posted against. She removed one Dalcon invoice from the file and photocopied it, then shoved the copy into her pocket and put back the original. She was replacing the file on the shelf when the door swung open behind her. She turned sharply to see the office pervert, Reg, walking towards her.

'You made me jump,' she said.

He stopped, barely a foot away. 'I saw – a bit nervous, aren't you?'

'Not really.'

'Working at lunchtime? You're committed for a temp.'

'I like keeping busy.'

With his eyes on her chest, he said, 'Are you enjoying working here? You're very quiet, like a little mouse scampering around. So sweet.' He was standing too close and she stepped back, but he just took a step forward, practically pinning her up against a filing cabinet. 'They're looking for permanent staff. Maybe you should apply. I could put a good word in for you, if you want me to,' he offered.

Tessa wasn't good in social situations but she was too old and experienced to be bothered and intimidated by Reg. She'd have been more scared if he'd asked politely to take her out.

'They're small, aren't they?' she said.

'What?'

'My boobs, breasts, tits, whatever you want to call them. They're small, almost non-existent.' Her eyes dropped to his flies. 'If you don't mind moving out of my way, I think I'll go and have a cup of tea.'

He stepped aside and she smiled then picked up her papers and walked away.

Back in her own office she laughed aloud. Adrenaline was rushing through her. Being brave was addictive. She felt euphoric, as if nothing could hurt her. This was where she started living. She was so caught up with her elation that she forgot all about Dalcon Trading and it was only at five to two, with everyone expected back, that she finally took out her copy of the invoice.

On her computer she tried to log into the debtor history ledger but 'Access Denied' flashed up on the screen. She had an idea. She got up and walked round to Sharon's desk – good, she'd left her computer on. Tessa clicked on the debtor history ledger and this time got straight in, her hands trembling. In the various search fields she selected the last six months and typed 'Dalcon Trading'. Immediately a list of every invoice received from them was on the screen. Tessa's eyes narrowed. The invoices had all been posted against the miscellaneous expense account. But management fees were never categorized on that account and especially not a hundred and thirty-one thousand pounds' worth. Hearing footsteps outside she exited and rushed back to her own desk, the invoice back in her pocket.

As she sat down Sharon walked in and launched into the latest gossip that she'd heard at the pub. Then Tessa told her about the episode with Reg. Sharon laughed uncontrollably and looked at her with amazement. 'You're a dark horse,' she said.

'I'm only just realizing that.' Tessa went on to tell her about her feelings for John, and Sharon suggested ways to make a move on him; she told Tessa what underwear to buy, how to do her hair, even what perfume to wear. That afternoon they chatted away like old schoolfriends.

At four forty-five Tessa remembered Dalcon Trading. Maybe Sharon knew something – she seemed to know everything else that was going on in the company.

'Sharon, what do Dalcon Trading do?' she asked.

'Why? This section has nothing to do with them.'

Tessa shrugged. 'No reason. I was bored at lunchtime and flicked through some purchase orders on the screen. Their name came up a few times, that's all.'

Sharon glanced at the door then leant forward. 'All I know is a pretty young foreign-sounding blonde woman named Rula, with expensive tastes, visits Harry from Dalcon every now and again. Rumour has it that she's a high-class prostitute that they hire to entertain the clients. Reg knows her. She probably looks after both of them – if you know what I mean.'

'She can't be. One hundred and thirty-one thousand pounds is a lot of sex in six months.'

Sharon stared at her suspiciously. 'What have you been up to?'

'Nothing, I was just bored and a little nosey.'

'Like I said, you're a bit of a dark horse.'

Tessa tried to laugh it off but Sharon remained

serious and wary looking. She picked up a heap of invoices and left the room.

The last ten minutes of the week were the worst. Sharon was such a gossip she'd be bound to tell someone about Tessa's questions. At any minute Harry and Reg might storm in and grill her on who she was working for. I've blown my cover, she thought. Crap spy! Even though she had enjoyed it, she guessed she wouldn't be coming back to Benchmark.

39

'Tessa, you're a star, a bloody star,' said Amy, and gave her a hug, then rushed over to her laptop with the Dalcon Trading invoice. George Clooney was sitting on it so she scooped him up and put him on the floor.

Tessa pulled up a chair beside her. 'A company search, right?'

'Damn right. Find out who the directors are,' said Amy, logging on to the Internet. She knew that Dalcon Trading, as a limited company, would have lodged its last set of audited accounts at Companies House. Not that she expected to see Greg Hamilton-Lawrence's name listed as a director. That would be too careless but you never knew: maybe Lady Luck was shining down on her.

'It might not be anything,' said Tessa, 'or it might just be some tax dodge unrelated to Greg or CEM.'

Amy was eagerly tapping the company registration into the search engine. 'It's definitely something. Sharon's comments tell us that.'

'But grapevines aren't always to be trusted.'

'But this is exactly what I was looking for. They'd need a company to generate invoices to get the money out of Benchmark's books. Then this company could make payments to Greg. They're covering their tracks. Sometimes there's a whole string of companies. Dalcon could be making payments to another company, which pays Greg. It's just a case of following the trail.'

'Well, I'm not going to work at Dalcon if that's what you're getting at,' said Tessa resolutely. 'My days as a spy are over.'

Amy was waiting for the company information to

appear. When it did she saw that Dalcon Trading had two directors – Rufus Tidmarch and Rula Broknizt. The company was registered as a group of management consultants; a detailed set of accounts would be posted within twelve hours on receipt of forty pounds. A brief summary showed that their last annual turnover was four hundred and fifty thousand pounds yet they declared a profit of only thirty-two thousand. A small profit meant a small tax bill, Amy knew. At a guess she expected the accounts would show that the bulk of the company's expenditure went on salaries, possibly those of foreign nationals or paying invoices from a company registered abroad; there were many ways to make money disappear off the balance sheet.

Tessa was thinking along the same lines. 'Well, Rula Broknizt must be the blonde pretty one who's supposed to be shagging Harry, Reg and their clients.'

'She's not shagging them. There's more going on here than some expensive call-girl racket.'

'The thing I don't understand is, this amount of money is huge to us, but to someone like Greg who's about to marry a billionaire's daughter, it's surely peanuts,' said Tessa.

'He's addicted to taking risks. You're the psychologist, haven't you picked that up yet? He lives for kicks.'

Tessa sighed. 'Well, I've done my bit. If you truly want my opinion – which I know you don't but you're getting it anyway – I think that although something's going on it's not backhanders. Just some tax dodge that most companies do. They create a few invoices to get the profit line down and therefore pay less tax. Dalcon Trading tells us nothing.'

Amy read every last detail on her screen, then printed a copy.

'And anyway,' continued Tessa, 'let's just say a miracle happens and you trace this to Greg. What then? He sounds like the sort of person who'll just move on and get another job.'

'Miranda's father is supposed to be a puritanical control freak. He's in international banking and all bankers have to be cleaner than clean. I just need to prove that Greg received financial incentives to award business to an overpriced company knowing it to be at the detriment of CEM. That's corrupt dealings. If I could expose him before the wedding, I bet you Miranda's father would make her call it off.' Amy's eyes sparkled. 'Greg wants to be a member of their family. I could stop that. It's one of the few things that would hurt him.'

Tessa looked doubtful. 'CEM wouldn't want a fuss. They'd let Greg go quietly so the father would probably never hear of it.'

'Oh, he'd hear of it, all right. You can be sure of it.'

Tessa shook her head, frowned and stood up. 'I have to be going.'

'Stay for a glass of wine. A celebration of your successful week.'

'No, I'm tired. And I want to call in at John's, give him the latest update. You should chat to him too. He understands all about business and might come up with a suggestion.'

'I'll see.'

'He was with me for over an hour last night,' said Tessa. 'Watch this space, Amy. I just know something's going to happen. In fact, I'm going to arrange a little dinner party for the three of us. Maybe next week.'

'Why include me?' said Amy, frowning at the wall.

'I'd be too nervous to eat alone with him.'

'Can't you invite Hilda as your chaperone?'

'*No way!* And I believe you owe me big-time. Anyway, it's just while we're eating. After the meal I want you to find an excuse and leave. It'll give John the perfect opportunity to make a move on me.'

Amy swung her chair round to face her. 'You're suffering from a love obsession. He might not be all you think he is.'

Tessa was indignant. 'He's *everything* I think he is – and more. And a love obsession is better than a hate obsession, which is what you're suffering from.' With that she smiled, turned sharply and walked out.

Tessa lit two large candles and an incense stick, then lay down on her sofa. She was exhausted from her week's activities.

Now that she was within the safety of her apartment, she allowed herself to relax. The fear had taken its toll and every muscle in her body ached.

But it had been worth it.

She wanted to smile, but even that felt like too much effort. She guessed it would be at least three days before she had fully recovered.

When she woke up she heard footsteps at the back of the house. Thomas, clearing up again, maybe . . . *What if it was John?*

Exhausted or not, she bolted upright, jumped up then ran to her rear window. John was kneeling by a flower-bed, putting in some plants. Her heart fluttered and a warm sensation travelled through her whole body. Suddenly she had to talk to him. She ran to her front door, but grew nervous about just walking up to him. I need an excuse to go out there, she thought.

I'll take the rubbish out! But she'd already done that. She peered out of the window to check that he was still there. Oh, no! He was getting to his feet. Instinctively she grabbed a black bin-liner and darted back into the living room. She flung into it any old newspaper or magazine that she could find, then blew out the candles and tossed them in too. She glanced around for anything else to throw away. Nothing. Unless . . . Her eyes were on her ruby and gold embroidered cushions, a present from Amy. Guiltily she threw them in. Forgive me, Amy, it's an emergency. Tessa tied the top of the bag, grabbed her keys, dashed out of the front door and ran round the side of the building. Then she stopped, took a deep breath and proceeded to walk casually towards the wheelie-bins.

'Hi, Tessa.'

She faked a look of surprise. 'Oh, hi, John. I didn't see you over there.'

He was leaning against a tree in the evening sunshine. 'I've planted some fuchsias.'

'Just throwing out my rubbish,' she said. 'It's amazing how much one person can produce. Second bag today.' She rolled her eyes then opened her bin and threw in the bag. She planned to retrieve it when it was dark and rescue the cushions. Now she strolled over to him. Her stomach was turning over with nerves. 'Beautiful evening.'

He nodded. 'Yes.'

They both gazed up at the sky and Tessa wondered what to say next.

John took the initiative. 'How was your day at Benchmark?'

'I found some unexplained invoices, which I've given to Amy. I shan't be going back, though. My days as a spy are over. I found the week quite an ordeal.'

'I suppose that's understandable, but what you've done is admirable, really.'

Bashful, she looked down at the flower-bed.

'What's your next mission? Infiltrating MI5?' he said, with a smile.

'I think I'll go back to the quiet life for a while.'

For several seconds he stared at her through narrowed eyes, deep in thought. Feeling under his gaze she felt unable to look up, instead focused on a pink geranium. Then she said, 'I'd better go.'

'Why don't you sit down for a while?' he asked.

Again, the warm sensation flowed through her, leaving her limbs like jelly. Mustering every ounce of courage she sat down, and began to pull at blades of grass.

'Is Amy pleased with your findings?'

'She's on the Internet now looking up the company history.'

'Let's hope she finds what she's searching for.'

A long silence ensued. Then Tessa said, stuttering a little, 'Actually, I wanted to ask you something. I'm going to have a little dinner party. Well, not a party as such, just you and Amy. Would you like to come?'

There was a pause and she feared he was about to say no, but when she glanced up at him she saw that he was staring beyond her. 'I think smoke's coming from your bin,' he said.

She turned round and, sure enough, thick smoke was billowing out of it. *Oh, no! The cushions!*

John ran over and threw back the lid. Large flames swooshed upwards. He ran to the outside tap and filled a bucket with water, then tore back and poured it into the bin. The flames got bigger. He ran to refill the bucket. Suddenly Tessa was galvanized: she grabbed a flower-pot that was standing by the tree, filled it with water, rushed across the garden and hurled it into the blaze.

Four buckets and three pots of water later, the fire was out. All that remained of the cushions were shreds of blackened fabric and grey ash.

'I wonder how that happened?' said John.

Tessa shrugged her shoulders.

'Were you chucking out some clothes?'

'Yes. At least it's out now, that's all that matters.'

'It was lucky we were around.'

'I'd better go in. Thanks for your help.' She began to walk away, downhearted.

She was just turning the corner when he shouted, 'Yes.'

She looked back at him.

'The dinner,' he said. 'I'd love to come.'

'Hello, Janis, how are you?' asked Amy.

'Fine. And you?'

'Couldn't be better.'

'So, the launch is nearly upon us,' said Janis – no hint of embarrassment over her indiscretion with Greg. 'I hope everything goes well.'

'I'm confident it will. After today's tour I believe you will be too.'

'I'm sure. Greg's done a wonderful job.'

'Yes,' said Amy boldly. 'He's good, isn't he?'

'Exceptional.' Janis moved on to greet the rest of the forty or so people who were in the Great Hall at the Olympia exhibition centre in London, where everyone had gathered to preview next week's presentations. After a week at Olympia the roadshow would tour across the UK and Europe.

Most people were sipping coffee now, waiting for the tour to begin. Janis, with numerous marketing and commercial managers, had arrived from TGA with a team of twelve flight attendants who would be working in the hospitality suite. Greg, William, Sally, Daniel and fifteen girls from Operations were representing CEM, and Paul was there with his team from the inhouse production company. Harry Jackson from Benchmark had arrived with three of his catering managers. Lastly a film crew was recording the preparations for the huge event. They would also film next week's presentation and the edited version would be used by CEM as a sales aid to show what CEM was capable of organizing. From a distance, Amy watched Janis and Greg greet each other with a professional handshake; no one would have guessed that they had been lovers. Soon Sally joined them and the three continued to chat easily between themselves. Amy was keeping an eye open for Mark Greenshawe. This would be the first time she'd seen him since the night in his mask room. At that moment he marched in with an air of impatience and went straight to William. They began what looked like an intense conversation.

Soon Greg, Sally and Janis joined them. When Amy went over to them she was blocked out of the group by Sally, so she stood aloof from them. Mark was talking about invitation-acceptance ratios and was concerned that a larger number of clients than they had calculated would not turn up, leaving rows of empty seats. 'What's the point in having the best event in town if our clients don't see it?' he asked.

Sally tried to reassure him, and when she fell silent, Amy leant in and held out her hand. 'Hello, Mark,' she said. 'How are you?'

He glanced down at her hand, then shook it.

'We were talking about attendance ratios,' he said, and returned to questioning Sally.

'We invited twenty per cent more people than we need, Mark, as we agreed,' said Sally. 'Your marketing team knew we were working to that figure.'

'It should have been thirty per cent,' he snapped.

'It's too late now to send out more invitations,' said William.

'No-shows could ruin the atmosphere. We want this arena to be buzzing with excitement but rows of empty seats will make it look like a West End Show that's flopped.'

There was a heavy silence. 'Why don't we get the telesales team to telephone every client on the day before they're due to attend to ascertain whether they're still planning to come?' Amy suggested. 'Hopefully that will encourage them to turn up. I don't believe there will be rows of empty seats, but if when we telephone, we find that fewer than the required numbers for each presentation are going to be there, we'll get some TGA and CEM staff on hand to fill the seats. No one will know and it'll create the right atmosphere.'

'Excellent idea.' William beamed at her. 'I'll doubt we'll need the TGA staff but it's a good safety-net.'

Mark nodded. 'Yes, we'll run with that,' he said, and walked off to his marketing managers with Janis in tow. Greg and Sally wandered off too, which left William and Amy alone. He excused himself and headed off to talk to Harry.

Amy grabbed a coffee and drank it while she watched Harry and William on the opposite side of the room. It had been such a frustrating week. Unfortunately, her enquiries into Dalcon Trading had proved fruitless. She had viewed their audited accounts, which revealed nothing untoward. She had even driven to their registered address, which turned out to be a serviced office in Old Street just north of the City of London: Dalcon Trading rented one small room on the fourth floor. When Amy telephoned, an answering-machine asked her to leave a message, which, of course, she didn't. From the set-up Amy knew that something strange must be going on – successful management consultants don't work from a one-room office – but she couldn't find any connection between the company and Greg. Maybe Tessa was right and it was just a tax fiddle. She was at a dead end with her investigations, and Interested Party hadn't sent her any more emails. Simon had programmed her system with a tracking device but it could only be activated by another incoming email.

A few minutes later Sally was standing on the podium, asking for everyone's attention. She explained that the tour would begin and led everyone down two newly constructed long silver tunnels into a huge sphere with a painting of Planet Mars as a backdrop.

'The guests will be asked to register at one of these desks, which will be manned by a TGA promotions team member. Once they've registered they'll be offered a glass of champagne and shown to the hospitality suite,' said Sally.

Everyone followed her down another shorter walkway into a large room, which workmen were still in the throes of completing. 'This room will be identical to the new TGA airport executive lounges, with sofas, a bar, tea and coffee facilities, television sets and computer terminals. We're even going to have fake windows with an illustration of planes docking outside.'

'With TGA's logo on their tails, I hope,' said Mark.

'Of course.'

Mark and his team asked a few questions, and then the tour walked through a final tunnel, which was dark apart from star-shaped lights set into the black walls. The TGA advertisement signature tune was playing quietly in the background.

Soon they arrived in a theatre and sat down to watch a short film, introduced by a senior TGA manager, who gave a talk on the airline's strategy and commitment to service. When it ended the theatre went dark – until a spectacular laser-light show exploded around the audience. They gasped when the seating area swung round in a semi-circle to reveal an exhibition area with the aeroplane fuselage. At this point they were invited to walk around it to view the new interior of the planes.

Throughout the hall there were exhibition stands,

where the chefs prepared the in-flight gourmet menu, or a selection of the wines that would be served on each flight was available for tasting. Boeing were displaying new aeroplane designs: over the next five years most of the TGA fleet was to be replaced.

Mark Greenshawe seemed impressed with what he'd seen and everyone breathed a sigh of relief. If he was happy then his army of marketing drones would be too. 'Excellent job, William,' he said. 'The whole industry will be talking about TGA next week. You have an impressive team with Greg and Sally.'

Amy was standing next to William but remained silent.

'Amy's done an excellent job also,' said William nodding at her. 'She controlled the overall appearance and feel of the set. We're very pleased with the result.'

'Along with our own marketing department,' said Mark. He moved to Greg's side, leaving William and Amy alone.

'Thanks for that,' said Amy.

William looked at her with a stern expression and whispered discreetly, 'The question is, why didn't Mark want to acknowledge your contribution?' His forehead creased. 'Although I knew that there was some bad feeling between certain members of staff at CEM, I had always thought you got on well with the clients. I'm now concerned that this might not be so.'

Amy was speechless.

'Getting on with people is a huge part of this job,' said William.

'I do get on with the clients, William, and I was fine with Mark Greenshawe until . . .' She paused.

'Until?'

'Until he tried to sleep with me and I turned him down.'

Matchstick Love

She had expected William to react but he seemed unmoved, just said coolly, 'Misunderstandings happen. It's your job to see that they don't.'

'I didn't lead him on, if that's what you mean.'

'These things happen in business, Amy,' he repeated. 'There is a skill in turning someone down gently so that neither party is offended. Diplomacy is king.'

'I'm very diplomatic, William. I find it insulting that you would think otherwise. Mark Greenshawe is—'

'A very important client.'

'But—'

'Excuse me interrupting,' said Sally, appearing as William's said, 'as I mentioned to you earlier I have an appointment with one of our suppliers. If it's OK I'll start to head off now.'

'Of course,' he said. 'I thought the tour went very well. In fact, I'll walk out with you. I have a meeting with the company solicitors. I'll meet you in the hospitality suite.' He turned back to Amy. 'You have excellent ideas, Amy. Don't take offence at what I've said. Do me a favour and think about it.' With that he walked away down one of the corridors and caught up with Mark and Greg.

Amy stood glaring at them as they turned the corner out of sight. Every bone in her body felt as if it was buckling with rage. *Diplomacy!* She was sick of this crazy company. Everyone was turning against her. In fact, she'd had enough of everything. She was going to tell William all about Mark Greenshawe and that weird room – and about Greg and his sick bet. It was time he knew the whole awful story. She might even express her concerns about backhanders and Dalcon Trading. She had to stop the constant erosion of William's support.

She burst into the hospitality suite but, apart from a couple of air stewards, it was empty. She hurried outside on to the private slip-road beside Olympia. There she glimpsed William and Sally as they turned the corner. Amy sprinted after them, but when she reached the main road there was no sign of them.

She started to walk away, and decided to speak to William tomorrow. Then she spotted William and Sally getting into the same cab on the opposite side of the road. It drove away heading west, out of town.

Strange, thought Amy. The company solicitors were in the opposite direction in Pall Mall.

41

Tonight's the night, thought Tessa. Tonight she and John would take the step out of friendship and into something delightfully more.

She was wearing a long, flowing red chiffon dress and black high-heeled shoes, both of which had been bought especially for tonight – from a catalogue, of course: high-street shopping was still too scary. She'd shaved her legs and even waxed her bikini line. The pursuit of love was a time-consuming business.

Tessa had straightened and tinted her curly hair auburn, and had spent an hour applying her makeup. Now, in the mirror, she could hardly recognize herself. Good! This is the new Tessa, she told herself. It was way overtime to start having some fun.

She went into the kitchen to check the dinner and gave the vegetarian dal a stir. She was proud of herself. Who'd have thought two months ago that she would be hosting a dinner party?

Within ten minutes there was a knock at her door.

'Hello, John,' she said. He was wearing a new pair of jeans and a blue shirt. He was clean-shaven but his blond hair had grown longer and it looked slightly messy. Tessa liked it that way – wild and untamed.

He was holding a bottle of red wine and for a moment didn't say anything as he glanced her up and down, looking surprised and taken aback.

'You look lovely, Tessa,' he said.

She glanced away shyly and stepped back to let him in. He followed her into the living room where she stopped and turned towards him. 'Amy hasn't arrived yet. She shouldn't be long.'

'Something smells delicious.'

'Thanks. I've made Indian food.'

'Hence the music,' he said.

Tessa blushed: the sitar CD had seemed a good idea at the time, but now she wondered if it was a bit cheesy. She had lit candles too, and they, with the smell of the incense, the spices from the cooking and her usual Bohemian décor, enhanced the quirky ambience.

'I brought you this.' He held out the wine.

She took it and hurried into the kitchen, praying that Amy wouldn't be long. Her chest felt tight, her palms damp with sweat. From out of nowhere, fear possessed her. *What was I thinking of?* A recovering social phobic hosting a dinner party! Her anxiety was spiralling out of control, all she could think about was ways to get him out of her apartment, so her panic would stop.

Enough! She stood up straight. She wanted John Smith to be there. She didn't want fear to control her life any longer. She would walk back into the living room and tonight would be special – the start of something good.

Within a few moments a composed-looking Tessa appeared in the living room with two glasses of red wine. John was sitting at one end of the sofa and she handed him a drink, then sat down in the armchair opposite. Her heart was in her mouth but she hid it. They sipped their wine, and occasionally their eyes met. They smiled at each other before looking away. Tessa sensed that even John was a little nervous, which was unusual for him.

He cleared his throat. 'I love Indian food.'

'That's good.'

'I wouldn't know where to begin to cook it.'

'I never have before tonight.'

'It's brave of you to have a go.'

'Yes,' she said firmly. 'It is. To be honest I'm trying to push myself more, take some risks. Life, after all, is for living.'

He toasted her. 'Congratulations. Taking risks can be hard. It's easy to fall into a rut.'

'Very easy. Thankfully, something came my way to wake me up. A person needs a reason to step outside their comfort zones.'

'That's true. What was yours?'

Tessa wondered what to say. This little scene was supposed to take place after dessert. She looked back at him, into his amazing crystal blue yes, and a new calm came over her.

'My motivation to break out from my fearful existence—' A loud knock interrupted her. 'I'll tell you later.' She went to let Amy in.

As Tessa opened the door, she said excitedly, 'He's here.'

Amy handed her a bottle of wine. 'You look fantastic,' she said, feeling guilty that she had made no effort: she was still wearing the emerald green jumper and black trousers she'd worn all day at work.

Tessa's smile ran from ear to ear. 'Thanks. Now, you mustn't forget what I told you. After dessert when I put on my Rod Stewart CD, that's the sign for you to leave.'

'I thought you said Ricky Martin.'

'Too fast. The Rod Stewart's got lots of love songs on it. I want to kiss him not salsa with him.'

Amy followed her into the living room where John greeted her with a lack-lustre nod of his head.

'Evening,' she said, and sat down on a hard-backed chair.

'I'll just get you some wine,' said Tessa, and disappeared.

A blanket of silence fell over the room. John sipped his wine, crossed his legs and stared into space. The seconds ticked away, but there was no sign of Tessa returning. Amy glanced at him discreetly. She'd like to get some scissors to his messy hair. 'I'll just see if Tessa needs some help.' She got up and went into the kitchen. 'What are you up to?' she asked.

'It's all under control.' Tessa handed her a glass of wine. 'You go back and talk to John.'

Amy didn't move. 'Sure I can't do anything?'

'Just talk to John. Don't leave him on his own.'

Reluctantly, Amy returned half-heartedly to the living room. She felt like the Wicked Witch of the West because she had kissed him. God knows what was going to happen tonight when Rod Stewart started playing?

'How have you been?' he asked.

'Fine. You?'

'Fine,' he said, with a touch of sarcasm.

'That's good. Everyone's fine, then.'

'Seems that way.'

'Your leg—'

'Better now.'

'Good.'

'Work?'

'The same,' she said. 'Yours?'

'The same.'

The burst of conversation was replaced with an uneasy silence. Amy studied the bookcase. John examined the floor. The Indian music sounded now as if someone was being strangled.

'I'm surprised you came,' she said quietly. 'Knowing what you now know.'

'Why wouldn't I come?'

'Well, it might be awkward.'

'For whom?'

'I just hope you let her down gently. She's quite fragile.'

His eyes narrowed. 'I—'

'It's ready,' said Tessa. 'Take a seat at the table and I'll start bringing everything in.'

'I'm impressed,' said John, half-way through the main course of dal, lemon rice, vegetable curry and *saag aloo*. They'd already eaten miniature *samosas*, onion *bhajis* and *pakoras*.

'It tastes amazing,' added Amy.

'Well, save some room for the Indian ice-cream I've made.'

'I'll eat it all. I haven't had such a good meal in ages.' John picked up his glass. 'To Tessa.'

'Tessa,' said Amy.

Tessa blushed. 'Oh, stop it, you two. Let's talk about something else.'

'I have some good news about my book,' he said.

Tessa's face was alight with excitement. 'What?'

'I have a publisher.'

Tessa squealed. 'I knew you'd find one. I just knew it! I can't wait to read it. When will it be in the shops?'

'Congratulations,' said Amy.

'Not for another year. They want it finished by October. It's a two-book deal so when I finish this one, I'm going to go travelling again, maybe New Zealand and Australia. Get some material for the second book.'

'How long will you be away?' asked a less-jubilant Tessa.

'Three or four months.'

'So you're giving up the unemployment office?' said Amy.

'No, I'm taking extended unpaid leave. I haven't had a huge advance, so I'll still need to work.'

Awestruck, Tessa raised her glass to him. 'It's your turn to be toasted. To John Smith, our famous neighbour.'

John began to tell them about his meeting with the publisher and his plans for the second book. Amy noticed how animated he had become, how thrilled he was to be able to continue writing. It was good to see someone so in tune with their life. She got up, and headed for the bathroom.

When she returned John and Tessa were laughing.

'John was just telling me about one of his adventures in Africa.'

'Really? Tell me too. I could do with a laugh.'

He shrugged. 'It wasn't that funny.'

Tessa squeezed her hand. 'It's your turn to be toasted now, Amy, so tell us something good that's happened.'

Amy proceeded to fill everyone's glass. 'Nothing to celebrate, I'm afraid.'

'So work isn't going that well?' asked John.

'Actually, I've decided on a change of tactic. Tomorrow I'm going to have a long chat with William Halson, the MD, about everything that's been going on.'

'I told you to do that ages ago,' said Tessa. 'It's for the best.'

'A risky move,' said John.

'I have no choice. William's losing his respect and trust in me. I know Greg's discrediting me. Nearly everyone at CEM is against me, even my secretary, Beth. I think she blames me for Simon not seeing her again.'

'Well, you did ask him not to,' said Tessa

'Can you blame me?'

'Of course not.'

'Tessa told me about the invoices she found. What company was it again?' asked John.

'Dalcon Trading.'

'And their accounts showed nothing?'

Amy shook her head. 'They have two company directors, Rula Broknizt and Rufus Tidmarch, but I've found no link with Greg.'

'They're unusual names,' said John thoughtfully. 'I suppose I could do an NI search on them.'

'What's that?'

'Nothing may come of it. It's just that when claimants don't know their National Insurance number, we can search the national computer. Everyone in the country is registered.'

Amy's eyes widened.

'Don't get too excited. It doesn't give much information and you really need a date of birth to ensure that you've got the right person, otherwise you could be searching hundreds of records. However, those are unusual names so hopefully there won't be too many of them.'

'But what sort of thing can you find out?'

'An address, date of birth, NI number to start with, but also a spouse's name, maiden name, PAYE record – or, rather, what companies they've worked for as an employee. Not as a director, unfortunately. It's a long shot but if I did manage to find the right people, maybe one of them has worked for a company Greg's been with. It would be a tenuous link but at least it would show that they know each other.'

'Definitely. Please give it a go,' said Amy.

'"Giving it a go", as you put it, could lose me my job. Misuse of classified information is a serious offence.'

She was desperately disappointed, and it showed.

John relented. 'Write down the names for me and I'll see if an opportunity presents itself. I'll also run a search on Greg.'

'Thanks, John, I really appreciate that.' She gave him a heartfelt and grateful smile.

'You're one of Amy's spies too, John. We'll compare tactics later.' Tessa giggled.

After dessert and coffee Amy and John moved across to the sofa and Tessa curled up on a beanbag.

'I'm so stuffed I won't be able to eat for a week,' said Amy.

'Me neither.'

'Nor me.'

The earlier tension had passed, and they were easy with each other.

'I think I'll put on Rod Stewart now.' Tessa smiled.

'Rod Stewart?' said John. 'I wouldn't have had you down as a fan of his.'

'He's sung some beautiful love songs,' she replied, 'but I could put something else on, if you like.'

'Is that a Cranberries' CD?'

'Yes, it is.' Tessa turned to Amy. 'I am putting on the Cranberries instead of Rod Stewart.' Her eyes widened at her before she turned and inserted the disk.

Amy knew that her moment had come. 'Unfortunately, I have to make a move. I've got to make plans for tomorrow.'

'It's still early,' said John.

'I'm exhausted.'

Tessa put on a sad expression. 'You do look tired but are you sure you can't stay any longer?'

Amy smiled.

'I'd love to but I mustn't. Enjoy the rest of your evening.'

Tessa showed her out to the front door and thanked her for leaving on cue. 'I'll tell you about it tomorrow,' she whispered.

Amy looked worried. 'Don't be too disappointed if nothing happens.'

'Why do you say that?'

'I just don't want you to get hurt. He might not see you like that.'

Tessa winked at her. 'I'm no fool. That man likes me.'

John and Tessa sat together on her sofa listening to the Cranberries belting out their songs. It wasn't quite the atmosphere she had hoped for but John said he was a big fan. He was telling Tessa more about his plans for the second book and his travels. Part of her was pleased for him but she was worried too that she'd never see him again. In her vision of their future together she would travel with him also, but not in October: it was too soon. She'd only just managed to travel three miles to Croydon and New Zealand was on the other side of the world — all those hours on an aeroplane, trapped with people. It would be impossible.

A doubt crept into her mind about their compatibility. Maybe Amy had been right and he wasn't interested in her. Maybe she had misread the signs. With the onslaught of negative thoughts her shoulders rounded and her happiness drained away.

'Are you OK?' asked John. He'd obviously picked up on her sudden depression.

She didn't even look at him, instead stared at the floor, feeling her heart, so abandoned and out of practice, starting to pain her. With a false nod of her head she continued staring at the floor.

'What is it? What's wrong?'

She couldn't answer him, and felt a sudden urge to run away – but she was already at home: there was nowhere else to run to. John took her right hand and squeezed it. 'Don't shut me out. What's wrong?' he asked.

Her eyes were glazed with tears. 'I – I—' She looked into his eyes. 'I so want to kiss you,' she said.

For a moment neither of them moved. Tessa couldn't believe that those words had come out of her mouth. If quantum physics had been more advanced, she would have gone back in time and unsaid them. She waited for him to make a polite excuse and leave. Instead he leant towards her and kissed her briefly on the lips. She was dumbfounded: John Smith had just kissed her. It wasn't a dream. It was real.

He smiled, and stroked the side of her face. Then he kissed her again, for longer. Her whole body quivered and tingled under his touch. Instinctively she kissed him back.

42

Amy's face lit up with relief. Ha! Got you! She clicked on the email that greeted her at work. '*Update*', from 'Interested Party@Hotmail438'

> Amy,
> I take it you've found nothing. Time is running out. Major restructuring is on the cards. Tell me anything — I want to help.
> Interested Party.

She grabbed her mobile and punched in a number. 'Got one,' she said, when the call was answered.

'Good morning, Amy,' said Simon. 'Do I take it your mysterious friend has emailed you?'

'Damn right.'

'I told you, there are no guarantees.'

'I'll keep my fingers crossed.'

'Keep everything crossed.'

She smiled. 'Thanks, I appreciate this.'

'Enough to have dinner with me?'

There was a noticeable pause. 'Isn't that emotional blackmail.'

'Well, how else am I going to get you to agree?'

'OK.'

'I'll be in touch.' He hung up.

Her office door opened and Beth walked in.

'Good morning,' said Amy, with a smile.

'Morning,' replied Beth, with a definite lack of friendliness. She went straight to her desk, and hung her full-length leather coat on the hook behind it.

That girl has either won the lottery or run up huge

debts to be able to buy so many expensive new clothes, Amy thought. Every day there was a new outfit. The other girls in the office came from wealthy backgrounds but Beth didn't.

'Could I have a word with you?' said Beth, approaching Amy's desk.

'Of course.'

She sat down in the chair opposite, crossed her legs and rested her hands in her lap. 'There's an opening for a secretary in Operations. Bridget is leaving. I hope you don't mind but I'd like to apply for it.'

Amy marvelled at Beth's transformation. Everything that had made Beth herself, had gone, leaving the perfectly manufactured CEM girl who sat before Amy: cool, polished, oozing confidence. She hardly even blinked. Not a hair was out of place. Even her teeth had been capped. She was just like all the others.

Amy clasped her hands and rested her chin on them. At least a minute passed before she spoke. Then, 'Beth,' she said calmly, 'are you aware that you've turned into Princess Anne?'

Beth's jaw dropped.

Amy nodded. 'It's true, I'm afraid. You're not the same girl who started here.'

Beth's mouth moved but no words came.

'Of course I don't mind you transferring to Operations. In fact,' said Amy, 'I would like it if you did.'

Beth stood up indignantly and stormed out of the room.

Amy grimaced. No doubt this little episode would be around the company within two minutes. By the time she had her meeting with William he'd probably know all about it. More ammunition for him against her lack of diplomacy. Well, fuck diplomacy. Fuck them all.

Ten minutes later a now tense and guarded looking Amy walked into William's office.

'Is everything OK?' he asked, from behind his desk.

'Actually, no. That's why I asked for this meeting.'

He indicated the two sofas in the corner of his office. 'Let's sit over there. It's more comfortable and less formal.'

They sat on the same sofa, a little distance apart. 'So what's troubling you?' William asked.

She took a deep breath and in a calm yet resolute manner stated, 'I had hoped not to involve you with this,' Amy began, 'but it's got to the point where I have no choice but to tell you of a few unpleasant things that have been going on at CEM.'

He sat upright, his expression serious and alert.

Amy continued before she could change her mind: 'As you know, when I first arrived here I was not welcomed by Greg. In fact, he made it clear to me both directly and indirectly that he thought my appointment was a waste of money and that my role should have been incorporated into Sales and Marketing.'

William nodded.

'He went out of his way to make my life difficult. Then, out of the blue, he changed towards me and became helpful, friendly and even charming. I felt it was because he'd got to know me and no longer saw me as a threat. Unfortunately there was a sordid explanation for his change of heart. I didn't know that at the time and I stupidly became attracted to him. He made it clear that he was attracted to me . . .'

William looked uncomfortable with the direction of

this conversation. He scratched the back of his neck.

'There is a reason why I'm telling you this, William. Unknown to me, Daniel and Greg had made a disgusting bet. If Greg managed to sleep with me within three weeks Daniel would have to pay for Greg's skiing trip.'

'*What?*' William was horrified. '*No!* You must be mistaken.'

'I wish I was.'

'Are you sure?'

'Quite sure. Ben told me. Anyway, foolishly, and I'm incredibly embarrassed about it, I did sleep with him.' Her fists clenched so that the whites of her knuckles showed. Amy went on to tell him about Greg's comments after his promotion and his subsequent difficult behaviour, listing various examples of it.

'Have you asked Greg outright if the bet existed?' asked William.

'Of course.'

'Did he admit it?'

'To me, yes. However, he made it clear that he'd deny it to anyone else. He wants me to leave, which of course I have no intention of doing. Unfortunately, he is so popular with everyone that I'm having difficulty with Daniel and Sally too.'

William sighed heavily.

'I also wanted to tell you about Mark Greenshawe.' She went on to explain about the mask room and his bizarre behaviour. 'Of *course* I tried to turn him down diplomatically, but he was insistent and, quite frankly, frightening.'

William was staring at Amy with a strange expression, which she couldn't identify.

She added, 'When I was leaving Mark's, running away from him, in fact, I opened the wrong door and found Greg and Janis having sex together.'

'I'm an MD, not some vicar responsible for people's morals,' he said, exasperated. 'If two consenting adults want to have sex then that's their business.'

'But *I* wasn't consenting – well, I wouldn't have if I'd known it was a goddamn bet, a trick.'

'You should have come to me before.'

'I felt I could handle it on my own. Anyway, what could you have done?'

'The question is, what do I do now? You do realize it's your word against his?'

'And Ben's.'

'And Daniel's. They'll both deny it. Ben was leaving, so it could be suggested that he wanted to stir up trouble. I understand he and Greg didn't see eye to eye on a few matters towards the end. Litigation is a messy business with no winners.'

'That's why I don't want to go down that route. I'm fully aware of the pitfalls.'

William rubbed his forehead with his thumb. 'Sorry,' he said, sounding calmer. 'I'll speak to him. I'll hear what he has to say, and I'll leave him in no doubt about my feelings on this. But how do you want this handled? How can you possibly continue to work together?'

'Can't he be encouraged to move sideways into a sister company?'

'Not if the allegation can't be proved against him.'

'I'm not saying I won't work with him, but I want you to warn him to back off. I want you to understand what I've had to put up with. I've had to fight my corner, which is why my manner might not have been as friendly or professional as I would have liked.'

There was a long silence, which Amy felt William should have been filling with support for her and disgust for Greg, yet he was staring into space.

Eventually he looked back at her. 'Thank you for bringing this to my attention. I need to give it some serious consideration, and talk to Greg. The three of us may have to have a meeting together. The fact is, you have to work together closely at times. If that isn't possible, then as managing director I will have to consider what action to take.'

'I understand.'

He raised both hands in the air. 'I'm shocked, Amy. I'm no fool when it comes to Greg, but what's a woman like you doing sleeping with him? I'd have thought you'd have more sense.'

Her eyelids lowered. 'Yes, so did I. I didn't want to involve you in this, William, but I felt I was losing your support.'

'Absolutely not.'

She felt relieved to have got it off her chest, although the outcome was by no means certain.

William nodded at her and offered her a supportive smile. 'I'll get back to you within a few days.'

She stood up, then immediately sat down again. 'Actually, there was something else.'

He raised both eyebrows, obviously concerned at what else she was going to say.

Amy fidgeted uncomfortably on the sofa. In a less resolute manner she said, 'Did Sally ever get back to you with the price-comparison exercise over Benchmark?'

'Yes, of course.'

'Was everything OK?' she asked, when he added nothing else.

'Mostly.'

'So they aren't charging us ten per cent above their competitors?'

William frowned. 'You've brought this subject up a

Matchstick Love

few times. Is there something you've discovered that I should know about?'

She hesitated. 'This is very much off the record, William.'

At that moment there was a knock and Charlotte, William's PA, walked in. 'There's an urgent personal call for Amy. I said you were in a meeting but a John Smith insisted he had to talk to you now.'

'You can take it at my desk,' said William. Charlotte left the room to transfer the call.

'Hello,' said Amy.

'Amy, it's John.' He sounded alarmed.

'What's happened?'

'It's about the NI search I did.'

Amy's eyes widened. 'I'm in a meeting. Can I call you in twenty minutes?'

'No. You need to know this now, before you talk to your MD. What's his surname again?'

She looked over at William who glanced at her oddly, obviously wondering what the big emergency was. In a relaxed manner she said to John, 'I really think I should call you later. I'm in a meeting with my MD.'

'Oh, shit! Well, is it Halson? I think you said that.'

'That's right.'

'I thought so. Just listen. You need to watch yourself. I searched for a Rula Broknizt. There are actually eight different Rula Broknizts with addresses in the southeast of England. Anyway, I looked through them all in case anything stuck out. Nothing did. Then I did a search on Rula Broknizt as a maiden name.' He paused momentarily, breathing heavily. 'This could be a crazy coincidence, but I found that Rula Broknizt is actually Veronik Rula Halson. Broknizt is her maiden name. She's married to a William Halson. From his date of birth that would make him fifty-three. They live in Chelsea. Does that sound about right?'

Every muscle in Amy's body was paralyzed apart from her eyes, which travelled across to William. He pointed to his watch. She nodded, and her eyes travelled to his desk where there was a photograph of his wife with their two young sons. Amy knew his wife was Polish and called Veronik. Sharon at Benchmark had mentioned a pretty woman with a foreign accent to Tessa.

'Are you still there?' said John.

'Thank you for that.' Amy said in an exceptionally calm manner. Inside her heartbeat began to race. Her stomach felt as if it was turning 360 degrees. Her legs were wobbly. This was insane. There had to be a reasonable explanation.

'I have to go,' said John. 'Watch yourself. I'll see you tonight.'

Very slowly, Amy put down the phone. She turned around and smiled broadly at William before walking over to him.

'Is everything OK?' he asked.

'He's had to take my cat to the vet. A car hit him.'

'Oh, I'm sorry.'

'He'll be fine.'

William indicated for her to sit down again, which she did. 'You were about to tell me something.'

'I was just concerned about the control of costs again. I know it's not my area but with pressure for more profit I wondered if we were getting the most competitive prices.'

'You really must let that go, Amy. Stepping on people's toes won't help anyone. And it seems to me you have enough to worry about without that as well.'

'So, as MD you've got full confidence that no

improvement can be made on price negotiation and the awarding of contracts?'

'Improvements are always possible, but Sally is the best person to deal with that, and I have every confidence in her.'

Amy smiled and stood up. 'I'll head off, then. Thanks for your support over the issue with Greg.'

'You've left me with an awful lot to think about. Give me a few days to work something out, but I want you to know that you can count on me.'

43

'High Holborn, please,' said Amy to the driver as she got into the cab. She grabbed her mobile from her bag and punched in Simon's number. She got his voicemail. 'Simon, I need to see you. It's urgent. I'm on my way over. I'll be there in fifteen minutes.' She hung up. This was crazy! What the hell was going on? She clutched a red A4 file tightly to her chest. It contained the Dalcon Trading invoice, their audited accounts and her own price comparison exercise, which she had expanded to numerous other events, producing graphs and tables to highlight the price discrepancies between Benchmark and their competitors. She had taken the file to work that morning, toying with the idea of showing it to William. Thank God she hadn't. As soon as she had left William's office, she had dashed back to her own room, grabbed the file and shouted to Beth that she had a client appointment.

Now Amy took a deep breath. What she was about to do was risky, possibly foolhardy.

Fifteen minutes later she walked into the Lazlo Manco headquarters. It was a large ten-storey building in Holborn, and the company occupied all ten floors. The marble-floored reception area alone covered over a hundred square feet, decorated with waterfalls and small trees in pots.

She went straight up to the front desk and asked for Simon Delaney. He wasn't in his office and it took the young receptionist several minutes to locate him. 'He says he's in a meeting with his staff at present,' the receptionist told her.

'Tell him it's urgent,' stated Amy defiantly.

The receptionist did so, then hung up. 'He'll be down shortly.'

Amy signed in and was asked to take a seat, but she couldn't settle. Instead she walked up and down until Simon stepped out of the lift. She hurried over to him. 'What's going on?' he asked.

'Is there a room where we can talk?'

They took the lift to the fourth floor. Simon asked her again what was going on, but Amy remained silent. The lift pinged, they got out and walked down a long corridor to a small meeting room. Simon sat down at the table, but Amy went over to the window and looked down below, before turning around and taking a seat next to him.

In a quiet yet ominous sounding voice she said, 'William's in on it too.'

His eyes narrowed. 'On what exactly?'

Amy launched into an account of why she suspected Greg Hamilton-Lawrence of taking backhanders from Benchmark and possibly other companies. She explained about the Dalcon Trading invoices, Rula Broknizt and John's NI search.

When she'd finished Simon said, 'There might be an acceptable explanation for this. Maybe William's wife was doing some unrelated work for Benchmark.'

'I've considered that, but with everything else – the overcharging, William's lack of interest in it and the strange emails – I'm convinced something's going on.'

He gazed at her for several seconds, twisting his mouth while he thought. Reluctantly he said, 'I think you should talk to Richard Jacobs.' He was the group financial director.

'You think I've got enough to approach him with?'

'That's your call.'

'What would *you* do?'

'I think an off-the-record chat with him is an appropriate course of action to take.'

'Let's do it.'

They headed out of the room and back to the lift. Simon pressed the button for the directors' floor. Amy glanced into the mirror and tidied her hair. Then she applied some lipstick. When the doors opened she stepped out determinedly. They headed towards Richard Jacobs's office. His PA met them and showed them into the boardroom. They had passed the point of no return.

'Yes, but how did you come across this Dalcon Trading invoice?' asked Richard Jacobs.

'As I said, I would prefer not to answer that,' said Amy.

'And you say a hundred and thirty-one thousand pounds' worth of these invoices have been raised?' That was the third time he'd asked her.

'Over a six-month period, yes.'

'But you don't have copies of them all.'

'No, just the one in your hand.'

'We would have liked copies of them all,' he said, peering over his glasses at her.

'That wasn't possible.'

Amy was sitting at one side of the rectangular table and Simon was beside her. Opposite sat Richard Jacobs, Philip Meyers and Peter Burchard, all senior directors at Lazlo Manco. There was also a dark, bearded, Greek-looking man in his fifties, whom she'd never seen before. He was sitting a little distance away from everyone else and scribbled notes constantly.

So much for the off-the-record meeting she'd hoped for – this had been a formal two-hour interrogation; at times it had felt as if she was the guilty party. Unperturbed, she had given them a concise statement of everything she knew about the possible backhanders.

Richard was now tapping the table with his pen. 'You said you haven't discussed this with anyone at CEM.'

'No. I wasn't sure who I could trust. As I said, I suspect William, Sally and Greg are behind it. However, others could be involved too. I'm not sure. All I know is that Benchmark is overcharging CEM and no one seems to care. I initially put it down to inefficiency, but CEM isn't inefficient. With the TGA contract alone, we could be talking about a couple of hundred thousand pounds going astray. Someone is making a lot of money out of this. When I found that William's wife was a director of Dalcon Trading, I felt I needed to bring it to your attention.'

'But why can't you tell us how you found out that Rula Broknizt was Veronik Halson?' asked Peter Burchard abruptly.

'I'd prefer not to say. A friend put his job on the line to access the information,' she said.

Richard looked sideways at the bearded man, and for the first time in two hours he spoke: 'Her maiden name is Broknizt, Rula Veronik Broknizt. Age thirty-six, born in Warsaw, moved to London aged twenty-one, worked as a model. She and William Halson met eight years ago through their mutual friend Harry Jackson, married two years later, two young sons.'

The other three men exchanged guarded looks and Peter Burchard whispered something in Richard's ear. Amy suddenly realized that they were already aware of something. An uneasy feeling descended on her.

'What's going on?' she said.

'I'm not in a position to say at present,' Richard told

her. 'If you could just continue to answer our questions.'

'I've told you as much as I know.'

'Just a few more.' He turned to a fresh piece of paper in his file. 'How long were you at Protea Software?'

She was unsure what direction this was going in. 'Three years.'

'I believe you were very successful.'

'I increased turnover threefold over three years. I hope to make a comprehensive impact on the bottom line at CEM, but my investigation into these irregularities has, at times, been distracting.'

'Of course. But returning to Protea, for a moment, can I ask why you left?'

She glanced at Simon. 'I wanted a new challenge. It was time to use my skills elsewhere.'

'So you're ambitious?'

'Very.'

'Do you like the event-management industry?'

What was the purpose of these questions, Amy wondered. Then it came to her. They were interviewing her. Of course. With William and Greg gone, the position of MD would be vacant.

'I love this industry and have many ideas on how to increase profitability. I have felt hindered by the underhand dealings, but I'm very excited about my next year at CEM. For the record, if people are suspended, fired, whatever, and it is necessary to appoint a temporary MD, I'd like to do the job. I'm fully qualified for the position and will apply when a permanent replacement is sought. I know I can deliver the profit margins that Pablo is looking for. I have a proven track record and I'm totally committed to the Lazlo Manco group.'

'Your request is noted. However, let's not jump the

gun. We need you now to return to CEM and say nothing to anyone. Carry on as before.'

'But they know I'm suspicious.'

'It won't be for long. We'll probably be speaking with you again some time later today.'

'I have my company medical this afternoon.'

'What time will that finish?'

'Around four.'

'Please ensure you head straight back to CEM after that.'

Amy nodded and the four men stood up. The three directors shook her hand, then left the boardroom immediately. The bearded man lingered behind. His cold eyes seemed to pierce right through her. 'I'd like you to write all this down in the form of a witness statement. Don't leave anything out. Have it ready by tomorrow,' he said.

'We've not met before,' said Amy. 'Where do you work within the organization?'

'I don't.' With that he turned and left.

Alone in the room both Amy and Simon exchanged intrigued and open-eyed looks.

'At least they've taken it seriously,' said Amy.

Simon looked worried. 'There's something bigger going on here. They already knew something. Those directors wouldn't give two hours of their precious time without good reason. I suspect the bearded guy is something in security, some form of investigator,' he said.

Part of Amy couldn't believe this was happening. It felt surreal. She was shocked by William's involvement, but on the other hand Greg would soon be out of CEM – out of her life! Torpedoes away! Then the uneasiness swelled inside her again. She looked at Simon. 'When will you hear back from the guy about the email?'

'Later today, hopefully.'

'Richard said they knew nothing about them.'

'There must be another suspicious person within CEM.'

She bit her lip. 'Something doesn't feel right.'

'Like what?'

'Don't know.'

'It sounds like you won't have long to wait.'

'I've been praying for this moment. Greg's put me through hell, Simon. One day I'll tell you what he's done, and you'll understand why I hate him. I'd like a front-row seat for the production of *Greg Hamilton-Lawrence Gets His Comeuppance*. Don't you love karma? It might take a while, but if you shit on people you'll suffer eventually.' She stood up. 'I have to be going.'

'I'll come down with you.'

'Thanks for your help with all this.'

He held the door open for her. 'That's OK. Just don't forget that you've agreed to have dinner one night.'

'I don't know why you'd want to go out with me.'

'Unfinished business,' he replied with a smile then walked off towards the lifts. Amy followed a few paces behind, looking troubled.

'Amy, might I have another word?'

She and Simon stopped and turned round to see Peter Burchard and the Greek guy standing in an office doorway. Amy walked towards them, Simon following her.

'Privately,' said Peter, staring at Simon.

44

It was raining, but Amy didn't mind: London smelt fresh in the rain, which washed the grime from the streets. It was gone four o'clock and she had just left the Nelson private health clinic in Charing Cross. She was walking unnaturally slowly, head lowered, eyes unfocused and dazed looking. Everything and everyone around her faded into a hazy blur. Even the noisy traffic was muted, as if the volume had been turned down. She wandered around the outskirts of Trafalgar Square and headed towards Haymarket, on her way back to the CEM offices in Piccadilly. She was late and would usually have jumped into a cab, but she had elected to walk. The rain soaked through her jacket and saturated her hair, which stuck to her scalp. People ran to seek shelter, yet Amy stopped in the middle of the street and stared up at the sky, letting the rain hit her face.

A part of her was reluctant to arrive at her destination; wandering no-mans-land was a necessary escape, a time to think and plan. Hadn't she lived her life by planning, trying to control every last thing; nothing could be left to chance. Sheer folly! Nothing could be controlled.

Half an hour later she arrived at CEM. Going up in the lift she gazed at her pale reflection in the mirror and grimaced. Soon the doors opened and she walked into the reception area.

'My goodness, you're soaked,' said Gillian, the receptionist.

Amy merely smiled, then walked down the corridor, peering into the other offices as she went by. The CEM drones were working away, tapping into laptops and bellowing into phones. At this moment everything was as usual. Nothing had happened.

When she went into her office Beth glanced up. 'I've been trying to reach you since this morning,' she said curtly. 'William was looking for you and he wasn't pleased when I told him your mobile was switched off.'

Amy ignored her and took off her wet jacket. Her blouse was damp in places but she didn't notice.

'Shall I tell William you're here?' asked Beth.

Amy shook her head and prepared to wait for whatever was going to happen.

Half an hour later it began. Tink appeared in the doorway. 'All these people from Lazlo Manco have arrived,' she said breathlessly. 'They pushed right past Charlotte demanding to see William. They're in with him now. What's going on?'

Amy shrugged her shoulders. Disappointed by her lack of response, Tink ran off to tell everyone else.

Within five minutes the intruders had invaded every department. Each manager was taken into a separate room and interviewed by two or three people. Everyone else was escorted into the boardroom where they were asked to wait for an announcement, which would be made in due course. Soon everyone was coming up with outrageous theories as to what was going on. Issy was convinced it was all a practical joke instigated by Greg and Daniel. 'They've probably planned an office scavenger hunt and are planting clues up and down the corridors.' Everyone giggled.

Beth joined the other girls in the boardroom but Amy was allowed to stay at her desk. Not that she did any work.

At half past five Amy was coming out of the ladies' cloakroom near Reception when she saw William being

Matchstick Love

escorted off the premises by three men; one was the Greek-looking guy. William saw her and stopped. He looked pale and shocked, and she felt a tinge of sadness for him. He started to say something but stopped himself and left the building. Amy returned to her office, slumping down in her chair.

Fifteen minutes later, the same three men walked with Sally along the corridor. Sally was crying. As she passed Amy's office she shot her a look of fury. Amy stood up to watch out of the window. Soon she saw Sally being escorted into the back of a waiting car, which drove away, but Amy continued to gaze out at the overcast sky. Twenty minutes later, she was still standing there when Peter Burchard appeared at her door. 'Richard would like to see you now.'

She followed him down the corridor towards William's office – William's old office. Just before they went in, Peter stopped and asked, 'Are you ready?'

Amy took a deep breath, stood up straight and nodded.

'Good luck,' he said, then opened the door and they walked in.

The atmosphere in the room hit her: it was tense and edgy. Several stern-looking men were sitting around the oval table: Richard Jacobs and Philip Meyers from earlier that day, Paul Burns, the commercial director, and Jonathan Hume, Pablo's right-hand man. There were two others she didn't recognize. However, there was one more familiar face – a face that shouldn't have been there. Greg Hamilton-Lawrence.

'Good to see you again, Amy,' said Richard Jacobs. He pointed to the seat opposite him, which she took. Peter sat down beside her.

Richard cleared his throat. 'I wanted to bring you up to speed with developments. It was two months ago that we were first alerted to possible wrongdoing within CEM. We took steps to investigate this, but the information you gave us this morning was something more concrete to act on.'

Amy nodded.

Richard continued, 'I am about to go into the boardroom to make an announcement to the other staff that William and Sally no longer work for the group. They resigned this afternoon. The staff will be told that their ideas didn't fit in with the future direction of Lazlo Manco and that we didn't feel the required growth would be attainable under their management. There'll be gossip, but that's irrelevant and will die out in time.'

'We don't want any of this getting out to the clients,' Paul Burns added. 'There'll be no police involvement. That wouldn't help anyone and would tarnish the reputations of CEM and Lazlo Manco. Everything will be dealt with internally. We have a more than capable security team. William was allowed to resign pending no further action. It may seem unfair but one has to look at the bigger picture.'

'Yes, I realize that,' she stated nonchalantly.

'Your suspicions were correct,' said Richard. 'William allowed Benchmark to overcharge, and in return the difference, several thousand pounds, was deposited with Dalcon Trading and then on to himself. We suspect that he received over three hundred thousand pounds. Of course, Sally was in on it too. Thanks to you and Greg, of course, we've managed to put a stop to it. It was Greg who brought this to our attention in the first place.'

Amy gave no visible reaction: she appeared at ease and unmoved. Her eyes were fixed on Richard's as he explained in more detail exactly what had gone on. She nodded in all the right places, not once glancing at Greg. However, a million thoughts and emotions whirled around inside her like a tornado battering her to the core. *Yet again Greg had come up smelling of roses!*

After several minutes Richard added, 'After consideration Greg's been appointed temporary MD pending the sitting of a permanent appointment panel, to which you, Amy, will be welcome to apply.'

The tornado gained in strength. She glanced at him and he smiled triumphantly at her.

'Congratulations, Greg,' she said, devoid of emotion.

'Thank you, Amy. You can't imagine what that means to me,' he said.

'I'll talk to you both in due course,' said Richard. 'Right now we have to make the announcement to the other staff. You two make a good team. We have optimistic expectations of CEM's performance.'

At that everyone stood up to leave, including Amy.

'Actually, I'd like you to stay, Amy,' said Greg. 'We have a lot to talk about.'

She sat down again, and focused through the full-length glass windows on the rooftop of the building opposite.

The others left and closed the door, leaving them alone.

There was silence. It was as if the world had stopped.

It was Greg who moved first. He stood up and walked over to William's desk, running his fingers over it, stroking it as if it was a woman's body. Next he sat down in William's chair, patting the armrests and gazing around the spacious office. Taking in a deep breath he exhaled loudly with a long pleasurable sigh. Then he let out a burst of laughter, which rang out and echoed off every wall.

'Oh, Amy! In a way I have you to thank for this,' he said. 'If it wasn't for your investigation I wouldn't be MD. Ironic, don't you think?'

Her blank expression gave away nothing.

'You thought it was me, didn't you?' He came and sat down at the table directly opposite her, blocking her view of the outside world. She continued to gaze ahead as if she could see right through him to the roof.

'Silly girl – as if I'd risk everything for a few hundred thousand pounds. That's chicken-feed where I'm headed. I merely let you do the donkeywork to get the proof I needed.' He pulled a look of mock-horror. 'Creating Interested Party kept you hooked. Have you not figured that out yet? Tut-tut. Off the record, I'd known about the financial kickbacks for a couple of years. But in business timing is everything. If I had moved on it earlier Roger would have been made MD. So I had to wait until he was out of the way. It wasn't in my interest to act sooner. My own agenda is far more important than Pablo's profit.' Another burst of laughter erupted from him. Again he admired the large office and beamed with pride. 'Yet another plan comes to fruition. I keep telling everyone, life is just too damn easy.'

Then his demeanour changed, his eyes narrowed in disdain. 'You women are a joke. You babble on about equality yet you're all too damned emotional to run the course. Business and emotion don't mix. If you want to play with us, wise up. Even hard-nosed Sally lost the plot. She used to be one of the better ones, until she fell for William. I don't suppose you know that they've been shagging for two years.'

Amy's eyes flickered.

'She'd have robbed a bank if he'd asked her to. So easily moulded, the lot of you. You're all plasticine in the right pair of hands. Some people disagree, but I've never been proved wrong. *Never*.' He rolled his eyes and shook his head as if she were totally pathetic. 'Your hatred of me has been your weakness throughout our brief encounter. But to me you're just another cog in the wheel that gets me where I'm going. Someone to be manipulated but certainly not worthy of hatred.'

Again she gave no reaction. Her vacant-looking eyes continued to gaze right through him.

His face twisted. 'Obviously we can't work together. I've tolerated your presence long enough. As managing director I will be closing Strategic Planning with immediate effect. Daniel is the new sales and marketing director. Obviously it would be unwise for me to sack you so I'm moving you to sales and marketing, and you'll report to Daniel. I believe you'll find that unacceptable so I expect your resignation within four weeks. Start looking for another job right away. To show that I'm gracious in winning – after all, I *have* won, Amy Lambert, in every respect – you'll be given a half-decent reference. I just want to be rid of you. You can go piss off some other man in the pantomime you call your career while *I* will delight in my role as MD, using it as a stepping-stone into the major league. I'll marry the billionaire's daughter, get the father to invest in my numerous ventures, screw the occasional Amy – because there are so many Amys in the world who are attracted to us bastards. It's only decent men who can't get laid.' He laughed boisterously, unrestrained even for him. He was in his element, his moment of ultimate triumph and humiliation of her.

Then he banged on the table. 'That's it, dismissed.' He waved her away, stood up, went back to William's desk and began to open drawers, as if she wasn't there.

Amy didn't move. She continued to stare at the roof

opposite. Then without turning her head, her eyes travelled slowly sideways in his direction and for the first time she fully focused on him. Her lips pinched. She stood up. Yet instead of making for the door, she walked slowly towards him, stopping by the chair opposite but not sitting.

In an unnaturally calm manner she said, 'Just explain something. Explain to me why you and Daniel made that bet.'

He looked up and scowled at her. 'For God's sake, move on. You're so boring.'

'Just explain. I need to understand.'

'What's there to explain?'

'Why me?'

'Why not? It was a laugh. It's just sex.'

'Don't you feel the slightest shame that you deliberately pursued me and slept with me within three weeks, just so that you could win a week's skiing holiday?'

He leant back in his chair and crossed his hands behind his head. 'Actually the holiday was for ten days in a five-star hotel. Most enjoyable. Now I've answered your question get out. As I said, dismissed.'

For the first time that afternoon Amy smiled. She stepped forward and put her hands on William's desk. 'Actually I believe it's you who are about to be dismissed.'

He rolled his eyes.

'Ironic,' she said. 'In screwing me you screwed yourself. I just hope Miranda and her father don't find out about your sacking. Then again, anonymous emails are an excellent way to spread information. I have a strong feeling that they'll both be receiving an email this evening. It really wouldn't surprise me if she calls the wedding off.'

'What the hell are you going on about? I'm not going anywhere. We've already been through this – it's your word against mine! Just get out,' he said abruptly. 'I don't have time for this crap.'

'Oh, but I can't leave,' she said smoothly. 'You see, any moment Peter Burchard and, no doubt, a couple of the security guys will be walking through that door.'

Greg looked at her as if she were insane. She gazed down at him and winked, then calmly sat in the seat opposite him, crossing her legs.

'*Get out now*. I'll call Security myself.'

'Wait one minute and they'll be here.'

'You're wasting my time. *Fucking get out!*'

'No.'

'Enough, goddamn it,' he screamed. 'I'll throw you out if I have to.' He jumped up but, at that moment, the door opened and in walked Peter Burchard, Richard Jacobs, Philip Meyers and the Greek-looking guy. They looked at Greg with disgust.

'I had hoped it wasn't true,' said Richard sadly.

Greg composed himself and beamed a friendly smile at them. 'What's going on, gentlemen?'

'A very sorry story,' said Peter.

Greg looked innocent. 'I hope this isn't anything to do with some allegations with which Amy has been trying to blackmail me. I deny them fully and I'm sure, once you've heard my side of events, you'll be in agreement with me.'

Peter Burchard stepped forward. 'Forget it, Greg. We have it all on tape.'

Greg's smile remained yet he shifted his weight from one leg to the other. 'I'm at a loss, gentlemen. Please explain.'

'Don't make a fool of yourself by denying anything. We all heard the conversation you've just had with

Amy – not just your admission over that deplorable bet, but also the fact that you knew about the financial backhanders for nearly two years but did nothing about it. Something about your own agenda is more important than Pablo's profit.'

Greg's smile disappeared. He stood deathly still, staring at the men with a stunned this-isn't-happening expression. Amy watched the spectacle unfold before her.

'After you came to us, Greg, with your concerns,' continued Peter, 'our internal security service took whatever measures they deemed fit to ascertain evidence against William. Bugging his office was one of them.'

'Illegal,' said Greg.

'As we said to William, do you really want to go down the legal route?'

Slowly Greg's mouth fell open. He raised his hands a couple of times then let them drop to his sides. Then, as if hit by a bullet, he slumped into the chair, dropping his head into his hands and exhaling loudly. A couple of times he looked as if he was about to say something, then stopped. There was quiet as everyone watched the previously regal Greg, now bent and defeated. Then, as if at the flick of a switch, he sat bolt upright and locked eyes with Amy. His mouth was twisted, like a snarling dog.

She smiled.

'Looks like I managed to sink your boat after all,' she said.'

Venomous hatred shone from his glaring eyes.

'Amy, I want you to act as temporary MD pending the full employment panel,' said Richard.

'It will be a pleasure,' she said.

'That's ridiculous,' Greg burst out. 'My methods

may be questionable but I would have got you the results you wanted. I know everyone in this industry. Without me CEM will lose half its client base.'

'May I remind you that your contract of employment states that you cannot work for a competitor for two years,' said Peter. 'I assure you that we will take the necessary steps to enforce it. Now, if you don't mind, you'll be escorted back to your office where we'll require you to hand over your entry and car keys, then answer a few questions. I believe it's in your interest to co-operate. We'll get you to sign a contract of termination, which will include a secrecy clause. There'll be some severance pay as an incentive to sign.'

'Fuck the lot of you,' Greg spat out. 'Let's get on with this farce.' He stared down at Amy, who wondered what he might do. He said, threateningly, 'I strongly advise you not to send those emails.'

She brought a finger to her lips. 'Oops. They've already gone.'

His face contorted with rage. 'Fucking bitch,' he yelled, and stepped towards her.

The Greek guy blocked his path.

'Don't make this any worse, Greg,' said Richard. 'At this point you may still get a half-decent reference.'

Greg looked Amy up and down with loathing. 'You women are all the same,' he growled. Then he marched out.

The other men followed him apart from Peter Burchard who hung behind. 'I can't believe what a conniving creep he turned out to be. The things he said to you. We were all stunned.'

'It might have turned out very differently.'

'I'm just glad I heard your conversation with William this morning about the bet. Otherwise it would have been your word against his, and Greg is a very convincing guy. Pablo had high hopes of him. He'll be shocked when he hears of all this.'

Amy cringed. 'Does he have to?'

'Afraid so.'

'I feel so stupid with everyone knowing what a fool I was.'

'Hey, go easy on yourself. Thanks to you, the top layer of corrupt managers have all been kicked out of CEM. Daniel will be asked to leave too. And you're now MD.'

'Temporarily.'

'I suspect it'll be made permanent.'

'Greg was right. CEM will lose some clients.'

'You'll have to win new ones. You said you like a challenge.' Peter looked at her curiously. 'I'd have thought you'd be more happy. Relieved.'

She stood up. 'I just want to go home. It's been a long and exhausting business.'

'At least it's over,' he said.

Amy looked at him blankly, then turned and walked out. Tears glazed her eyes. It wasn't over. In a sense it was just beginning.

45

Hearing a knock on her front door, Tessa dashed out into the hall to answer it. She knew it was Amy – she'd just seen her park her car, and couldn't wait to tell her all about last night. She ushered her friend inside and pulled her into the living room. 'You won't believe it.' She was giggling like an over-excited child. 'Wait till you hear this.' She was about to launch into a detailed version of how it had felt to be kissed by John, when she suddenly noticed that Amy was as pale as a ghost, and her eyes were red from crying. 'What's happened?' she asked.

Amy's mouth opened, but no words came. She looked rigid with shock.

'My God! What?'

Her mouth moved yet there were still no words.

'*What?*'

Amy held her stomach as if she might be sick. In an almost inaudible whisper she said, 'I'm pregnant.'

A deathly silence filled the room. Tessa stood completely still, staring at her in disbelief.

'Pregnant?'

Amy nodded.

'How? Who, for God's sake?'

Tears began trickling down Amy's face. 'Greg.'

'No!' gasped Tessa. 'How? When? Don't tell me you slept with him again?'

'Of course I didn't. I'm three months pregnant.'

'You didn't know?'

'I thought I was run down. I've had two light periods since then. It can happen that way, they said.'

Tessa was shaking her head and frowning incredulously. 'Didn't you use anything?'

'He had two condoms, but we did it three times.'

'You fool!' shrieked Tessa. 'How could you?'

Amy buried her face in her hands and began to sob uncontrollably. Tessa sat down and put her arms round her. 'Oh, Amy,' she said.

Amy continued to sob, overcome and exhausted by all the day's events and the news from the clinic that afternoon, that she was pregnant, which at the time she had acknowledged by a blank-faced nod of her head.

Tessa wanted to say it would all be OK, but those words were meaningless and possibly untrue. 'Have you thought about what you're going to do?' she asked.

It was several minutes later before Amy even managed to sit upright. Her face was swollen and covered in red blotches, and still the tears trickled down her cheeks. 'I don't want his child,' she said, her face suddenly contorting with disgust and fury. 'His fucking monstrous offspring growing inside me. His child! His genes. I feel sick. I don't want it. I want it out of me. I hate him – I hate *it*.' She was thumping her stomach.

Tessa watched in horror. 'Amy, stop, please! Wait.' She grabbed Amy's hands, but Amy yanked herself away.

Gradually she became calmer. 'It's got a heartbeat,' she said. 'They did a scan. I have a little baby growing inside me.'

Tessa's head lowered and for several minutes they sat in silence. Eventually Tessa took her hand and said softly, 'You know I'll help you.'

'How?'

'If you have it.'

'How can I have it? *Greg!*'

'Don't tell him.'
'I'd rather die than have him in my life.'
'He doesn't have to know. It's your baby. Not his.'
'He'll find out.'
'You'd have to leave CEM.'
'He's been sacked.'
'What?'
Amy went on to summarize what had happened.
At the end Tessa was smiling. 'You did it, Amy. You got rid of him. You'll never have to see him again. He'll never know about the baby. He's out of your life for good.'
'I'll have to leave CEM. It's filled with his spies.' Her fists clenched. 'I finally get what I want, Greg's gone, I'm MD. *And now this!* If I have this child I'll have to give it all up. And who'd employ a pregnant woman? My life, as I know it, is over for good.'
'Would it be so bad?'
'Yes, horrendously bad. It's all I know. How would I live? I'll need money.'
'I'll look after it,' said Tessa 'Once it's born you can get a less pressurized job.' She squeezed Amy's hand. 'There's always a way – we just have to find it.'
Amy's head hung over her knees, as if she might vomit. For some time she sat there, while Tessa rubbed her back. 'What would I tell the child?'
'You'll have a few years to work that out.'
'I never want to see him again. Never, ever.'
'You won't have to. Don't see this child as his. It's yours. *All yours.*'
'What if it turns out like him? A woman-hating, manipulative monster?'
'It won't. Not with you as its mother. It's your baby, not his. It's nothing to do with him. You can bring it up however you like.'

Amy shuddered.

For the next hour they talked about all that had happened and how Amy would cope if she had the baby. Eventually, worn out, Amy said she wanted to go home.

'Are you sure you'll be OK on your own?' asked Tessa.

Amy nodded and stood up.

'Call me any time, night and day. Even if my hall light is off, just knock. I mean it.' Tessa took Amy's hand again. 'I want you to know that you don't have to go through this alone. I'll even be in the delivery room if you like.'

'*You* in a hospital?'

'If I can be a spy I can be a midwife.'

'You're a good friend,' Amy said, and kissed her.

Tessa reached for the latch but stopped. 'You probably don't want to know about this now, but I just have to tell you. I kissed John last night. I'll tell you about it at a more appropriate time.'

An hour later Amy was sitting on her sofa gazing at the television. The news was on, but she wasn't taking it in. She was drinking orange juice – no vodka now – and she had just eaten beans on toast.

She was thinking about her life and how she had lived it. She thought of all the jobs she'd had and the burning ambition that had driven her in the pursuit of success. But what was success? Neither she nor Greg would be MD of CEM. Neither had won.

She imagined life with a baby. It was terrifying. Bringing up a child alone. How would she manage?

Each time she contemplated having Greg's child, his face forced its way into her mind's eye. Of all the men in the world, she had to be carrying *his* child. He would haunt her for ever. The thought of him finding out and trying to have any influence on the child appalled her. She vowed never to let that happen. *As God is my judge, I'll kill him first!*

She began to think of all the men she had dated, what a sorry bunch they were. They, too, had been trapped in the hunt for success, gathering possessions around them to prove their worth. There was no denying that she'd had fun with some of them – and great sex. But that had just temporarily filled a void in her. That was the sum of her relationships: they had filled a void until one or both parties became bored and moved on in search of another temporary filler.

John Smith had been right: it was all 'matchstick love' – a momentary flame that extinguishes quickly. Everyone was in love with being in love. In this crazy world nothing meant anything any more. It was all about chasing the thrill, the little highs, the excitement. And she had been the worst culprit. She closed her eyes and found herself thinking of John. He was one of the few who were different, who had jumped off the treadmill and saw the beauty through the bullshit. *You're so stupid Amy*, she told herself. *Stupid and superficial for not seeing what a genuine, lovely person he is.* The tears welled up again.

Tessa was sitting in an armchair, sipping wine and thinking about Amy. She wanted to go up and comfort her but Amy needed to be alone. She would just have to wait and see what Amy decided: ultimately Amy always did what Amy wanted to do. *I suppose we all know what's best for other people but not for ourselves*, thought Tessa. But, then, maybe it would be all right.

A baby brought joy into the world and, regardless of the father, Amy would love it. Tessa admitted to herself that she'd like to look after it during the day. It was probably too late for her to have her own child but she'd be a damn fine auntie. And, after all, she believed in fate: there was a reason for everything that happened. Obviously Amy wasn't meant to be MD of CEM. Maybe having a baby would ground her.

Tessa knew that she was an incurable romantic but she decided there and then that Amy must have her baby and that she and John would be the godparents. They would take care of mother and child. Everything would be OK.

When she heard a knock at the door she leapt up and opened it. John was standing there. He was holding a bunch of azaleas and irises and his crystal blue eyes gazed affectionately into hers. His blond, curly hair looked neater today, as if he'd combed it, which she didn't like so much. She felt the desire to mess it up and let it run wild. She'd spent too much of her life trying to conform to society's norm and she'd had enough of it. *No more!* John was his own person, standing out from the crowd, and she loved that about him. She already knew that their future was going to be together, and that in time he'd see it. It was fate! There was no point in fighting it.

'For you,' he said, holding out the flowers.

'Thank you, they're lovely.'

'Would you like to join me for a candlelit takeaway?' he asked diffidently.

'I'd love to.'

'Give me an hour. I just have some things to sort out.'

She nodded. 'I'll see you then.'

Suddenly he bent forward and kissed her. 'I look forward to it.'

Matchstick Love

Tessa floated back into her living room. Yes, it was definitely fate!

Amy continued to sit on her sofa, staring into space and contemplating her life. All her mistakes glared her in the face. She hadn't a clue as to what the future might hold, but gazing at her stomach, she knew inside that although it was the worst thing that could have happened, she wouldn't be able to get rid of the baby: we reap what we sow.

She had stood up to fetch a glass of water when she heard a knock at her door. She opened it, expecting to see Tessa, but it was John.

'Can I come in for a second?' he asked.

Hesitant, she glanced away.

'It'll just take a second. I wanted to clear something up.'

She stood back from the door and he walked in.

'How did work go? Was it your MD's wife?'

'It was, but it's too complicated to go into it now. Another time. But thanks for your help,' she said quietly. 'I really appreciate it.'

He noticed her swollen eyes. 'You OK?'

'Not really, but I can't talk about it now.'

'I won't keep you. I just didn't want there to be any confusion,' he said. 'It's just that, you were right. We are from different worlds and we shouldn't have kissed. As you said, it was probably the alcohol. It would never have worked out between us. And . . . I'd like to get to know Tessa.' He smiled. 'She's a little zany, but I like her. She has such depth. I had no idea she was interested in me, but when you told me I started to look at her differently.'

Amy nodded and went to open her door.

'I felt I should explain,' he continued. 'I don't wish to be rude but I don't want you to think that Tessa is my second choice to you in any way.'

'I didn't,' said Amy.

'I was attracted to you, but not every attraction should be pursued. You're a lovely person but, as you said, we're worlds apart. I just wanted you to know that. I don't want it to be weird between us.'

'It won't be weird.'

'Best if she never knows.'

Amy nodded.

'I hope we can be friends, Amy.' He walked towards the door. 'You need some dynamic, wealthy, ambitious businessman, who can show you a bit of excitement. That obviously isn't me. I hope you'll find him.' He smiled at her, then left.

Amy shut the door and slid into a huddle on the floor. Tears filled her eyes and she cradled herself like a lost child. In a defeated sounding whisper she said, 'Excitement isn't everything.'